STATE OF EMERGENCY

JACK EMERY 2

STEVE P. VINCENT

First published by Momentum in 2015

This edition published in 2017 by Steve P. Vincent

The moral right of the author has been asserted.

A CIP record for this book is available at the National Library of
Australia

State of Emergency

Cover design by Xou Creative

Edited by Kylie Mason

Proofread by Laura Cook

 Created with Vellum

To all those who have resisted the excesses of tyrants in ways big and small and often at great personal cost.

PROLOGUE

"Twenty seconds." One pulled a balaclava over her head. "Gun it."

The driver nodded and put his foot to the floor, the engine roaring as the vehicle sped across the Harvard Bridge and onto Massachusetts Avenue. The windows were tinted, so the pedestrians who glanced at the vehicle as it sped past couldn't see the deadly cargo inside.

"Ten seconds. Everyone check in."

As the van took a hard right onto Vasser Street, the rest of One's team checked in. The team – four in the van with her and one located strategically on a rooftop near the campus – were as slick as ever. One smiled under her mask. She didn't need to do the check and knew they'd be ready, but fifteen years of habit was hard to break.

One was jolted in her seat as the van mounted the curb and then pulled to a stop. Two slid the door open, climbed out and broke into a run. She too was running as soon as her feet hit the ground. Three and Four would follow, while Five would stay at the wheel. As she moved, there were squeals of panic from nearby students. She ignored them. They were irrelevant unless they got in the way.

The team crossed the sidewalk and reached the entrance of the Massachusetts Institute of Technology Electrical Engineering and Computer Science Department in seconds. She pointed at Four and he moved into the building with his submachine gun raised. The others followed him in and they split into pairs.

"Remember, we're looking for Daryush Daneshgahi." She paused. "We need him alive."

From the foyer she went left with Two, while Three and Four went right. They had intelligence that Daneshgahi was a creature of habit and would either be in his office or his lab. She had her weapon raised and was moving briskly when an alarm started to wail. It was a surprise it had taken this long.

Her headset crackled. "One, this is Six. Campus police are starting to arrive."

One spoke into her voice-activated microphone. "Copy."

They reached Daneshgahi's office and took up positions on either side of the door. One waited as Two turned the handle and pushed the door open quickly. She entered the room and swept from side to side with her submachine gun, then quickly lowered the weapon. The office was well lit and empty. There was nowhere he could be hiding.

She cursed under her breath and the distant boom of a high-caliber rifle seemed to punctuate her profanity. Six was on the rooftop, tasked with keeping any police away from them, and he'd started the boom boom. While a few officers weren't a problem, with each passing second more would arrive.

She left the office with Two in tow as she spoke into her headset. "He's not in the office. Moving to check the cafeteria."

As she rounded a corner, a shot boomed. She flinched but kept moving toward an MIT police officer, who stood with his pistol drawn. He looked about fifty and very scared. Her silenced weapon barely made a sound as it delivered two rounds into the officer's chest. His eyes widened as crimson blossomed on his blue shirt. His pistol fell to the floor with a clattering sound and his body followed. One fired once into his face and didn't break stride as she stepped over him, with Two behind her.

Her headset crackled. "This is Three. We've got him. We have the target. He was in the lab."

"Good job." She felt a mix of relief and satisfaction. "Begin exfiltration."

She pictured the entirety of the exfiltration in her head as she moved. The snatch teams would move through the buildings and then onto the lawn, southeast across the campus. Five would drive to pick them up, while Six would shift position to cover Killian Court and their escape route before withdrawing. The whole team would be in and out with Daneshgahi in less than seven minutes, as planned.

She waved at Two and they moved south through the building and out into the courtyard. Once outside, they kept moving, scanning their surroundings and the top of buildings for shooters. The few students that remained ran when they spotted the armed commandos. Maybe MIT grads were intelligent after all. Smarter than their campus police, anyway.

She looked at her watch. By now Six would have taken his final shots. He'd be abseiling down the Maclaurin Building and moving to meet them at the extraction point. Radio silence meant no hitches. It had gone reasonably well so far and they were in the last minute of the operation. Nobody challenged One and Two as they reached the edge of the campus and crossed Memorial Drive.

She glanced at Three and Four, who were already crouched with weapons raised and facing outward. Two joined them in a covering position while she looked at Daneshgahi, face down on the lawn with his hands cuffed behind his back. She lifted him up. His face was the illustration of terror, but he kept quiet. It looked like he was pretty smart.

A shot drew her attention and she turned towards it. She needn't have bothered, because her team put down the police officer quickly. A few seconds later, Five pulled the van to a stop in front of them. She slid the door open, bundled Daneshgahi inside and climbed in. Their prisoner gave a small whimper of protest as the rest of the team joined them.

Six arrived at the van just as One was closing the door. The sniper's breathing was heavy and something had obviously taken longer than it should have, but he'd made it. She didn't need to ask and he didn't need to answer – if he hadn't made it, he'd have been cut loose. That was the business they were in.

As the door slammed shut and the engine roared, One looked over to Daneshgahi. The Iranian computer scientist was watching the floor and she could feel the fear radiating off him. She took the hood that Two was holding out to her and placed it over Daneshgahi's head. He started to cry.

ACT I

1

FEMA would like to assure the public that, despite the recent terrorist attacks, its ability to provide disaster assistance remains intact. Staff are working hard to provide coordinated relief to all locations affected by these attacks. Citizens in need of support or those with something suspicious to report are encouraged to contact the new National Security Hotline.

Federal Emergency Management Agency
News Release

J ack Emery stared at the news bulletin as the massive Reuben sandwich in his hand continued to sag. Though he was meant to be on vacation, you couldn't take the news out of the newsman. He took a bite without taking his eyes off the screen, his brain working overtime to process the ramifications of what he was seeing. A half-dozen attackers – good ones – had gone to a lot of trouble to snatch one MIT student.

A chunk of corned beef and a dollop of sauerkraut breached the edges of his sandwich and fell onto his lap. He cursed, placed his lunch back on the plate and mopped at the mess with his napkin. It didn't help. He looked like a freshman who'd been touched in the nice place by a cheerleader. Jack shook his head and looked back at the screen as he picked up his Coke.

A hand on his shoulder made Jack jump and spill the drink. He looked around, angry, until he saw Josefa Tokaloka's smile beaming down at him. Though it had been only a year since they'd seen each other, the large Islander looked like he'd aged a decade. Jack grinned widely and stood to wrap his arms around Jo's enormous shoulders. It felt like hugging a bronze statue.

Jo crushed him in a bear hug. "Making a mess as usual."

Jack laughed and pulled away. "It's good to see you, Jo. Meeting up was a great idea."

"No problem, it's been a while." Jo's smile slackened slightly. "Plus, I figured you could do with some human contact that didn't involve people shooting at you."

Jack nodded and jerked a thumb at the screen. "Can you believe it?"

"Given recent events?" Jo frowned. "Yeah, Jack, I can."

Jo had a point. Jack had only been back in the US for a few weeks, but in that time there had been a dozen attacks across the country, all professional and brutally successful, targeting critical infrastructure and public gatherings. No group had claimed responsibility and no suspects had been identified. Casualties were mounting, panic was spreading and the authorities seemed impotent to stop the attacks.

"They're all connected, Jo. I'm sure of it. If I didn't know any better, I'd think it was the Foundation reborn." Jack hated thinking it, but even though over a year had passed it felt like just yesterday he'd been fighting to stop Michelle Dominique and her corrupt think tank. He'd gone to hell and back to stop her, but not before Dominique had sparked a war, taken control of the largest media empire in the world and almost gained control of Congress.

Jo shook his head. "Doesn't fit. The FBI tore them to shreds and their entire leadership is dead or before the courts."

"Yeah, you're right. But these are professional hits." Jack sat back down and gestured for Jo to sit on the lounge chair opposite. "Makes Syria seem almost civil."

Jo laughed softly as he sat. "How was it over there? You did some good work."

"Tough. There's not a lot of hope." Jack had spent the last three months in Syria covering the siege of Homs. It had been hard, but had also provided a rich vein of stories for his new site, which focused on long-form investigative journalism that the rest of the news media could bid on to broadcast. It was the perfect deal for everyone: he had the skill and not very much money, while they had the chequebooks but had cleared out most of the journalists with the skill.

"So why Vegas?" Jo looked around at the table games and the slot machines. "Given your particular vice, I figured this would be one of the last places you'd want to spend time."

Jack followed Jo's gaze. While the attacks – and the fear of more – had subdued Vegas a bit, you could never fully clear out the stags and hens, the corporate getaways, the tourists and the addicted. They were like moths to a flame. While there was gambling everywhere, it didn't interest him. The booze did, though he was more in control of those temptations these days. But what really drew him to this particular desert in Nevada was the fact that it was probably the least news-conscious place in America. Day and night passed without notice here and if it didn't involve gambling, sport or entertainment then it didn't rate a mention.

He thought he'd needed that time away from the news. After he'd won his second Pulitzer for the stories he'd written about the Foundation, he'd spent months working to get his estranged wife's body repatriated from Shanghai and organizing her funeral. He'd thought that watching her casket being lowered into the earth would be a release, an ending. He'd been wrong – more pain had come up inside him. After that, he'd tried burying himself in his work. He'd thrown all of his effort into the new site. Then, needing stories to tell and an escape, he'd traveled to Syria. Upon his return, he'd wanted some time away from the news. In theory.

"I like it here." He exhaled slowly. "Hell, I'm just glad to be back in the States, to tell you the truth. The site is going well and I've hired some other contributors. It was time for a break."

"Glad to hear it." Jo smiled slightly. His face looked gaunt and tired. "EMCorp wasn't the same when you left, you know that?"

Jack raised an eyebrow. "Wasn't?"

Jo's smile widened. "I retired a few weeks after you left, Jack. I'd love to say it was because you weren't there, but it was actually the love of my life who forced me to quit."

"Your wife?"

"My heart surgeon." Jo laughed and tapped his chest. "This fucking thing should have killed me, but the good people at New York Presbyterian kept me ticking a bit longer."

Jack couldn't believe it. Jo was the toughest hunk of meat he'd ever known. "Sorry I wasn't there, mate. Why didn't anyone let me know?"

"Well, I was too busy being cut open. I think Celeste wanted to tell you but Peter stopped her. He said you had to be left alone to heal. I don't think she was very happy about it."

Jack winced at the mention of her name, but before he could reply a drinks waitress approached. Given the length of her skirt, it was a good thing she had a beaming white smile and cute eyes, or else Jack might have struggled to look anywhere else. They made small talk for a moment before Jack ordered a beer. Jo went with ginger beer. As she shuffled off to get their orders, Jack's eyes were locked onto her legs.

Jo gave a long, booming laugh. "Fall off the horse, Jack?"

Jack turned back to Jo, feeling himself flush red. "I never stopped liking women, Jo."

"The booze, I mean."

"I limit it to a couple these days." He shrugged. "Hard to be a saint all the time."

"GOOD AFTERNOON, ADMINISTRATOR." The young White House staffer held out her hands in apology. "The President has been delayed, but you're welcome to wait."

Richard Hall frowned. He reached up to his nose and slid his glasses back into place. "Okay, please let me know when they're ready."

He moved to a sofa and sat with a sigh, his back aching as he did. While Richard had lorded over the entirety of the Federal Emergency Management Agency for a decade, his boss was the most powerful woman on the planet, so delays were to be expected. But within a few moments he looked up to see the President striding down the hallway with members of her staff, each trying to get a word in. The scene was akin to hyenas stalking a wounded lion. The lion might be the most powerful, but the hyenas were legion. It made the lion vulnerable. The thought made him smile as he adjusted his tie.

President Helen Morris offered a tired smile as she approached. "Good to see you, Richard. I hope you haven't been waiting long?"

Richard stood. "Not at all, Madam President. Only a few minutes."

Morris didn't stop walking. "I'm heading to the Situation Room now. Care to join me?"

Richard nodded and followed her to the lift, where the staffers were repelled by some invisible force field. Apparently none of them were senior enough for a jersey in the big game. After a short ride and some small talk, they exited into the cavernous, 5000-square-foot Situation Room. Dominated by a mahogany table and leather chairs, the room was a high-tech dungeon used by the most senior members of government and the military to deal with any crisis abroad – or at home. The other members of the National Security Council were already seated as the President sat at the head of the table and Richard took a chair to her left.

"Thanks for coming in, everyone." Morris opened her leather folio and quickly perused her papers. "What do we know?"

Richard knew the answer: Nothing. He glanced up to the large screen at the far end of the table, which showed a map of the continental United States with digital pins marking the locations that had been attacked in recent weeks. When displayed in such a way the enormity of the situation revealed itself. Though the attacks had resulted in carnage, the authorities had identified no pattern, no logic, no leads and no suspects. He kept his mouth shut and others adopted the same strategy, though there were a few nervous coughs to punctuate the awkward silence. He sat back. The failure did not belong to him, though the solution might. Forty years of public administration had taught him patience.

Finally, Walt Clarke – the President's National Security Advisor – leaned forward to speak. "The attack on MIT was precise and astonishingly fast. They were in and out in less than eight minutes. Local police had only just started to arrive."

"That's it?" Morris peered over her glasses and down the table at Clarke. It wasn't a kind look. "I know all of that. I watch CNN and read my briefings. I want to know who? Why? Where next? What're we doing about it?"

There was a muted sense of tension in the room. While Morris was quite inexperienced, she wasn't regarded as a pushover. Richard doubted anybody in the room had seen her react this icily to their advice. Though she'd been in office for nearly a year and Richard had hardly been overwhelmed by her competence, this was the first time she'd seemed panicked. Richard knew there was opportunity for whoever could explain the attacks and provide a path forward to stopping them.

Clarke was visibly shaken by the President's bluntness. "I can't answer that. We have some footage, but it gives us nothing. We do know they kidnapped a computer scientist – Daryush Daneshgahi – and then swapped vehicles a number of times and disappeared."

Hayley Penbroke, the Director of National Intelligence, cleared her throat. "While I can't speculate on the who, the why is clear. Daneshgahi is a genius."

Clarke scoffed and turned towards Penbroke. "I doubt he grew up with running water. He can't be worth all that effort, surely?"

Penbroke glared at him, then turned back to the President. "We smuggled him out of Iran and gave him a full scholarship at MIT. He can pop the hardest encryption like it's bubble wrap. We keep a pretty close eye on him and he's never given us reason to doubt him. He's a good kid, really. Whoever has him is now a huge threat."

Morris frowned. "In practical terms?"

Penbroke didn't hesitate. "Any computer system is

vulnerable. The Stock Exchange. Power grids. Air transportation safety systems. You name it, he can crack it."

General Mike Cooper, Chairman of the Joint Chiefs of Staff, raised his hand and interrupted. "Nuclear launch codes?"

"No, not those, General." Penbroke crossed her arms. "Pretty much everything else is in play though. This is more dangerous than some missing ammonium nitrate."

"Okay." Morris placed her hands flat on the table. "While everyone keeps trying to figure out who's behind all of this, what're our options? We can't just sit and wait."

Cooper spoke. "Madam President, give the word and we can have troops on the street in every major city in the country within twelve hours. We can also increase the cover at major infrastructure. I can't guarantee that these measures will stop the attacks, but they will make the bastards think twice."

"No." Morris's voice was sharp. "I don't want the army on Sixth Avenue. If there's one thing that'll panic people more than attacks across the country, it's a visible army presence. Besides, there's no possible way we have enough troops to cover everywhere that needs it. Deploying the military just gives these bastards a victory."

Richard gave a small smile. He'd underestimated the depth of the President's dissatisfaction with the other arms of the Federal Government. While she'd no choice but to rely on her advisors, she clearly wasn't putting much faith in them getting results. He couldn't blame her. The attacks had rocked America and her advisors weren't coping. They were overwhelmed and predictable, offering nothing that would work, nothing that would influence the situation or America.

It was time for him to speak. "Madam President, if I may?"

Morris gave a small nod. "Go ahead, Richard. That's why you're here."

He leaned forward. "While I agree with the desire for additional security, and concede that combat troops may be needed if this continues, there's another option. FEMA can use the State Guard to provide more security at key facilities. It's a middle ground – more protection, but without tanks on street corners."

Morris's face was expressionless. She seemed to consider his words for a few moments before she held her hands out. "Thoughts?"

Richard looked around. His plan earned a few nods and a lot of silence. Only Cooper seemed opposed, sitting with his arms folded. Most importantly, nobody raised any objections. Truth be told, they were all out of answers and probably happy for someone else to take the heat for a while. That suited Richard just fine. He was banking on the fact that he'd been in his job for a long time, while many of the people at the table had clocked less than a year in theirs. Rolling up the Foundation for a New America had taken a scythe through the upper ranks of government and the end of the Kurzon administration had removed more still. Richard had kept his head down and his hands clean, and was now considered a trusted broker by many, including Morris. He decided to press his luck.

"At the same time I can ramp up the support that FEMA is providing. All it will take to get this up and running quickly is a budget allocation." Richard sat back in his chair and looked at Morris. "That will take me to the limit of what FEMA is able to do, at least without the declaration of a state of emergency."

Morris sighed, removed her glasses and closed her eyes. While he knew she was a strong believer in civil liberties and loathed any discussion of the state taking more of a role in daily life – like deploying troops into cities – she also must know that doing nothing was not an option. Personally, Richard thought the choice was obvious – cut down on freedoms, ramp up surveillance, saturate the streets with assets and it just might be possible to win this thing. He could understand her hesitation, however. This was one of the largest decisions of her young administration so far and she was clearly fighting an internal struggle over it. She massaged her temples, looking every bit as old as her fifty-eight years. Finally, she opened her eyes again and ran a hand through her greying hair.

"Richard, make it happen. Dial it up as high as you can go without that declaration. Get the State Guard protecting our most important facilities and increase the relief FEMA is providing across the country." She exhaled heavily. "But I want FEMA talking to the rest of the administration. Protect us and help our people."

"Not a problem, Madam President." Richard nodded and sat back with a small smile. He'd won the hand, but in Washington things could go backward as quickly as they went forward. He knew when to gamble and when to take his winnings. He'd been trying for months to get FEMA dialed in to the main game as a legitimate player rather than just a mop-up agency at the call of others. He'd succeeded, now he kept quiet.

Morris stared down the table at the rest of the council. "Let me make this clear, ladies and gentlemen. While Richard beefs up our defense, I want the rest of you on offense. We have the most elaborate national security apparatus on the planet. I'd like to see some of it put to use. Find these bastards."

～

THE SOUND of the rotors slicing through the air was One's constant companion. Her team sat in silence as they edged closer to their target. The briefing, walk through and gear check had all been done on the ground and each member of the team knew their role, except for Daneshgahi. The Iranian computer scientist sat in his seat with his head downcast, with Two and Three seated on either side of him captive. It was all quite relaxed.

One looked down at her watch: 2159 hours. Right on time, the helicopter started to descend. She waved her hand at the rest of the team and held up one finger. The other five members of the team gave a thumbs-up in return. With thirty seconds to go, she lowered her night-vision goggles over her eyes and stood. The others joined her, Two and Three hauling Daneshgahi to his feet. The second her watch ticked over to 2200 hours, the helicopter touched down with a light thud.

She slid the door open and jumped the short distance from the helicopter to the ground. She took a deep breath. The cool evening air was both a shock and a thrill. It was her first time in Nevada and her first visit to the Hoover Dam. Once her team had finished disembarking she slid the door shut, raised her carbine and started to move along the causeway. Once they were clear of the helicopter it lifted off again, to take up station overhead and act as their eyes in the sky.

"This is Big Bird." The team was about halfway between the landing zone and their target when the helicopter reported in. "Three armed sighted targets ahead of you."

"Confirmed." One crouched and the rest of the team did the same. She kept her eyes peeled, but couldn't see the threat. "Move up."

She moved forward slowly with the others, leaving Three and Five to guard Daneshgahi. Losing the Iranian was not an option. Though she couldn't see any targets yet, they must be near the concrete structure that housed the entrance to the control room. Whoever was guarding the dam had hastily constructed some basic cover and fortifications. A boom broke the silence of the night – some sort of rifle.

"Three targets visible." Six's voice came over the network. He was slightly ahead of her.

"Get rid of them." One crouched and raised her carbine, but she didn't have a clear shot.

More shots roared from the other end of the causeway. Their foes weren't very good, shooting from extreme range and with no real accuracy. It was possible they didn't have night-vision gear and were shooting in hope, but she couldn't bank on that. She started to move forward, but was forced to drop low again when more fierce gunfire erupted. She heard a grunt in her earpiece.

"I'm hit." Six sounded like he was in pain. "My hand. Not too bad though."

She cursed under her breath. "Confirmed."

She heard a whoosh as Four – the squad's grenadier – fired the underslung grenade launcher on his carbine. A large explosion lit up the night and One heard a roar as the grenade struck home. Hardly stealthy, but effective. Flames licked at the cover that dam security was using and one of the guards staggered forward. She raised her carbine and fired a burst at the exposed guard. He dropped.

She hadn't expected much resistance and it was over and done with now. When nobody reported further hostiles, she started forward. "Move up."

They reached the large steel door that separated them from the command center, paying little attention to the three bodies scattered among the crates they'd used as cover. She knocked on the door and whistled softly to herself. The door was too thick to blow up and its electronics had recently been upgraded to make it independent from any network. Luckily her employer had provided the answer.

"Three, Five, move up with Daneshgahi." She turned to Four. "Do it."

Four nodded. He let his weapon hang by its strap and dug into a pocket on his combat vest. One smiled as he held the electronic access card to the reader until it beeped, flashed green and unlocked the door with a clunk. She'd half expected the card to fail, foiling their entire operation, but it turned out her employer could be trusted. Some dam employee somewhere would soon be very rich.

Four swung the heavy door open with a grunt and led the way inside with Two. One waited as Three and Five moved up with the scientist and followed the lead pair inside. She waited a few moments until she was satisfied things outside were under control, then followed with her carbine raised. She left the wounded Six on guard outside. He was hurt, but could hold their rear if any trouble came along.

They moved quickly through the corridor, alert for any threats. In a few moments they reached the expansive control room, which had a bank of computer terminals, large monitors and status boards on the walls. The capacity and flow of the Hoover Dam were managed from here, along with the key safety systems and contact with the outside world. One lowered her carbine as the team checked for any threats.

Five examined the terminals. "The systems are in lockdown."

Two's spoke up from across the room. "I've got a pair of civilians."

One walked to where Two was standing over a pair of workers, cowering under a terminal. She crouched. "You have five seconds to override the lockdown."

"Please, just leave us alone." A young woman shrank back further. "We just look after the systems in the evenings. I don't know how to do very much."

One stood, raised her carbine and fired a single silenced round into the woman's skull. A spray of blood escaped from the woman's head and she slumped to the ground as the shell casing pinged off the floor tiles. One believed her – she was just a console operator, unable to help the team out of their predicament. She turned to the older man, whom she had a hunch knew more than his dead companion. She pointed at him.

The man nodded and One stepped back as he crawled out from under the terminal. Without speaking, he took his seat and started to type. He was shaking like a leaf in the wind as a password command box appeared on the screen. One held her carbine to the back of his head as he typed the command in slowly, then hit Enter. The password box disappeared and the screen flashed red with a warning that an alarm had been triggered.

"How disappointing." She sighed and pulled the trigger.

As his body dropped to the floor, One let her carbine fall to her side. A quick glance at the terminals told her all she needed to know. The facility control room had now gone from being locked to completely inert – even if a member of staff wanted to unlock the systems, they'd be unable to. She hated heroes. With a sigh, she approached Daneshgahi and lifted his chin with her index finger.

"I can deal with the override, so long as you have the equipment I asked for." His voice had a tremor and his eyes kept flicking to the dead man. "Just promise I'll live."

She smiled and held out a small kit bag that had been on her combat vest. "You deliver on your promise and I'll deliver on mine."

He nodded frantically and snatched the bag from her hand. One was alert but curious as he opened it, drew out a small device and plugged it into a USB port. Daneshgahi's hands danced across the keyboard, command prompts and lines of code flashing on the screen at dizzying speed. She didn't understand it, but she didn't have to. Her employer had assured her that Daneshgahi had the skills to do what was needed.

After less than a minute, he stepped back from the terminal and smiled at her. "The lockdown is no longer in effect. The control panel is back to normal."

One looked at Three, who nodded as he held a carbine to Daneshgahi's side and whispered into his ear. Daneshgahi's eyes went wide and a deep look of worry crossed his furrowed brow. Finally, Daneshgahi looked down at the console, hit a few keys, turned to her and nodded. She stepped up to the terminal, where a box on the screen was asking for confirmation of the command.

"Everyone ready?" She looked at her team and saw nods in return. She hit the Enter key. Klaxons started to wail and lights flashed red. "It's time to go."

Daneshgahi looked as if he'd burst into tears at any moment. "I've done what you wanted. Please, I want to go home."

She ignored Daneshgahi and spoke into her headset. "Big Bird, we need extraction. Two minutes."

"Confirmed." The helicopter pilot's voice was calm. "No sign of further hostiles, but there's some radio noise coming out of Nellis Air Force Base. Suggest you hustle."

She jerked her head toward the door. Daneshgahi started to move and she followed him and the other four members of her team toward the main door and out into the cool night air. She looked over the side of the dam, and though she couldn't see the water in the darkness, she could hear it. As they waited for their ride, Daneshgahi moved a few steps closer to her, a look of frightened conviction on his face.

Four raised his carbine. "Back off, buddy."

The Iranian didn't buckle as he ignored Four and

addressed One. "I gave you access. I've done what you wanted. I want to go back to Boston. You promised."

She smiled at Daneshgahi and nodded once. Without a second's delay, Three and Five grabbed him from behind. As they manhandled him closer to the edge, One followed. His eyes were frantic and kept flicking back and forth amongst the team as he fought to free himself from their grasp. She casually drew her pistol and placed it against his skull. His eyes widened as she pressed down with some force.

Daneshgahi became a dead weight in the arms of her men as he started to wail. "Please, I gave you what you wanted. You can't. You promised."

"You've been a great help, for whatever that's worth." She squeezed the trigger.

2

With unprecedented flooding across several states following the attack on the Hoover Dam, FEMA has mobilized to assist cities, towns and rural areas in need of support. Until this support can reach affected locations, citizens are reminded to beware of areas that are flooded, to secure their home but be cautious of electricity around water, to avoid driving and conserve food.

Federal Emergency Management Agency
News Release

J ack looked out over the serene water contained by the Hoover Dam as he sipped his coffee. He found it difficult to comprehend the devastation it had caused just a day earlier. Though the dam wall was physically intact, the terrorists had opened a pair of spillways, freeing an enormous amount of water. Half-a-dozen large towns downstream had been flooded and thousands were missing, presumed dead.

Jack ran a hand through his hair and resumed his walk along the causeway. "They did a job on this place."

"It was surgical." Josefa frowned. "If they can pull an attack like this off, there's really not a safe location in the entire country."

Jack shrugged but said nothing as they neared the operations center. There was a score of maintenance staff on the causeway, repairing damage caused by the gunfight. Though they could do little to help the towns flooded and lives ruined downstream, they were doing a fair job of hosing away the blood. Milling around, far less busy, were some Nevada state troopers, police and some security contractors.

Josefa snorted. "Upping the security seems a bit pointless."

Jack laughed. "Like waiting until after the shot clock has expired before shooting."

They had already passed through a security cordon at the entrance to the dam, but there was another checkpoint near the entrance to the operations center. Jack was glad that, at times like this, he had friends in high places. Given he'd very publicly assisted US authorities to foil the Foundation for a New America, he was able to access areas that would be denied to others. It was time to make use of it.

He gave his widest smile and held up his press pass as he approached the two guards standing outside the operations center. "Hey, guys."

The security guards looked at each other and then one of them scrutinized the pass. "You've got no business inside."

Jack sighed. "Bill McGhinnist, Director, Federal Bureau of Investigation, would have something to say about that. Should we give him a call?"

"I don't care if you've got the King of England on speed dial, pal." The guard didn't seem impressed as he tapped the clipboard. "No name, no entry."

Jack was about to point out there was no male monarch currently straddling the British throne, but he saved his breath. Another man approached them, dressed in chinos and a polo shirt that bore the logo of the US Bureau of Reclamation. He had the look of someone deeply troubled, a guy pushed into the deep end and struggling not to drown – Jack knew a source when he saw one. He stepped forward.

"Good morning, sir. I'm Jack Emery." He flashed his pass. "I've been given permission to cover the story of the dam attack. This is Josefa Tokaloka, my... assistant."

"Eric Waterford." The other man smiled weakly and jerked a thumb toward the guards. "Don't mind these gentlemen. You're not on their list, but you are now."

"Thanks." Jack smiled at the guards. One of them glowered, as if resenting the challenge to his unassailable authority.

Jack snorted and followed Waterford and Jo inside. Though there were signs of conflict outside, there was no apparent damage to the inside of the facility. They walked in silence down a short corridor and into a cavernous room dominated by a few rows of computer terminals and wall-mounted screens. It was pretty clear that this room had been the focus of the attack. The scene of a mass murder.

"We're here." Waterford turned and held his arm out, showcasing the computer terminals. "This is what lives were lost for. This is where your story is, Mr Emery."

Jack took a few more steps into the room. "Can you tell us what happened?"

"They hacked in and compromised the spill gates." Waterford looked close to tears as he pointed at a terminal. "A lot of water rushed out of the dam very quickly."

Jack paused, then joined Waterford and put a hand on his back. It was time to change tack. "Why are you talking to us, Mr Waterford? Why give me the story?"

"I know who you are and what you did for this country. You'll call it fair." Waterford shrugged. "Plus, I owe it to the people who died here. I'm lucky to be alive myself."

"You saw the attacks? As in, eyeballs on what they were doing?" Jack was excited by the thought of an eyewitness account.

"No." Waterford cast his eyes downward. "But I heard it. There's a supply cupboard in the hallway. I hid in there once I heard the gunfire."

Jack nodded. Waterford's mess of emotions was clearer now. "There's no story here. You're not giving me anything CNN doesn't have. I need something exclusive."

Waterford gave a sad-looking smile. "I can do you one better. They cut our security camera feeds, but we've got a hard-wired network. We caught it on tape."

Jo whistled. "Can we see it?"

Waterford nodded and walked over to a cabinet against one of the walls. He chose a key on his oversized key ring and unlocked it. Inside the cabinet there was a small monitor. Jack watched with fierce curiosity as Waterford's hands danced across the keys and the wall-mounted monitors came to life with some dark but decent footage. He could barely contain his excitement at the size of this scoop.

"You got it. The whole thing." Jack couldn't believe such an elite team could be so careless.

The video showed six figures wearing balaclavas, weapons raised and alert as they led a seventh man – Daneshgahi – across the causeway. Before long, they'd paused and were exchanging fire with the security team. Jack watched in awe as they met the attack with cool professionalism.

Waterford pressed a key. The vision switched to above the external door, where three bodies were sprawled like dolls discarded by a raging toddler. Jack winced. The attackers were at the door and managed to unlock it easily. Five of them moved inside with Daneshgahi while a single figure remained outside.

"Wait a minute." Jack's eyes widened and he looked at Waterford in confusion. "How the hell did they get in so easily?"

"An inside man." Waterford shrugged. "I don't know who, or why, but it's the only way they could get through that door so quickly."

"Okay." Jack nodded. "I need these tapes and I need to get back to Chicago. This is going to explode."

CALLUM WATKINS CROUCHED low as he moved through the foliage, careful not to step on any dried twigs or knock his rifle against a tree or sapling. He held up a gloved hand, his fingers balled into a fist, to stop his companions from advancing any further. He listened, alert for any sound or sign of their target, but heard nothing. With a smile, he lowered his fist and edged forward slowly. He lived for this.

He winced when he heard a small crack from behind him, and turned his head to see one of the others holding up a hand in apology. Callum glowered, but moved on without further rebuke. They weren't in Fallujah this time and mistakes didn't mean death, but it still annoyed him when others screwed up. He brushed aside some shrubbery as quietly as he could, then inhaled deeply.

There he was. Callum crouched as low as he could and lifted his rifle. Square in front of him was the mother lode – the largest male stag he'd ever seen. It was an amazing beast. When its haunches were locked squarely in his iron gun sight, Callum breathed. In and out. In and out. He aimed, concentrated on his breathing then squeezed down on the trigger slightly.

The sound of a steam train whistle broke the serenity. Callum flinched involuntarily, just as the rifle boomed in response to his caress. He'd missed and the deer was spooked by the barrage of sound. It broke into a run, crushing twigs underfoot as it disappeared deep into the forest. Callum stared at where the stag had been, his mouth agape, then lowered his weapon and looked around.

"What the hell?" Callum locked his eyes on one of his companions. Though Todd Bowles was a friend, right now Callum wanted to shove a branch down his throat until leaves sprouted from his ass. When the other man didn't look up from his iPhone, Callum placed his rifle against a tree and marched over to him.

Todd looked up from his phone. He gave no sign that he understood the enormity of his screw up. "What? It's important."

"So is the biggest deer this side of the Rocky Mountains. I had it lined up!" Callum pushed Todd off his feet and onto his back. "Who brings a phone hunting?"

"Hey, calm down!" Todd took a half-hearted swing at Callum as a few of their friends dragged him away. "I had the phone set to ring only for an emergency. It rang."

Callum fought off the hands of his friends and sat on the ground. "What do you mean? What's the matter?"

"It's from my buddy in the Secret Service. We were together in Kandahar. Word is that all the state defense forces are being mobilized."

Callum paused. It was no small deal if true. The Illinois State Guard had been reconstituted after the war between the United States and China, along with those from other states that had long ago abolished them. A rung below the National Guard, they were a small force under the command of the state governor. Every state in America now had one, armed with surplus military equipment.

Like many in the guard, Callum was ex-army and attracted to the pay and conditions that they offered for part-time work. It seemed a good way to keep in touch with the life and career he'd known for his whole adult life. He could keep his pension and work for them tax-free, which sure beat packing groceries at Wal-Mart or cleaning windows in the Illinois winter. He'd signed on and kept his sergeant rank.

"That's a big deal." Callum started to stand. "Must be because of the attack on the Hoover Dam yesterday."

While the attacks across the country had been severe and showed no sign of slowing, Callum hadn't expected them to lead to the mobilization of any arm of the military. Even the activation of the state defense forces showed that a large number of people in the highest levels of command were taking things pretty seriously. He wondered if there was more to it.

"Wait a minute." Mark Pettine looked up from the ground, deep in thought. "Who's doing the activating? We're under the governor's authority."

Callum and Todd looked at each other and shrugged, before Callum started to walk back to his rifle. "Doesn't matter. We better pull up camp. We'll get the call soon."

MARIPOSA ESPOSITO PAUSED BRIEFLY and then clicked confirm, sending thousands of pounds of relief supplies from warehouses across Illinois to towns devastated by the Hoover Dam flood. She stood, walked to a whiteboard near her cubicle and drew a line through a name on the board. She smiled, proud that she'd now helped all of the towns she'd been assigned to assist. It was a good thing, because while FEMA Area V had deep resources to call upon, most relief supplies in Illinois had now been trucked off.

Mariposa walked back to her desk and sat heavily in her chair.

She struggled to stifle a yawn and looked to the left of her monitor. She'd pinned a photo of her seven-year-old son, Juan, on the cubicle wall. His close-cropped hair was ruffled from play and his smile was so wide that it plumped up his cheeks. Best of all were his chocolate brown eyes that made her heart melt. She looked back at the screen, but before she had the chance to do any work, one of her colleagues walked over and parked his rear on the edge of her desk. She looked up with a smile still on her face. Murray Devereaux looked as tired as she felt.

"You're cheery." He took a sip of his coffee and looked up to the board. "Nothing left to dispatch?"

"Just pressed go on the last lot." She patted his leg. "How're you holding up, Murray? How's Di?"

"One step closer to a divorce." He gave a tired shrug. "Things were going better until we had to start working these double shifts. Back to where we started now."

Mariposa gave a sympathetic nod. FEMA officers had been working hard since the beginning of the attacks a month ago. All leave had been canceled and many of the staff had been spending more time at the office than at home. She'd had to hire a sitter. But the attack on the Hoover Dam had nearly broken their backs, with the work stepping into overdrive in the past twenty-four hours.

"I don't know what to say, Murray." Mariposa grabbed his hand and gave it a squeeze. "Except that we're helping a lot of people."

His expression darkened. "Fat lot of good it's doing. As soon as we react to one attack they cause chaos elsewhere. Each time, our supplies run a little lower."

She nodded. "And it doesn't feel right that we're leeching all of our supplies, given Chicago hasn't been hit yet? I get it."

He exhaled for a long few seconds. "There's no point thinking about it – it's all on the back of trucks now. We better just hope the hammer doesn't fall here."

"Amen to that."

He raised his coffee cup in salute and then lowered it to consider its contents. "Running on empty, you want one?"

She glanced at her cup but didn't get the chance to answer as her computer made a sound that drew her attention. Only emails from a select few people made that sound, Murray among them. She leaned forward, clicked on the new arrival and scanned the contents of the email quickly. Murray read over her shoulder and let out a soft whistle.

"Big wigs incoming." He scoffed. "Arriving just in time to congratulate themselves."

Mariposa let out a short laugh then reached up to cover her mouth. "You're terrible."

"Not wrong though. Catch you later." He smiled and walked back toward his desk.

Mariposa put her headphones in and started answering the emails that had built up while she had been coordinating relief supplies. As she worked in rhythm with the music, the distractions of the rest of the office vanished. Most of the emails were routine and many were complete junk, but all had to be dealt with. She liked to go home with an empty inbox.

Something hit her in the head and she jumped with a start. She looked down at the eraser which had settled on her desk, then looked up to see Murray beaming a smile in her direction from his desk. She frowned, until he jerked his head toward the break area, where a bunch of men in suits were waiting and the rest of the staff had started to gather.

She checked the time and was shocked that a full hour had passed. She stood and stretched again, unsure about what could be so important that it required a full gathering of the staff. It was late, everyone was tired and the work was mostly done. People deserved the chance to finish up and go home for a while before it all started again tomorrow.

As she approached the break area, she sized up the two men from management: one of them was very slick but also very young, while the other had a few more laps on his tires. Yet the aura of power radiated off them both in a way that surprised her. These were very important people. She crossed her arms and waited for them to begin.

"Thanks, everyone." The older of the two, a completely bald man, smiled and held his hands together. "I'm Frank McCaskey, here on behalf of Administrator Hall."

That got everyone's attention. Richard Hall was a god to the men and women who worked for FEMA. He'd taken over the organization after Hurricane Katrina, when it had been smashed by criticism about the effectiveness of its response. Since then he'd quietly gone about fixing the problems, building morale among the staff and making FEMA more influential than ever.

McCaskey smiled. "The executive team wants to express our thanks for the incredible effort over the past month or so. If this were the private sector, we could give you bonuses, but it's not, so we can't. All I've got to offer is our thanks and the assurance that you're making a difference. You're saving lives and helping people.

"Unfortunately, we're going to need to ask more from you all. From tomorrow, FEMA is going to full mobilization. Code Red." McCaskey paused. "I know this sounds unusual, but it's in response to the unprecedented challenges that the country is currently facing. We have a huge role to play."

Mariposa looked around at her colleagues. They appeared as concerned as she felt. The last time the organization had gone to Code Red had been for Katrina, and that hadn't gone well. A full response to one geographic location was one thing, but to achieve it across the entire United States felt like an impossible dream. It would mean longer hours, more stress and more work.

"I'd like to introduce my colleague." McCaskey pointed to the young man. "This is Alan Benning, he's going to take charge of Area V for the duration of the emergency."

Benning offered a grin and a wave as half-hearted applause greeted the news. "As far as you'll all notice, not much will change."

Mariposa looked at Murray, who'd raised an eyebrow. She knew that look.

Everything was about to change.

3

All available support has now been dispatched to the areas flooded following the attack on the Hoover Dam. FEMA is pleased to announce that all Critical 1 incidents have been responded to and the agency is working in collaboration with local authorities to respond to Critical 2 and Critical 3 cases. The President will address the media today at the White House and provide a full update on the situation.

Federal Emergency Management Agency
News Release

Richard had never set foot inside the White House Briefing Room before, despite four decades of public service. It was testament to the type of work he did that, on the odd occasion he spoke to the media, it was from the site of some disaster or another. Yet here he was, seated alone and off to the side as he waited for President Morris to arrive. Circumstances had changed – for the very first time he had a place in the center of major conversations taking place in America.

Camera flashes and the low hum of conversation

interrupted his daydreaming as President Morris arrived with her press secretary and a Secret Service agent. Morris was wearing a blood-red jacket that strongly contrasted her graying hair and pale skin. It had probably been chosen by her political handlers to project strength. The press secretary whispered into her ear and left her alone at the lectern, while the agent stood off to the side. Richard watched her intently.

"Good morning, everyone." The President looked straight ahead with as much conviction as Richard had ever seen from her. "Today I'm here to speak to the American people about the most severe threat we've faced this century."

Richard smiled as some of the journalists looked up. The White House press corps gathered here nearly every day to hear the routine affairs of state, but it was rare that a briefing would begin with such a blunt statement. Given the events during that time period – 9/11, wars with Afghanistan, Iraq and China and attempts by the Foundation for a New America to control the country – it was a bold claim. Yet Morris wasn't wrong.

"The terrorist attacks that have swept our nation are unprecedented. We've been attacked before on home soil, but we've never before seen a chain of coordinated assaults like the one that we're currently facing. The damage has been immense, from Cowboys Stadium to MIT to Walt Disney World. The attackers are well trained, well equipped and deadly. No group has claimed responsibility and we do not know their motive.

"It pains me to admit that while the authorities are doing their best, they've made little progress. While investigations continue, I've had to escalate our response, to provide more security for our critical installations and on our streets. In doing so, I've tried to balance security against the impact on the daily lives of Americans. But it's clear to me that traditional approaches aren't working to protect us."

Richard felt a surge of satisfaction. For Morris to publicly admit that her administration was powerless in the face of such assaults was huge, and he knew better than anyone how far away they were from results. Since she'd authorized the deployment of the State Guard at the NSC meeting, he'd been working overtime to get things moving. Since the meeting, the attack on the Hoover Dam had only escalated things further.

The previous evening he'd been working late into the night to get the State Guard deployed when Morris had called. She'd skirted around the issue at first, until she'd finally swallowed her pride and asked him what more could be done. It was the moment Richard had been waiting for. They'd talked for an hour about the possible contingencies and he imagined that her speech notes for this morning had been changed significantly after their conversation.

Morris gripped the lectern. "The atrocity at the Hoover Dam was the final straw for me. That attack looks to have killed thousands and is the latest sign that nothing we're trying is working. Given that, I've consulted with my advisors and searched deep into my soul to look for new ways, new ideas, to keep our people safe. We think we've come up with something, but it was a hard decision to make."

Richard snorted. Morris had been speaking to her advisors for weeks, since the commencement of the attacks. They'd come up blank and their inexperience and lack of imagination had cost the country dearly. In truth, he knew that he was the only one she'd consulted the previous evening, and was glad that his experience was finally being taken into serious consideration. He'd been available to her from the very start, but she'd neglected to seek out his advice. He'd served America for decades and only wanted it to be great.

He sighed. It was a shame so few Presidents were up to the challenge. Most floated through their time in office like so much driftwood on the high seas, achieving nothing except in occasional, deferential nods to the Constitution, the Bill of Rights and the founding fathers. They told Americans what they *deserved*, but not what was necessary for them to have it, or to keep the country safe and prosperous. They ignored the fact that, sometimes, foul-tasting medicine was needed to fix the body. Occasionally, a President was forced to face this fact.

Morris shifted her gaze and stared straight down the cameras. "Prior to entering this room, I signed orders declaring a state of emergency across America and executed a number of executive orders pertaining to our government, legal system, economy, media and critical infrastructure. The current situation necessitates this action and I don't take this step lightly. Actually, please come up here and join me, Richard."

Richard was surprised at the invitation, but composed himself quickly. He stood and walked to the front of the Briefing Room, going over their conversation from the previous night in his head. They'd discussed the mobilization of the State Guard and the extra options Richard had hinted at in the NSC meeting. He'd told her about a number of long standing executive orders that were on the books, ready to be activated in an emergency but an afterthought to nearly everyone in America. Nearly.

In the time it took him to reach the President, she had given the assembled media the highlights of his career. He was surprised with how gushing she was in her praise, but perhaps shouldn't have been, given he offered her a life raft to save her administration. The advisors she'd hand picked to be part of her inner circle had failed so she'd turned to him, a career bureaucrat with decades of service to a half-dozen presidents. He smiled. If he was her chance at absolution, she was the key to his legacy. If she could be persuaded.

"Thank you, Madam President." He stood beside Morris, adjusting his eyes to the lights and mentally preparing – for the first time – for the spotlight. "Good morning."

Morris smiled. "Richard is a colleague and friend with immense experience in disaster management. Commencing immediately, he's in charge of a coordinated response to these attacks. He's in charge of the basics – transportation, power supply, food distribution – as well as security and the investigation."

The assembled members of the press corps looked up from their notepads and tablets and just stared. Every set of eyes bored into him like a drill, as the realization of what they were witnessing sank in. He'd never actively sought the limelight, but to achieve his goals it was a necessary next step. Others had proven incapable of such responsibility, but he was up to the job.

Hands shot into the air and questions started to fly. Richard looked to the President, who smiled slightly and waited. She'd done this before. It was a process that Richard didn't quite understand, but it seemed to work. Morris waited patiently for the initial boilover to calm down to a low simmer before one journalist drowned out the others. Morris pointed to the man.

"Tim Gossinge, *Washington Post*. Madam President, you're handing over the reins to FEMA? How will it work and why are you taking action of such severity?"

The President smiled. "Thanks, Tim. The orders that allow me to place much of the administration of our country under the control of FEMA have been on the books for years. After much thought, I've decided that we need a new approach. We need everyone singing from the same sheet, and Richard is the finest conductor in the country. All arms of federal and state government will report to him."

Richard swallowed, shifted forward slightly and waited for the President's nod to speak. "If I could just add, coordinating all parts of our campaign against these terrorists will take a huge effort – from security to first response to disaster relief to investigation to arrest to prosecution. FEMA's involvement will get everyone pointed in the same direction and, when that happens, we can't be stopped."

Gossinge persisted. "That doesn't explain the need to take over things completely unrelated to the attacks though, does it?"

Morris frowned. "Come on, Tim, you're not that stupid. These attacks target our way of life and we must protect that way of life. Americans expect the lights to turn on, food on their supermarket shelves and gas in the pump. This reality is under threat. It's Richard's job to protect it. I don't back away from my decision."

"Madam President. Elena Winston, *Chicago Tribune*." Another reporter cut in, as she tapped a pencil against her leg. "What resources will FEMA have to do this job?"

"Whatever they need." Morris's reply was blunt. "Pretty much the entirety of the federal government will be at Richard's disposal, except the military."

Winston scribbled furiously as she spoke. "Without the military, how do you expect to protect anything? Beat cops and private security too fat to chase anybody?"

Richard stayed silent. It was best for the President to fend away the shots at his authority, including questions that dealt with the extent of the new powers that FEMA had been granted. Given the enormity of the job, bringing the entire country under the administration of FEMA and the protection of the State Guard, he'd have enough threats and challenges in the coming days. He didn't need to step into the line of fire unnecessarily.

"The state defense forces will also be providing security at our most critical infrastructure and rapid response to any attacks that occur." Morris glanced at Richard and then continued. "These forces were recently beefed up following the war with China. It gives us the force we need at the right time."

"The right time?" Winston leaned forward in her chair. "And how long will these controls be in place? Isn't this a breach of our democracy?"

"No. I was elected to solve problems, and that's what I'm doing. As for how long? These orders are effective immediately. It's possible we may quickly reach a point where things can return to normal, but after a year of operation, the executive orders will be reviewed. You'll be briefed accordingly throughout this period."

The room erupted.

Morris held up her hands. "The orders also cover control of the news media. We're keen to ensure terrorists don't gain exposure for the attacks, so we must take this step."

The President's press secretary, clearly unhappy with the uproar, stepped forward. "That's all for today, ladies and gentleman. Thanks."

Morris started to step away from the lectern and put a hand on Richard's back. He went with her, the Secret Service agent in tow. As they approached the exit, Richard heard the press secretary deliver the final zinger – that the press briefing packs would detail the changes and how they would work, but that all reports from now on needed to be cleared by the Press Office before printing or publication on the internet.

The roar that filled the room was only silenced once the

door closed behind them. Richard took a deep breath. He didn't like the chaos of the mass media and it would be one of the first things he'd get under control. It still amazed him that America could shift to virtual totalitarianism with a signed document and a press conference. The changes gave him the opportunity to bring order and stability back to America. It would be his lasting legacy.

He turned to the President. "Well, I think that went alright?"

JACK CURSED as the amber light switched to red just as he drove through it, causing a camera to flash. Though he was in no hurry, he'd been sucked into what he was listening to on the radio and hadn't been paying attention. He didn't look forward to a traffic fine from the good state of Illinois, though he did wonder how the executive orders applied to such things. He'd just have to wait and see if FEMA were as efficient at stamping out traffic offences as they were at taking control of society.

The more detail he heard about exactly what FEMA would be in charge of, the more worried he became. Worse, he suspected the stale reports were being read straight from approved media releases. He'd flown out of Las Vegas early after publishing his story on the Hoover Dam, so he had been in the air when the bombshell from the White House had dropped. By the time he'd landed, the screws were already starting to tighten.

Now, as he drove down West Adams Street toward his hotel, it was clear that FEMA had been prepared for kick-off. He tooted his horn as a black Illinois State Guard Humvee cut him off. The vehicle held four uniformed troopers with their weapons clearly visible, but Jack had seen enough men with guns in recent months to not be intimidated. It was for naught anyway – they didn't acknowledge his presence as they continued down the street. So much for courtesy among motorists.

He sighed and pulled the vehicle to the side of the road, right out the front of the Club Quarters Hotel. It had been his home away from home in Chicago since his return from Syria. It wasn't palatial, but it was cheap and comfortable until he found a place of his own. He'd thought about returning to New York to live, but there were too many memories there. Too much pain. He killed the engine, reached into the back seat for his duffel bag and climbed out of the car.

A valet rushed over to him. "Welcome back, Mr Emery. Good to see you, sir. Can I take your bag?"

"No need, Mo." Jack smiled at the familiar routine and handed over his keys. "Take care of the car though?"

"You got it." Mo took the keys and started toward the car. "Unlucky for you that you're so late. We've had issues with check-ins since noon."

Jack hefted the duffel bag over his shoulder, confused by Mo's words, and crossed the sidewalk to the hotel entrance. Once inside he slowed and then stopped entirely. A uniformed Illinois State Guardsman stood in the foyer sporting a bored expression. He didn't even look at Jack when he entered. Jack swallowed hard and approached the reception desk, behind which sat a cute brunette he knew well.

"How's it going, Maggie?" Jack rummaged around in his pocket. He pulled out a cigarette lighter and placed it on the counter. "I got you that lighter."

"Oh, thanks! I didn't think you'd remember." Her eyes lit up. "Did you have a good time in Vegas?"

"It was great until the Hoover Dam got attacked." Jack pulled out his wallet and extracted his credit card.

"Yeah, isn't it terrible? Those poor people." Her

expression darkened. "I've organized your normal room, but I'm going to need to register you."

Jack frowned. "What do you mean?"

She jerked her head toward the guardsman and then lifted a piece of paper. "New rules. Everyone on this list has to go through enhanced check-in. You're on the list. I'm sorry."

Jack looked at the list. It contained names, occupations and contact details. He laughed at the simplicity of it all. On the back of the huge data trawl that the National Security Agency had been conducting over the past few decades, FEMA had clearly been able to produce a list of people it was interested in keeping track of. As a prominent journalist, he was a prime target for such treatment, though he did wonder how far the list extended.

"Okay, let's get on with it." He gave her a small smile. It wasn't her fault. "What do I need to do to be able to park my head on the pillow?"

Maggie smiled. "Oh, just the usual. But we've also been instructed to take copies of your license and all of your credit cards."

It took about ten minutes for Jack to fill in the paperwork and hand over every piece of ID he possessed. He shook his head as he took the elevator up – he had a bad feeling about where this was all heading. When society started to muzzle and track journalists, bad things tended to follow. He'd seen it in conflict zones overseas, but he'd never expected to see it in the United States.

Once he reached his room, he tossed the duffel bag onto the bed and pulled out his cell phone. He searched through his contacts until he found the name he was after: Celeste. He stared at it for a few long seconds, not sure that he wanted to make the call, and then pressed the green button. He put the phone to his ear and waited for what seemed like an eternity for her to answer.

"Hi Jack." Her voice was cold. "I think I hear from my dead grandmother more than you."

"I deserve that, but it's good to hear your voice." During the time he'd spent dealing with Erin's funeral, setting up the website and working in Syria, they'd barely spoken. He'd hoped she'd understand his need for distance, but clearly she'd taken it personally. He couldn't blame her. They'd gone through hell together, and as much as he'd needed space, it wasn't hard to imagine her needing something different. And he'd left her out in the cold.

Her sigh was drawn out. "What do you want, Jack?"

"I've just checked into my hotel and it seems there's a whole lot of shit that comes attached to being a journalist now. I wanted to make sure you're okay and let you know."

"It's happening here too, Jack." There was a pause. "There's New York State Guard troops on the streets. They're at Penn Station, Central Park, Yankee Stadium – you name it."

So it was happening all over America. It was amazing how quickly the executive orders were being implemented. The announcement had only been made four hours ago but already the troops were in the streets, the monitoring was in place and the tendrils of FEMA were expanding to embrace all of society.

"I reckon they've had this drawn up for a while." He sat on the edge of the bed with a sigh. "It's low key for the moment – dudes with rifles – but I wonder what comes next."

"It gets worse, Jack. The *Standard* offices got a visit from some FEMA employees an hour or so ago, explaining our place in the new world order."

"Oh?" He lay back on the bed, closed his eyes and did his best to imagine that she was in the room with him. He didn't dare say that though.

"Yeah. They basically told us to continue working, but

that all stories must be submitted for approval prior to publication."

Jack was appalled. "Did Peter go for it?"

"Don't know. We haven't got a response from the company yet, but it's hard to see them resisting."

Jack couldn't picture it either – the company was likely to toe the line even with Peter Weston in charge. EMCorp had been through too much in the past few years to put up much of a fight. The company was traumatized and the shareholders were jumpy. Any journalists that strayed from the strict conditions were probably on their own.

"Just keep your head down, Celeste. This is a dangerous situation. Stay out of it."

"Oh, I plan to." She laughed softly. "I've had my turn at the hero game."

Jack felt the same way, deep down. A year ago he'd have been outraged by all of this, but he'd rocked the system enough and had the scars to prove it. The trauma both Celeste and Jack had suffered during the war with China and at the hands of Michelle Dominique would be a long time healing. It probably also gave them a free pass to sit out of this battle.

"How are you doing, Celeste?"

"Alright. Busy. You should be here, Jack."

"I can't." He ended the call.

MARIPOSA FELT STRANGE, seated on a plastic chair on the grass of a high school football field while, in the bleachers, a few thousand people were gathered for a FEMA briefing about the executive orders. The same briefing was taking place in thousands of locations across the country. They were also being broadcast on television, radio and the internet. She wondered if the other briefings had the same feeling of tension as this one. She could feel the silent fury emanating from the mass of people as a Chicago Police Department lieutenant finished his briefing on the changes to law and order in the city. As he sat, there was silence from the crowd.

Mariposa tapped her lapel microphone to make sure it was on, then stood up and walked around the table. She wanted to project an air of calm and impress on these people that FEMA wasn't the enemy, talking from behind a desk. Following the police officer who'd laid down the law about curfew and potential punishments was a tough gig, but she needed to show them that FEMA were the guarantors of security, prosperity and order during this extraordinary time. As she moved toward the crowd, the State Guard troops and Chicago PD officers providing security tensed up, apparently uncomfortable with her proximity to the crowd.

She raised her hands, palms up. "Our final briefing concerns the impact on business. In short, we need to balance the maintenance of private enterprise with protecting essential services, social order and consumers. For the vast majority of you this will mean no change. You'll be able to run your businesses and make a profit."

She felt like a liar. The changes that had been announced and the restrictions to movement and activity would affect everyone. For most the changes were minimal, except for enhanced security and some restriction on accessing goods and services. But for business, the impact was enormous. Though there was no sense in causing panic before the measures were fully implemented, she was sure there'd be plenty of that anyway.

"However, for the minority of you involved in the production, distribution and retailing of certain goods and for those of you delivering essential services, there will be some changes. For starters, there will be price controls to protect consumers and prevent profiteering, along with random audits to ensure good conduct."

Her last few words were drowned out entirely as the stands exploded with outrage. She waited patiently, her hands clasped in front of her. The security detail inched forward slightly but kept their cool for the time being, though she noticed a few hands on weapons. The noise from the crowd started to subside after a minute or so, until a grossly obese man in the front of the bleachers got to his feet. His face was flushed red.

She knew what was coming and tried to cut him off. "There'll be time for questions at the end of the sessions, sir. We'd ask that—"

"Just who the fuck do you think you are, lady?" The man's voice was like rolling thunder. "This is America. I'll run my business however I like."

Mariposa did her best to keep calm, but she was scared. The security detail didn't reassure her. "I'm here to explain the changes, sir, and—"

He interrupted again. "Explain them, huh? You're going to cripple my business for no reason. Chicago hasn't even been attacked!"

Mariposa narrowed her eyes. She'd been briefed on the executive orders along with the rest of FEMA, but hadn't expected the changes to be so drastic. The outrage in the community was understandable. She felt some of the same reservations as the people in the crowd were expressing, but she trusted Richard Hall to get it right. "Let me be clear—"

Another man stood and interrupted her. "Oh, shove your bureaucratic bullshit, lady."

Mariposa needed to act. She couldn't allow this anger to overflow. She turned and looked at the police lieutenant, who gave a slight nod. Without warning, the State Guard troopers and local police stepped forward and raised their weapons. The men who'd been protesting stammered and then stopped speaking entirely. A stunned silence fell over the crowd. Peace at the end of a barrel. It had come to that.

"Let me be clear. These changes have been enacted across America until the attacks stop and order can be restored." She stepped forward and stopped a few feet away from the bleachers. "You don't have the ability to opt out. You'll comply or the police will shutter your business. Resist further and you'll be locked up."

She waited. The resistance was still there, but the appearance of guns had pushed it beneath the surface, hidden behind muttered comments and shaking heads. She couldn't shift the feeling that FEMA was trying to achieve something that was nearly impossible – bringing Americans to heel. But even though she didn't like it, she knew that it was the only way to stop the attacks.

She took a few steps back and walked toward the table as the roving microphones found the first person wishing to ask a question. An elderly woman stood and started to speak. Mariposa was worried she'd miss the question, given how much her hands were shaking under the table, but she caught the gist of it. As she started to answer, she hoped again that this was all worth it.

She hoped that Richard Hall knew what he was doing.

4

The President has declared a state of emergency and enacted a number of executive orders. The orders grant FEMA emergency powers over critical infrastructure and normal civil liberties. FEMA is well prepared to respond to this new demand with the support of its State Guard colleagues. All citizens, businesses and media organizations are encouraged to check FEMA.gov to learn what the new restrictions mean for them.

Federal Emergency Management Agency
News Release

C allum lifted his canteen to his mouth and drank deeply.

It had been a hell of a couple of days since American life had been turned on its head. For Callum it had been even worse. He'd had to drop his day job for full-time State Guard deployment and had spent the last few days as a glorified security guard as FEMA put the changes in place. Callum had been deployed with a handful of guardsmen to Bartlett, Illinois – a postage stamp–sized town of about 40 000 people.

This took the cake though. He was standing with Mark Pettine and Todd Bowles by their Humvee, carbines at the ready, as the local liquor store opened for the day. A small queue had already formed in front of the store. People must be stocking up, given liquor stores could only open twice per week. But as the queue formed he could feel a strange buzz from the crowd. Tension. Anger.

"This blows, Cal." Bowles ran a hand through his hair. "Where the fuck else in the world would you need guys with carbines covering a liquor store?"

"Russia?" Callum shrugged. "It's because they had some trouble here last time they opened. The locals just need to get used to their booze being rationed."

"At least we didn't draw duty patrolling the old folks' home." Pettine laughed as he leaned against the Humvee.

Callum groaned. Since the FEMA controls had been enacted, it was the medium and small towns of America that had experienced the most trouble. The cities had enough guardsmen and police to keep the peace, but in towns like this there was usually only the cops and, if they were lucky, a small State Guard contingent to keep an eye on everything. It had boiled over on a couple of occasions already.

"Show time." Pettine stood at his full height, one hand on the barrel of his carbine. "Let's see how this goes."

Callum nodded grimly as the door opened and the owner stepped out. They watched in silence as the man explained that, under orders of FEMA, purchase of beer was being restricted to one six-pack and purchase of cigarettes to one packet. Callum winced when he heard that the sale of spirits was being restricted entirely on the weekend. That sure was one way to win hearts and minds.

The collective mood of the crowd seemed to change

in seconds. Callum estimated that there were forty people in the line, ready to pounce on the booze for the hour that the shop was open. But as the owner finished speaking the crowd started to get vocal, jeering at the owner and shuffling forward. Callum sighed, walked to the back of the Humvee and opened the trunk. He dug around in the back, found the megaphone and turned it on.

He winced as the megaphone gave a squeal, then raised it to his mouth. "This is the Illinois State Guard. Stand down immediately."

His order seemed to have no impact. The crowd surged forward, pelting the shopfront with whatever they had at hand. Then, as if in slow motion, a member of the crowd reached into his jacket and pulled out a small pistol. Callum didn't have time to raise his own weapon before the gunman fired two shots. He glanced sideways at Bowles and Pettine, who had their carbines up.

"Firearm!" Bowles fired his carbine as the shopkeeper fell. "Put him down!"

The gunman was felled by the rubber rounds fired by his friends. Callum knew that rubber rounds had an equal chance of dispersing the crowd or enraging them further – he'd seen both reactions in Fallujah. As Bowles and Pettine moved forward slowly, Callum reached up to his vest for his radio.

"Command, this is Watkins. We've got a riot at our post. Shots fired. Requesting support."

The response was nearly instant. "Watkins, this is Command. There's no support nearby."

Callum couldn't believe what he was hearing. The command post had oversight of all FEMA operations for miles around and that was the best they could do? He found it nearly as hard to believe as rioting over restricted consumption of beer and smokes. But he had a job to do.

He joined Bowles and Pettine and started to move forward, raising his carbine and firing into the crowd.

As he'd feared, the rubber rounds did little to dim the outrage of the crowd. Some people scattered and ran, but others surged towards the liquor store and trampled the body of the owner. The majority of the crowd was now inside the store, taking what they pleased from the shelves and making a mess in the process. But a few had forgotten about the booze and turned on Callum's squad with firearms visible.

"Stand down!" He hoped the crowd could hear him over the noise. They didn't stop. "Stand down! Now!"

It didn't work. This was going to hell quickly and would get worse if his team came under fire. As one member of the crowd raised his weapon, Callum crouched to one knee, aimed at the center of the man's chest and squeezed the trigger. The man staggered, but he didn't drop his weapon. Until Callum hit him with two more.

The crowd surged closer, and Callum could feel cold sweat on his back. He fired at another target, a man leaning down to pick up a bottle. Then another, a woman who snarled at them like some sort of horrible dog as she pelted a rock at them. He aimed at her and fired, but his weapon clicked. His carbine was empty.

"I'm out!" Callum looked left to Pettine.

Pettine nodded. "Me too."

He glanced back to the woman, who was leaning down to pick up the gun the other man had dropped. Callum made his decision. He was out of rubber rounds, and there was only one other way to end the riot. He ejected the magazine and loaded the real thing. As his finger caressed the trigger, he shouted for the woman to stop.

Then Pettine's carbine barked from right next to him, and the woman dropped to the ground, a small mist of blood escaping her head. The few left in the crowd slackened, as if they couldn't believe what they'd seen. More shots rang out. Once the rioters realised what was happening, the attack was reversed. They screamed and ran as one.

The others inside the store took a second or two longer to figure it out, but once they did they scrambled to follow the pack, running from the store. Given the blood now flowing onto the road, Callum didn't much care that a bunch of the looters had cases of beer and bottles of booze tucked under their arms.

Callum and his team immediately ceased fire, though they held their positions. After a minute, there was nobody in the parking lot except the dead and the wounded, who writhed on the ground in agony. From what he could tell, there were two dead – the shopkeeper and the woman – and six wounded.

It was an enormous toll for a riot at a suburban liquor store. He turned to his team. "Keep the live rounds loaded in case they come back."

"I think that's the least of our problems." Bowles shook his head. "CO is going to freak."

Callum didn't want to think about that, though he didn't see any alternative to what they'd done. "We'll need some cops and ambulances."

Pettine nodded and then looked down at the corpse of the shop owner. "Poor bastard."

Bowles glanced inside the shop. "I'll drink to that."

MARIPOSA HATED THE CHIME, and whoever had designed it. As she stood and stretched her muscles, she questioned the need to have it ring again and again to call staff to a meeting. She thought an email would do the trick just as well, but the hourly five-minute standup staff meetings had become routine since the commencement of the executive orders.

"Come on, Murray." Mariposa leaned over the cubicle partition, where her colleague was still typing away. "Let's get this over with."

He sighed as he stood. "Yeah, my doctor usually says the same about my prostate exam."

She smiled but didn't speak as they gathered with about a hundred other staff in the meeting space. Nothing better illustrated the growth in staff numbers at the FEMA Area V Clark Street offices since the attacks and the declaration of the state of emergency. They'd grown from 160 staff to nearly 500, and their office was barely large enough for everyone.

Alan Benning, the new director, held up his hand. "Okay, thanks everyone. I want to keep this one short. You guys know the drill."

Under the standing agenda, Mariposa was first to report. She cleared her throat. "The city is quiet. There's only been a few minor reports in the last twenty minutes."

A few of the others gave small nods or smiles of encouragement. Mariposa and her team had been handed the toughest job of all: coordinating the control orders in the city of Chicago. It had gone fairly smoothly and the systems they'd long had prepared had held up to the real-life test. Chicago was probably safer than ever, given the number of cops and State Guard troops deployed throughout the city. There had been a few scuffles and arrests, but things had settled down.

Once she was finished her report, she listened as the other team managers reported in. There were no major issues. The medium-sized cities and larger towns were less secure but not too bad. Public utilities and transportation were secure and operating. Though the media was fidgety and a few organizations had rebelled, examples had been made of a few high-profile holdouts and most were toeing the line. All in all, the entirety of FEMA Area V was looking okay.

Benning looked toward Murray. "How's our distribution network looking?"

Murray smiled. "No trouble. The only angst has been around the vice rations."

Mariposa winced. Lost in the fine detail of the FEMA crackdown had been a strict reduction in the amount of booze and cigarettes people were allowed to buy. She didn't really see the sense in it. Given people were restricted from going out after midnight, she saw no harm in letting people cool off at home with a bottle. As it was, there were a lot of bored people unable to go out and without much to help them loosen up at home. It was a bad recipe.

"Okay, great." Benning knocked his hand on the table. "See you all next hour. Until then, let me know if anything comes up."

Mariposa started to walk away when a junior staffer ran into the middle of the gathering. "Hey! There's been a shooting in Bartlett. It's the State Guard."

Noise erupted in the room. Mariposa looked over at Murray, who gave a shrug and stood in silence. She watched as Benning held his hands up and did his best to be heard. A shooting was a dramatic escalation on their patch of turf and she found herself shaking at the thought. There could just as easily have been a similar incident at one of the community briefings she'd led.

"Everyone calm down." Benning finally managed to be heard above the noise. "What happened?"

"Some State Guard put down a riot at a liquor store. There's a few people dead." The junior looked like he was about to cry. "It's all over the media, despite the bans."

Mariposa's eyes widened. While the media had been told in no uncertain terms what was acceptable to report, the restrictions clearly hadn't sunk in fully. While other FEMA areas had experienced more trouble than Area V had, as far as she knew this was the first incident anywhere in America in which the authorities had had to put down dissent with lethal force. Mariposa felt a lump rise in her throat. The game had just changed.

"Okay, we'll need to handle this. You all know the drill." Benning looked at the manager responsible for media relations. "Get your dogs under control, Jim."

The team dispersed but Mariposa waited behind, a million thoughts running through her head. Though things had been relatively calm to date, she had no doubt that people were being suppressed, rather than carried along with the changes until the attacks were dealt with. If people were pushed so hard that they resisted and started to die, things had gone too far. She was about to move back to her desk, but found her feet anchored to the floor.

She swallowed and then approached the director. "Alan, do you have a second?"

"Sure." He gave a weary smile. "What can I do for you?"

She leaned on the edge of the giant table. "I've got some concerns, Alan. I think some of the changes we're trying to force are unnecessary, attacks or not."

"Come on." Benning reached up to massage his temples. "I've – we've got enough going on here without an attack of the morals, don't we?"

Mariposa wavered. She was not usually the one to speak out, but she felt she had an obligation to voice her concerns. "I don't agree. If we keep squeezing, there's going to be more issues that bubble up. I think we need to let things settle, not agitate them even more."

He sighed. "Things have been going fine here, Mariposa. But don't assume that's the case across the whole country. The south is ablaze. Let's keep our patch quiet."

"But—"

"No, Mariposa." Benning's eyes locked onto hers. "This is above your pay grade. Do your job and leave the rest to me. If you still want it, that is."

She wanted to fight, but Benning's threat was clear. She thought of Juan, at home with the sitter she could barely afford despite all the overtime. If nothing else, she had to make sure he was looked after. Others, more important than her, had put the country on this path. Who was she to argue? She sagged. "Okay, Alan."

He exhaled loudly and his posture softened. "I don't like running roughshod like this, but we've all got jobs to do. Go do yours."

She nodded and walked toward her desk with her head downcast, all fight gone from inside of her. She was still worried about the direction things were heading in, but felt that she'd pushed her luck about as far as she could with her boss. She sat down in front of her computer and reviewed her emails, which never seemed to cease. After a few emails she glanced at her phone, picked it up and dialed. It rang for a moment before being answered.

She mustered all the authority she could. "I want extra caution by city security forces. I only want live rounds in the hands of the rapid response squads."

She waited for the confirmation then hung up. She smiled. If there was no way she could impact the direction of the entire organization, she could at least make sure that the zone she was responsible for didn't go to hell. For now, she'd have to be satisfied that no police officer or State Guardsman inside the Chicago city limits would be firing off live rounds without her knowing, given the rapid response squads were under her direct command.

There was nothing else she could do.

～

RICHARD INDICATED, turned the wheel slightly and eased to
a stop outside his home. As he killed the ignition, he looked
out of the window and stared with pride at his house – a
fashionable and perfectly restored colonial in the heart of
Georgetown. After another second of indulgence he
grabbed his briefcase from the passenger seat and climbed
out of the car. He locked the vehicle and crossed the
sidewalk.

"Evening, Administrator." The Metropolitan Police
Department officer standing at the bottom of the stairs
greeted him the same way as always.

Richard stopped at the base of the stairs. "Good
evening, Frank. How are the wife and kids?"

The officer smiled beneath his cap. "They're great,
Administrator."

Richard fumbled with his keys. "Good. I'll be staying in
for the night."

"Okay, sir."

Richard nodded. He climbed the stairs, unlocked his
door, entered the house and closed the door behind him.
He knew that the police guard was probably unnecessary,
but since the attacks had started all department heads in
Washington had been given similar protection. From
tomorrow, he'd also have an armed driver picking him up
every day. He'd miss driving to the office himself.

He keyed in the code to the alarm and then pressed
another button on the same console. On cue, the curtains
started to close, the climate control fired up, some of the
lighting came on and soft classical music started to play. He
locked the door and hung his keys on a hook beside it, then
walked through to the open-plan kitchen and living area.

He paused at the entry to the living area and smiled as
he took in the scene before him: a large corkboard that
covered two whole walls in his living room, which he
otherwise kept sparse. He'd started the corkboard years

ago. He couldn't remember when exactly, except to say that it was at the point when he'd started to feel like America was off the rails and careening out of control. It had been an outlet for frustrations he could share with nobody.

But it had become more than that. Since that moment, he'd watched the leadership of the country flounder and fail, being all too easily led by the nose or bought off or sidetracked. Instead of being a diligent servant of pragmatic governments, Republican or Democrat, he'd instead watched with dismay as good public administration made way for partisan bickering, a deadlocked Congress and federal debt and deficit nearing catastrophe.

One full wall of the board was covered in a color-coded history of the past few years – news clippings, FEMA briefings and a map. It told a story of American dysfunction. Many of the more recent clippings were the fault of Michelle Dominique and the Foundation for a New America. He'd hoped that the near miss America had experienced with that lunatic would recalibrate the system, but many of the same problems remained.

As the years passed and as Richard entered the twilight of his career, he'd come to realize that his hopes for a leader to emerge in the mould of Washington, Lincoln, Roosevelt or the other greats were false. No great politician was coming to wash away the filth that was clogging the gears of effective governance. The country just lurched on, served by mediocre government, as it ever gradually approached the precipice.

Once he'd decided he needed to act against – rather than just catalogue – the dysfunction, Richard had tried to make himself available to President Kurzon and, later, President Morris. He'd offered innovative solutions to some of the deadlocks facing the country and his experience in managing disasters should have made him an invaluable support to a president. But he'd been ignored and pigeon-holed as the guy who cleaned up after cyclones.

This had forced him to take matters into his own hands. It had become clear to Richard that if no leader stepped forward, and if the incompetents already in power wouldn't take his help to learn and improve, then something had to give. He'd decided that he could get the country moving on the right track again – if he got the chance. He couldn't do it through election and campaigning, but there were other ways.

No, the answer was seizing control and solving difficult problems, even if those solutions required some extreme measures – restricted freedom, mass surveillance, a compliant media. Only then would the attacks stop. If he achieved that, then history would look upon him kinder than the parade of squatters and incompetents who'd occupied positions of power in recent years. His legacy as a man of supreme integrity and enormous public service would be secure.

He shifted his gaze. The other wall of board featured columns filled with the steps he was taking in clear stages. It had started with months of research into the power he had at his disposal as the Administrator of FEMA, along with the power the position potentially held in the right circumstances. All he'd needed was a catalyst, in the form of the deadly attacks sweeping across the country. He sat on the sofa and stared at the board.

Now events were moving him toward the middle of the board, which featured the steps he'd take to bring order and stability to the governance of America. He'd tried serving incompetents, waiting for the right leader. When that had failed, he'd proactively made himself available to those same incompetents, to steer and guide, but they'd not listened. Now the opportunity had arrived. He'd take more control. He'd solve problems. He'd reshape America. He'd secure his legacy.

He woke with a start and realized that he must have dozed off. He reached up and massaged his temples with his index fingers. He was tired and pushing himself too hard, but saw no choice but to continue on the current path. He'd told nobody else about his plan, trusting others with only enough information to play the role he'd assigned them. With a shake of his head to remove the cobwebs, he rose and made his way into the kitchen.

A glance at the clock made him wince at how late it was. He opened his fridge and took the assigned meal – planned and prepared a week in advance – and heated it up in the microwave, then sat at the table to eat. The food wasn't spectacular, but it was nutritious. He didn't take pleasure from much other than his work, so had no qualms with the bland pumpkin soup. There was nothing wrong with it that some fresh pepper couldn't fix. He ate slowly, taking pleasure in the music playing.

After another glance at the clock, he placed his dishes in the dishwasher and then opened his briefcase. He removed a single news clipping, walked to his board and pinned it to the wall. Satisfied, he started up the stairs to bed. He undressed, hung his suit and placed his dirty laundry in the basket. As he climbed into bed, he reached over to press the button that would turn off all of the lights in the house. He smiled as he closed his eyes.

ACT II

5

In the three months since the executive orders were enacted, the diligence of my staff and the cooperation of the American people have allowed these new powers to be introduced with a minimum of fuss. It is my hope that, for however long they're necessary to ensure security, the restrictions have the minimum possible impact on everyday people going about their lives and make the maximum contribution to our security and wellbeing.

    Richard Hall, FEMA Administrator
    Media statement

Jack's phone buzzed on the table. Unknown caller. He answered as he rushed to finish his bagel and wash it down with the dregs of his coffee. "Jack Emery."

"My name is Omega." The voice on the other end was being scrambled into an electronic mess. Jack swallowed hard and checked nobody was in earshot.

Captain Dan "Omega" Ortiz had been the commander of the squad of Marines that Jack had been embedded with in Afghanistan. Ortiz had saved Jack's life after Jack's exposure of isolated Marine Corps cooperation with a CIA torture operation. Though the full details had remained top secret, Ortiz had earned himself a chest of medals and a promotion and Jack had earned a Pulitzer for the story. If Omega was calling, something was wrong.

"I don't know anyone by that name." Jack was completely deadpan, not wanting to give away that he knew Ortiz to anyone tapping the call. "What can I do for you?"

"A lot. And soon. In the place my kids love." The line went dead.

Jack felt a bit of a buzz. For the three months since the commencement of the executive orders, he'd mostly kept his head down. Jo had flown home to New York and Jack had kept filing stories on his site, which were then purchased by national media. Despite temptation to do otherwise, he'd done the right thing and had everything vetted by the authorities before publishing. Though it grated on him, he had no desire to rock the boat.

Now he wondered what Ortiz had for him. He knew straight away where the meeting point was – Millennium Park. Ortiz had told Jack about the place on a long ride through the desert in Afghanistan. His kids loved the Millennium Dome, he'd said. Luckily Jack was close. He stood, exited the Starbucks and started to walk the few blocks to Millennium Park. He'd be there in a few minutes.

His heart was beating faster and he was uneasy about meeting his friend. Jack knew it was likely that he was being monitored – just as closely as Ortiz, probably, given the effort the other man was going to to avoid scrutiny. But despite the risk, Jack didn't hesitate. He owed Ortiz more than any other man alive and if he said jump, Jack asked how high.

He looked toward the park as he crossed North Michigan Avenue. He could see no sign of danger except for the armed State Guardsman scattered around, which was par for the course these days. He still found the sight of armed men on every second block off-putting. By the time he reached the Millennium Dome it felt like everyone was watching him as he paced back and forth next to it.

"Where is he?" Jack whispered, after he'd waited for about ten minutes. He was feeling as conspicuous as a pink battleship, until he spotted Ortiz approaching.

"Hi Jack." Ortiz held out his hand and sported a wide grin. "You've been busy since I saw you last."

"Yeah, tough gig, saving the world." Jack smiled as he shook the proffered hand and then pulled Ortiz into a hug. Jack was taller, but Ortiz was as solid as a tree trunk.

"I bet." They broke apart. "Good thing this humble one saved your not-so-humble ass."

Jack laughed. "Good to see you, Dan."

"I'm wearing a Cubs hat, in case you haven't noticed. I feel filthy."

"At least you've still got your quarterback good looks. How are you?"

"Just peachy." Ortiz nearly spat the words. "Get my ass shot at fighting for freedom only to find uniforms on the streets over here. I can't even buy a bottle of booze!"

"At least you can still work." Jack snorted. "I have to submit to Uncle Sam before I'm allowed to publish."

Ortiz laughed. "Pussy. What happens if you don't?"

"I'll get locked up. A journo I know tried that one on. Turns out FEMA isn't joking." Jack kept his voice low. "So what's going on in the world of the US Marine Corps?"

Ortiz shrugged. "Oh, about the same. The grunts are confined to base full time and the NCOs and officers can't scratch their ass without approval."

Jack was slightly surprised by this. Though he knew the troops on the streets weren't regular military – or even National Guard – it shocked him that the military was apparently on lockdown along with the rest of society. The situation stank, and Jack wasn't sure if there was any hope of a resolution any time soon. Though the attacks had slowed, they hadn't stopped entirely.

"So what can I do for you, Dan?" Jack looked around, paranoid they were being watched. "You've taken an almighty risk."

Ortiz shrugged. "Look, these pricks are clamping down on the country that I fought for. I want you to get the word out. There's regular citizens resisting all over the country, and even a couple of smaller military units, but they're isolated and being picked off by the State Guard."

Jack wasn't surprised. You couldn't just turn America into an armed camp and not have problems, but the government had kept news of the trouble quiet. "Where?"

"I need your promise that you'll report it."

Jack hesitated. "I can't promise anything, Dan. You know what I'm risking."

Ortiz smiled, a clear twinkle in his eyes. "You think I'd bust my way off base wearing this shit to meet with your sorry ass if I didn't have something decent for you?"

"Maybe?" Jack let it hang.

"Take this." Ortiz rummaged through the tote bag that he carried and held out a manila folder. "It's all the detail you'll need to cause at least a little bit of heartburn."

"How'd you get it?" Jack didn't take the folder right away.

Ortiz shrugged. "You don't need to know how. But it shows there's a bit happening across the country."

Jack looked at the folder for a few long seconds then let out a long sigh as he grabbed it. He owed Ortiz his life. "I'll do it. But I'm not sure it'll work."

"Just do your best." Ortiz gave a toothy smile. "It's no fun being a passive son of a bitch anyway, is it?"

Jack laughed at that thought for a long while as Ortiz

turned and walked away. As his friend disappeared into the crowd, Jack mused that if he had any sense in the world, he'd keep within the boundaries – as he had for the last few months – and toss the folder in the nearest bin. But Jack Emery wasn't known for his sense. It's why he kept getting dragged into warzones and conspiracies.

ONE WATCHED through her binoculars like a patient hunter stalking prey. At this late hour, the FEMA distribution center was quiet. They'd watched it all day and it had been a hive of activity, with trucks coming and going. At night, however, there was little except silence and shadows. Just the way she liked it. She smiled as she swept her gaze across the entire facility one last time. A chain-link fence topped with razor wire surrounded the facility, which was lit up by floodlights. The only way in – or out – was through one of three gates, each guarded by a pair of armed State Guard troopers. Inside the facility, another handful of security personnel strolled around with no particular routine.

She lowered the binoculars with a smile. The security looked tough, but she knew better. For such a critical facility, it had some of the slackest security she'd ever seen. This would be easier than taking on the student police at MIT – the easiest job she'd had in months. She looked to her left. Three other members of her team were prone in the dirt, alert for any threat and ready for action. Positioned further away, on either side of the base and out of sight, Five and Six would provide sniper support. She smiled. Though it was a pleasure to command them, dealing with such talented people made her feel a little bit redundant sometimes.

"Everyone, confirm ready."

It took only a second for confirmations to come in over her earpiece.

"Okay, cut it."

The floodlights cut out instantly. Though from this distance she couldn't hear the inevitable alarmed shouts from the security, she could imagine the carnage. Within moments a few tiny pinpricks of light started to illuminate the darkness as the security turned on their flashlights – a poor substitute for the floodlights' angry yellow illumination.

One lowered the goggles that had been resting on her head, taking a second to adjust to the night vision before giving the order to proceed. One and her team moved low and fast across the flat grassland that led to the distribution facility, making a beeline straight for the closest gate. She knew they'd be close to invisible in the darkness.

When they were a hundred yards out, One held up a clenched fist. Looking through his large scope, Five would see her signal and radio Six, and together they'd begin the count.

Three Mississippi.

One raised her carbine as she approached the guardhouse. Thanks to the night-vision goggles, her target was as clear as the sun.

Two Mississippi.

Another target was on the periphery of her gun sights, but she couldn't think about him. She had to trust that her unit mates would do their job while she did hers.

One Mississippi.

She slowed and took smaller steps. The target filled her sights. Despite the blackout, things seemed calm. If they'd been spotted, the base would be a hell of a lot busier.

One squeezed the trigger as the count hit zero in her head. At the same time, she heard the dull thud of suppressed weaponry from nearby and the booming reports of the rifles used by Five and Six – the sound traveling slower than the death it signified. Both of the State Guard troops in One's assigned gatehouse fell. Five and Six were taking care of the other gates. On cue, she heard another pair of thunderclaps.

"Gate A clear." She spoke as she moved inside the gatehouse, kicking away the rifle lying next to one of the corpses. Neither guard was moving.

"B clear." Five's voice was soft.

"C..." Six sounded unsure, then she heard another boom. "C clear."

"Commence phase two." With the gates assaulted simultaneously, she didn't envy the four State Guardsman still alive inside the distribution center: they would be confused, scared shitless and know they were outgunned. One moved outside the gatehouse to where Three and Four had already cut through the chain-link gate. With the power out there was no other way to open it. She waved her hand and the three others followed her through the hole.

They moved quickly through the distribution center, weapons raised and covering each other. She'd hoped that Five and Six would be able to reach out and touch the four remaining State Guard troops, but the maze of shipping containers would likely block their line of sight beyond the gates. Unless the snipers received a bit of luck, her ground team would have to deal with the final defenders up close and personal. It didn't bother her, it just made the situation a bit messier.

She followed Four around a corner, then ducked instinctively as a weapon barked from somewhere. She heard a grunt in her earpiece as she crouched onto the hard concrete, her eyes searching for the shooter. The shooter's mistake was peering up to see if he'd hit anything – in her night-vision goggles his head was easy to spot above the wooden crates he was using for cover. She put a round straight through his skull, then stood and scrambled to where Four had gone down.

"Two, Three, keep going." She crouched beside Four. "You okay?"

The other man nodded, though he gripped at his chest and was sucking in quick breaths. "Took one on the Kevlar, but I'm good to go."

"Okay." She nodded and they followed Two and Three. She rounded a corner and discovered they'd put down the remaining State Guardsmen.

"Commence phase three." She was moving as she gave the order. "I want the explosives planted and ready in four minutes."

The team split and she jogged toward the base of the first container stack. She let her carbine hang from its strap as she removed her backpack, threw it on the ground and unzipped it. Inside were enough explosives to land her in prison for several lifetimes. She pulled one of the compact bombs from the bag and secured it to the side of the container. Once she was satisfied, she raised the small antenna and flicked the switch on the device. A green light glowed.

She picked up the bag and moved on to the next stack. The bombs her team was busy planting were a mix of high explosives and incendiary devices, so whatever didn't blow would hopefully burn. They wouldn't destroy the entire facility or even all of the supplies, but they'd make a mess. It was all a small team could do to such a large facility. She was confident the result would be the same: a vital facility crippled, a state short of critical supplies further stretched and a nation stressed.

"Uh, incoming." Five's voice drawled in her ear. "A pair of State Guard Humvees are closing on gate B. They're a few minutes out."

She stopped in her tracks. They'd planned to be gone

before any reinforcements arrived. The nearest State Guard units should have been over an hour away, and local law enforcement wouldn't respond to such a dangerous situation. It was a problem. Given the amount of explosives they'd had to haul along, the team had packed lightly: they certainly weren't geared up for a prolonged fire fight with any sort of capable foe. She considered her options for a moment and then decided.

"Okay, Five, Six, stay cool for now. The rest of you finish up, then find some cover just inside gate B and await my order. You've got one minute."

She planted her last bomb.

CALLUM DRUMMED his hands on the back of the passenger seat as the Humvee raced along the road. Pettine was at the wheel, singing along to the song at the top of his voice, while Bowles simply laughed and shook his head. The newest addition to their small squad – a small guy named Tony Harrington – didn't seem to know what to make of the situation, so simply smiled and cradled his carbine. A second Humvee followed them.

They were all in good spirits considering the lack of sleep they'd all had. The order had come through that afternoon to redeploy from Bartlett, where Callum had spent three uneventful months since the liquor store shooting. Their new assignment was to guard one of the large FEMA distribution centers. They were nearly there, but it was almost midnight. Callum knew he'd be paying for the lack of a full night's sleep for days.

The car started to slow. Pettine turned his head. "Hey, Cal, there's something wrong."

Callum sat higher, leaned to his left and looked through the windshield. Up ahead the Humvee's headlights brightened the gatehouse of the distribution facility. It should have been flooded with light, even at this hour, and there should have been a pair of State Guard troops looking to share a joke before they were relieved. Instead, all they saw was a closed chain-link gate and an empty hut with blood sprayed all over the glass.

"Heads up guys, I'm going to call it in." Callum held his carbine in one hand and reached for the radio with the other. "Command this is Mobile Four."

There was a brief pause before the radio squawked back. "Go, Four."

"We've reached Distribution Center Echo. The lights are out, nobody's around and there's blood. No visible bodies but they can't be far away. Any info for me?"

"Standby."

Callum placed the radio handset on the seat beside him and checked his weapon. The carbine was cradled between his legs, barrel facing the floor. Callum ejected then reloaded the magazine and checked the safety. Around him, Bowles and Harrington had their weapons ready, while Pettine had one hand on the wheel and the other on his sidearm. Callum hoped that the troops in the other Humvee were ready as well.

The radio crackled. "Mobile Four, we've no reports of power outages at that facility and the guards haven't reported any problems."

Callum tensed. "Well, I'm staring at a problem. They haven't reported anything because they're most likely all dead."

"Move in with Mobile Three to investigate. We're routing Mobile Seven, Mobile Twelve and Air One to you." The voice on the other end was dispassionate.

"ETA?"

"Unknown. Will advise. The facility is critical. Repeat order: Move in with Mobile Three to investigate."

Callum nearly managed to mask his fury. Nearly. "We'll ride into the darkness. See if you can do anything about the power situation?"

"Affirmative, Mobile Four. Command out."

Callum looked around the vehicle. In the dim interior light he could see enough on the faces of his squad – his friends – to know what they were thinking. None of them had signed on for hot combat or for driving into an ambush, but both seemed on the cards in the next few minutes if whoever had attacked the compound was still around. FEMA taking over had changed everything: they'd gone from being glorified militia to soldiers again, eight men driving into the unknown.

The radio sounded again. "Mobile Four? What's the play?"

Callum picked up the radio again. "Mobile Three, we've been told to check it out."

"Affirmative, Four. We'll follow you in. Stay frosty."

Callum didn't bother replying. He returned the radio to its position. "Hit the gas."

Pettine nodded and the vehicle edged forward, headlights showing the way. Callum turned his head and saw the second Humvee start to move forward as well. Though they provided some protection from small arms fire, he felt very vulnerable. He had two Humvees and eight men to secure an enormous facility against god knew what. He didn't like the odds.

The chain-link gate buckled then gave way under the pressure of the Humvee's bullbar. Callum winced at the high-pitched squeal the gate gave as it shifted off its railings, then the loud crash as it crumpled in a useless heap on the ground. If the bad guys didn't know they were at the base before, they certainly did now. Pettine hit the gas and the Humvee moved inside.

They drove in, overlooked by shipping containers and

enveloped by shadows. Callum leaned forward, peering desperately out of the windshield for any sign of activity. A hundred yards inside, they rounded a shallow corner and found themselves in a large, open area used to house trucks. In the middle of the yard lay two State Guard troops in duty fatigues, unmoving on the ground.

"Fucking hell!" Bowles pounded his armrest as the vehicle ground to a halt. "They're dead, Callum."

Callum summed up the scene. It wasn't good. There was no sign of the attackers, even if they were still here, and limitless cover for a concealed foe. He had no tactical advantage and found it hard to believe that command had ordered them in, given the situation, but an order was an order and they had a job to do. He resisted the urge to tell Pettine to turn the Humvee around and get the hell out.

"Callum, we've got to pull back." Pettine's hands gripped the wheel. "We should wait for some light and some help."

Callum ignored Harrington's silent nod. "Our orders are to investigate. More than likely whoever made this mess is long gone. Probably just wanted some alcohol."

"And managed to take down ten armed guards and the entire base power grid to do so?" Pettine scoffed. "Come on, Cal."

"I don't want to hear it." Callum gripped the door handle of the Humvee. "We need to get out of these tin cans. Let's go."

Callum opened the door and climbed out of the vehicle. After a moment all eight Guardsmen stood outside the vehicles, scanning the surroundings. Then he heard a scream, followed by the impact of rounds hitting metal. Though Callum could see muzzle flashes from four different locations, he couldn't hear the shots being fired. It was as if he and his team were surrounded by phantoms.

He shouted at his team to find cover as he reviewed the

situation: his foe had suppressed weapons, good visibility – probably aided by night vision – and excellent firing positions overlooking vulnerable and lightly protected targets. It all added up to a hopeless situation. Callum ducked low and started to move around to the back of the first Humvee, which seemed safe for now.

As he moved, more rounds knocked angry welts into the door he'd been in front of just a moment ago. A few of his men raised their weapons and returned fire in the general direction of the muzzle flashes. As he slid down against the rear of the Humvee, in the dim light provided Callum could see Harrington writhing in pain, Bowles sprawled on the ground and members of Mobile Three similarly placed. Pettine was crawling toward him.

All this carnage, and he hadn't fired a shot. Callum screamed out for the last man from Mobile Three to hustle, then rose from his haunches and fired his weapon to cover him. It was no good. The man took a round to the head and dropped. Callum cursed, ducked his head around the corner of the Humvee and fired into the darkness. He may as well be firing spitballs at a tank, though, because each round was met with a withering response.

He inched behind the vehicle again. The only consolation was that they didn't seem to have the vehicle completely surrounded. It might let him hold out for long enough for reinforcements to arrive. But that would just mean another eight dead. He ejected his magazine and replaced it with his only spare. He slammed it home as Pettine slid down alongside him. His face was covered in blood, probably from one of their colleagues.

"You got any spare magazines, Cal?" Pettine's expression was grim.

"Nope. Last one."

Pettine cursed, threw down his carbine and drew his pistol. "Seen Bowles?"

"He's dead, Mark. We could try to make a run for it?"

Pettine wiped his brow. "You're kidding. We're done, my friend. Been nice know—"

Callum ducked down instinctively as rounds pounded the back of the Humvee. The attackers had shifted position. As Pettine gripped his throat, Callum raised his weapon and fired blindly into the night, without even the headlights of the Humvee to guide him. He emptied his magazine then started to draw his pistol, but didn't get the chance. He screamed in pain as a round hit him in the foot, then another in the chest. He fell backward.

Despite the pain, he could feel the cold concrete against his skin. He tried to move but couldn't seem to coordinate his limbs. The blackness of the night had left the stars shining brightly. He wondered if he'd follow Pettine, Bowles and the other members of his team toward one of them.

6

Following the attack on the FEMA distribution center in Illinois, the agency would like to express condolences to the families and friends of the following FEMA staff and State Guard troops, killed while performing their duty: Mark Pettine, Todd Bowles, Tony Harrington, Lamaar Price, John Fitzgerald, Stephen Welles, David Sales, Craig Anderson, Dean Worthington, Daniel Yee and Greg Laselle. The only surviving victim of the attack, Callum Watkins, remains in critical but stable condition in hospital.

Federal Emergency Management Agency
News Release

Jack turned his head to check for cars, thinking that if there was something to be said for an authoritarian crackdown, it was improved traffic. He crossed the street, getting ever further away from his hotel room. He'd spent the days since his meeting with Ortiz frustrated. He'd struggled to resist the allure of the information he'd been given – intelligence reports about a few units in the south going rogue, along with some reports about gun-nut militias. Resistance to FEMA control was a good story.

An hour ago, he'd tossed the folder onto the bed and gone for a walk. He'd made several attempts to circumvent the censorship and anonymously post details of the files he'd been given online, but all had failed spectacularly. He didn't know enough about navigating the darker shadows of the internet to get it out that way, meaning his only choices were to find someone who did or to put his name to the story and submit it for approval.

Jack stopped dead in the middle of the road. There he was again, the man in the green shirt, for the third time in the past half-hour, alongside a less conspicuous and better-dressed female companion. Jack started walking again. Unless the pair was walking as listlessly as he was, there was no explanation that would satisfy him that they weren't on his tail. Though he hadn't broadcast the information yet, maybe the authorities had noticed his attempts and put a tail on him.

He began to snake his way through the city randomly: he turned down a street, entered a shop, did a lap then walked out again. No matter what he tried, they followed. He reached up and wiped the sweat that was starting to bead on his forehead, then turned sharply and stared at his pursuers. The man in the green shirt looked away, but Jack locked eyes with the woman. He knew in a second that they were after him. He needed to get somewhere well populated and try to lose them. He turned and made his way to Navy Pier. It was the best he could come up with under pressure.

Jack entered the building, weaving past dawdling children and families. He looked over his shoulder and couldn't immediately see his pursuers. He tried to lose himself in the food court. Though it was after lunch, there were still enough people milling about to give him a chance. He left the cavernous building next to the *Spirit of Chicago*, a white cruise ship with several rows of windows, then cut left and walked further along the pier. It seemed counterintuitive to corner yourself at the end of a pier when being pursued, but he was counting on that assumption. He smiled with relief.

He walked, slower now, past another pair of cruise ships. He was just starting to think he might have evaded the pair when he looked behind him and saw that horrible green shirt. Jack turned, his anger building up like a tempest. Though the shirt was terrible, the man inside it was a good size. Jack could see no sign of a weapon, but that didn't mean there wasn't one. Even if he was unarmed, Jack doubted he could take the guy. His only chance was escape.

Jack looked around frantically and eyed a tour boat about to depart. He started to walk toward it when the woman stepped into his path. She wore a serious look and had a hand inside her purse. He guessed she had a weapon, but hadn't produced it because there were kids about.

Jack sighed and held up both hands. "I don't want any trouble and I don't want to scare the children. Let's take it easy."

The pair looked at each other, then the man in the green shirt smiled slightly as he spoke. "I don't know what you think is happening here, Jack, but that's not it."

"Well, if it's all the same to you guys, I'm going to get out of here. I've had quite enough of spy versus spy." He started to walk away but the man reached out and grabbed him by the wrist. Jack didn't hesitate. He caught the man's hand and stepped into the hold, twisting behind him and yanking the man's arm up.

Jack was about to ease off, his warning heeded, when the woman had stepped forward and held a flick knife at his throat. "Let go of him."

Jack's eyes widened and he eased off on the pressure slightly. "Get that away or I'm going to break his arm."

"That's worth a slit throat." Her voice was deadpan and her emerald eyes flashed naked fury. "Let go of him."

"If you think you intimidate me, you're sorely mistaken." Jack twisted a little harder, causing lime green to inhale sharply. "Tell me why I shouldn't break his arm."

She took a deep breath, but the knife didn't move an inch. "I can't tell you who we are, not yet, but you need to trust us."

"No, I really don't." Jack applied slightly more pressure.

The man gave a yelp and spoke through gritted teeth. "We're from Guerrilla Radio."

Jack laughed, but he did relax the pressure slightly. Amateurs. "From where?"

"Guerrilla Radio. We're part of the resistance that's forming. We're trying to get the word out, report the truth and support others opposed to FEMA control."

"Using *actual* radios?" Jack released the man's arm. "What sort of name is Guerrilla Radio, anyway? Been listening to a bit too much Rage Against The Machine, guys?"

"We can't tell you much just yet." The woman glared as she lowered her knife. "But it's just a name. We're—"

"Forget it." Jack held up his hands. "I don't care. I shouldn't have asked. Just leave me alone."

The man rubbed his arm. "We saw your report from the Hoover Dam. It must have raised questions."

"We need help." The woman had a hint of desperation in her voice. Jack couldn't figure out her angle. "We need *you*, Jack."

He ignored them, turning away. The last thing he wanted was to be involved in trying to topple the authorities. Battling Michelle Dominique and the Foundation for a New America had nearly cost him his life

– *had* cost the lives of some dear to him. He was uneasy about the control being exercised by FEMA, but he was still a far cry from getting involved in a two-bit resistance movement.

"We've got your friend Simon Hickens helping us." The woman's voice called from behind him, tempting. "He said you're not the sort to walk away."

Jack stopped dead and closed his eyes. First Ortiz now Simon Hickens. She might be lying, but if he was involved it changed things. "Why me?"

Lime green spoke this time. "We admire your work. You need an outlet, we need another reporter. We don't know everything but we know some, and it's critical we find out more. People have started to die. The attacks are just the start. FEMA has started to flex its muscles and enjoys the President's unqualified support."

The woman gave a cheeky smile. "You're too much of a newsman to walk away. I'm Elena Winston. This is Matt Barker. Let's get a beer and you can hear us out."

Jack stood for a long few moments. Every ounce of good sense told him to walk away, but his feet remained rooted in place. Barker had a genuine smile on his face, despite his terrible taste in shirts. Winston intrigued him more. She had a fierceness about her and her name was familiar for some reason, though he couldn't place it.

He turned to her. "I know your name. Where are you from?"

"I was a White House Press Corps reporter for the *Tribune*, but I quit the moment the paper agreed that all stories would go through the FEMA censor."

Jack nodded. At least she was a journalist. "Fine. A beer. And you're paying. And you're also going to use your networks to distribute some info I'm sitting on."

∾

MARIPOSA NURSED her coffee mug with both hands, glad for its warmth and the fact that, with her hands occupied, she was less likely to fidget. Across the table from her sat Alan Benning, eyes glued to his tablet as he swiped and zigged and zagged with his finger, his work never done. They were in one of the few enclosed meeting rooms that had been retained in the cubicle jungle that was the Clark Street home of FEMA Area V Command.

"He's late." Benning didn't look up from his tablet. "His prerogative, I suppose, but hardly the best use of our time, is it?"

Mariposa muttered something to the affirmative. She wasn't in the business of gossiping about her superiors, especially Richard Hall. He was in town and his assistant had organized a meeting with Benning and herself. Now he was late and Benning was irritated. For her own part, she winced at the thought of how much work was building up while she waited here. It just meant more hours in the office and fewer at home with Juan.

Before she could say anything else, Administrator Hall strode into the meeting room. He was an old and foppish-looking man, but his reputation and the power he now held was undeniable. She stood a moment faster than Benning, who'd been distracted by his tablet. Hall gave them a curt nod and stared for just a moment too long at Benning. As she sat back down, Hall took the vacant seat at the head of the table.

He looked up. "Thanks for meeting with me, both of you."

"No problem at all, Administrator. Mariposa and I were just discussing how much of a pleasure it is to be able to show you the great work we—"

Hall held up a hand. "This isn't the time. We've got seventeen dead on your watch. I want to know what happened."

Mariposa was shocked by his bluntness. She looked to Benning, who reached up and stuck a finger between the collar of his shirt and his neck. He pulled, loosening it a bit. It was an obvious gesture, but a mistake. It showed both the administrator and her that he was nervous. Already unimpressed, Hall's eyes narrowed at the delay, as if he was making an assessment of Benning. If Mariposa was a betting woman, she wouldn't wager on it being a positive one.

Mariposa spoke first. "I think there's been a misunderstanding, I look after Chicago. The incident happened—"

Hall glanced at her. "You're here because I want you here. But first I want to know exactly what happened."

Benning finally managed to find his words. "Uh, that one was on me, Administrator. We changed the duty rosters but there was an oversight. The distribution center sent half of their security detail on to the new posting at the correct time, but the changeover was very late. By the time help arrived, it was too late."

"I'm aware of the details, Alan." Hall's glare could have obliterated concrete. "I want to know *why*."

"It's my fault. I didn't make sure the order was followed through." Benning looked down at the table. "It was just a mistake."

Hall seethed. "A mistake that led to one of my most critical facilities going up like a bonfire? A mistake that left seventeen State Guard men dead and another critical?"

Benning stammered. "Yes, Administrator, but—"

Hall slammed the table. "It's hard enough for me to keep the country united as we deal with this threat. Mistakes like this sap my ability to do so."

Mariposa had heard that Richard Hall was a level headed man, but he was showing he had a temper. She couldn't blame him. State Guard casualties had always been a possibility with an undertaking of this scale, but this was more than that. It was a wipe out of several squads. Hall needed the Guard ready to jump into burning buildings, but already she'd heard whispers about their capacity and new restrictions on their operations.

Benning looked shellshocked. "All I can offer is my apology."

"No, it's not." Hall stared straight at Benning. "I had high hopes for you, but you've let me down. You're resigning, Alan."

"But—"

"This isn't a conversation. You're resigning. Immediately. Get out."

Benning looked like he might protest, but the administrator's stare put a halt to that. Benning went pale and gripped his tablet like a life raft, not looking at either of them as he stood and moved to the door. Mariposa started to stand as well, more confused than ever about why she'd been in this meeting, when Hall cleared his throat. She glanced at him and he shook his head slightly. She paused then sat back down and waited.

Hall ran a hand through his hair as Benning left. Once it was just the two of them he spoke. "I've heard good things about you."

"I'm just trying to keep things as stable as possible, despite the restrictions." Mariposa looked at her hands, then up. "It's a hard situation for everyone."

Hall smiled thinly, no hint of teeth. "That it is. I'm appointing you to replace Benning in charge of Area V. I need someone who considers their actions and is thorough."

Mariposa didn't know what to say. She squeezed out her words. "Thank you, sir. Alan is a good man, but I won't let you down."

Hall sighed, finally seeming to cool down. "We're

stepping up our timetable. Most of the country is now compliant with the orders, but the south is ablaze. A resistance is rising and there's underground media. The attacks have slowed, but not stopped, and each additional niggle we get makes it harder to achieve our core mission."

Mariposa nodded, but kept quiet. The rise of a resistance and underground media was not surprising, given the scale of the changes involved. But it was also a set of problems that Hall seemed willing to apply force to to stop. The underground media was probably the more difficult to deal with. They could be anonymous, dispersed and effective. As damaging as poison; as elusive as quicksilver. A problem.

Hall continued. "I was hoping some low level enforcement would be enough to deal with these problems, but they're growing nonetheless. The President is getting very impatient and I'm going to start leaning harder on my area commanders for results. That includes you from now on."

"I understand, sir. I'll do my best." Mariposa swallowed hard. "We've had some success here, but there's more we could be doing."

Hall smiled like a hyena. "That's exactly what I had in mind. The great thing about the executive orders is the level of autonomy they allow us to get the things that need doing done. I'm always available for a call if you have new ideas on how we can achieve this. Now, come with me."

She stood and followed Hall out. Promotion had been the last thing she'd thought about when she'd walked into the meeting room. She knew about the distribution center attack, but it was the latest attack among many. It seemed strange that the Administrator of FEMA would take such exception to this one that he'd promote her in its wake.

Once outside the meeting room, she saw the entire staff gathered. Murray Devereaux gave her the thumbs-up as

Hall gestured for her to stand alongside him. Mariposa kept her head down as the conversation buzzed. A hundred whispers with a thousand different theories swirled around the room, but to most it would be obvious – Benning was gone and Mariposa was standing next to Hall.

"The incident at Distribution Center Echo was unforgiveable." Hall spoke over the chatter, which died down. "While we can't completely prevent these terrorist attacks, at least not yet, nor tie down our bases so tightly that they're impregnable, a mistake by this office contributed to the death of seventeen of our people."

Mariposa noticed the shuffling of bodies and the sideways glances. It wasn't every day an organization head was quite so blunt. Richard Hall was clearly not a man who suffered failure. He was a legend within FEMA, so he'd earned that right. It made her dread the idea that the buck now stopped with her. If a firecracker went off it would be her fault.

Hall shifted on the balls of his feet. "We now don't have critical supplies for half the Area. Your colleague, Mariposa Esposito, has performed admirably in her duties in securing the downtown area of Chicago over the past few months. By all reports, there have been few issues with the administration of her area of responsibility.

"This is no small feat, given the potential for conflict in dense urban environments – as we've seen in Salt Lake City and other places. As a result, after Alan Benning's resignation, I'm promoting her to leadership of FEMA Area V. I expect her to bring the same level of professionalism, diligence and results to her new role."

There was a buzz from among the staff, until Murray guffawed. "Go on, don't keep the boss waiting."

Mariposa shook her head and stood slightly taller. "I'd like to thank the administrator for the faith placed in me. While the incident at the distribution center was terrible, it's a blemish on an otherwise faultless performance by our office. I strongly believe we can get back on track."

She paused. This was her opportunity to speak out, to tell the administrator in front of a large number of their colleagues of the wrongs being done in his name. That the restrictions, the violence and the oppression were just making things worse and that they were lucky there hadn't been worse incidents. That the changes taking place in America weren't ones that she wanted for her son, terrorism or not.

She didn't get the chance, as Hall started to speak again. "I'd like to thank Mariposa for agreeing to take on this responsibility. It won't be easy, but with such a fantastic team around her, I've no doubt you'll get the results that are needed. The way we stop these attacks and restore order is through doing our jobs well.

"I'm spending the next few weeks traveling around the country, to oversee the response to problems in many of our areas. While, by and large, the entire organization has done a great job in securing America, there have been patches of bad performance. I intend to rectify these. Personally."

If Hall's ruthless treatment of Benning were any sign, then whoever was causing Hall problems would be best to quit before he arrived. He'd taken over a shattered organization and within a decade was leading the response to the largest wave of terrorism in US history. To Mariposa, he didn't seem to be the kind of man who let a problem go unsolved, but more the kind who'd beat one into submission.

JACK WIDENED his eyes and blinked a few times, trying to will away the tiredness that threatened to make him a car accident statistic. He'd never realized how dull driving on straight, empty roads at night could be. He'd been going the same speed in the same direction with nothing but the reflector strips on the road for company for hours now. He couldn't even play the radio or wind down the window, lest he wake up his passenger.

Elena Winston was curled up in a ball on the seat beside him. He admired her ability to sleep in a moving vehicle. He remembered such effortless sleep – these days, his sleep was interspersed with nightmares about Erin, his torture at the hands of the Chinese or the other pain inflicted upon him by Michelle Dominique. Yet Elena seemed undisturbed by the world or her mind. He sighed and drummed softly on the steering wheel.

They'd left Chicago just prior to the city being locked down for the evening curfew. Elena had arrived at his hotel with mixed news: Guerrilla Radio had broadcast Ortiz's information successfully, but because of Jack's earlier attempts to disseminate the report it was important that he leave town. She'd offered him a car and now, less than twelve hours after meeting her, he was leaving Chicago with her, bound for New York.

One of the things FEMA had outlawed but couldn't really police was travel on interstate roads at night – America had too many roads for that. It was a risk, but they were trying to get the hell out of Dodge before some flunky figured out that Jack was behind Guerilla Radio's story about the nascent resistance. He cursed himself again for trying to post the story. While he wasn't safe anywhere, he would be safer elsewhere.

He failed to completely stifle a yawn as a truck approached from the other direction. The amount of light that filled the car increased until, right at the point of passing, the inside of Elena's Chevy was lit up like day. It turned out Elena was human after all, as she stirred and sat up beside him. The darkness enveloped them again, but she was already awake. She sucked in a deep breath and scratched her head for a moment.

"Welcome back."

"Did I fall asleep?" She ran her hands over her face.

He laughed. "The minute we left the city."

She pulled down the visor, which had a small light and a mirror. "Sorry. Tired."

He cast a glance sideways and smiled at the hair matted to her face. "Classy."

"That's me." She fixed her hair.

"Tell me how you got that story out."

She looked at him as if she were summing up whether she could trust him or not and then shrugged. "Easy. We release everything we gather and can verify through all of our channels: shortwave radio, the Darknet, underground lectures. Even printed pamphlets, in some places where it makes sense."

"Why not just use the Darknet exclusively?"

"Could do, but there's not enough people using it. We need a mass movement of organized resistance. What we're trying is nothing that hasn't been done before when the shadow of totalitarianism casts itself over society. We have to try. Our reach is modest, but growing. Thanks to people like you."

Jack let that one go. He still wasn't entirely comfortable with helping Elena. If he'd been thinking straight, the issues he'd had while trying to disseminate Ortiz's information and the danger Elena had put him in by broadcasting it herself would have sent him running in the other direction. Instead, here he was, digging himself deeper. But at least he was asking questions. He didn't get a chance to probe her further, because her phone started to ring.

"It's my fiancé." The pride in her voice was palpable as she looked down at the screen. "Do you mind?"

Jack smiled and shook his head, but struggled to suppress the darkness that rose from the pit of his stomach. Losing Erin still hurt, though less these days. Despite her cheating and the distance between them in the final months of her life, he still felt like he'd been robbed of something. He didn't begrudge anyone their happiness, he just found it hard not to think of what he'd lost.

She answered the phone. "Hey, babe, how're you?"

Jack listened to the conversation, though he tried not to. She sounded so in love, so committed to the man on the other end. Yet she also seemed to have another passion – reporting against the menace that was creeping across America and recruiting others to do so. He admired her resolve. He'd felt the same once, a passion for both his wife and for fighting injustice. He wasn't sure he still had it in him, but he liked to see it in others.

Finally she hung up and turned to him with a smile. "Sorry, hope I wasn't too soppy. It's been a while since we've seen each other."

Jack smiled slightly and turned his head to glance at her. "It's fine. What's his name? What does he do?"

"Brad." She beamed. "He works deep in the physics dungeons at UCal Berkley. I don't really understand what he does, but he's a great guy."

"Sounds wonderful." Jack turned his eyes back to the road.

"He's the only reason I hesitate to do what we're doing." She sighed.

"What do you mean?"

She laughed softly. "If we make a mistake and we're exposed, they'll go after us hard. Is there anyone they can use to get to you?"

Jack thought about it, and conceded that Elena was

probably right. FEMA were clearly growing restless and intervening into American society with an increasing vigor. So far journalists had been some of the worse treated, and growing dissent increased not only the risk for the journalist but also their loved ones. Guerilla Radio and the fledgling resistance were the very definition of such dissent.

"No, my wife died last year." Jack thought of Erin again, then his mind flicked to Celeste. Did she count? He wasn't sure.

"That doesn't protect you. All it will take is one mistake and you'll be exposed. It nearly happened in Chicago. If you're joining us, think hard."

He considered her words. His entire family was in Australia – out of reach. The majority of his friends were journalists and, while he had feelings for Celeste, he wasn't sure what to call whatever they had. Regardless, if his friends were keeping their heads down, they'd be completely fine. If not, he couldn't help them anyway. But he had no way of knowing if they were wrapped up in all of this. No phone call was safe from interception.

"If you're in, *really* in, I'll need your help in New York. We need people we can trust. Hickens trusts you, so you're in."

"I've committed to going as far as New York. I need to think about anything more than that."

A few seconds passed in awkward silence before Elena turned to him. "We've got a few stops to make along the way."

"Don't trust me enough to tell me where?"

She laughed. "You've got plenty of time to make the right decision."

7

FEMA has issued a cease and desist order to a number of media organizations around the country. These organizations have been complicit in reporting mistruths that aid terrorists and other agitators in making life and the administration of the country more difficult. These orders require the immediate removal of all censored material and carry with them significant financial and custodial penalties for any proprietor, editor or journalist in breach into the future.

Federal Emergency Management Agency
News Release

J ack kept his eyes closed as his ears strained to confirm what he'd heard. He knew the sound of light machine-gun fire like he knew the bottom of a whisky glass. He looked at the alarm clock beside his bed. It was early and they'd arrived in Indianapolis late. Despite wanting nothing more than to go back to sleep, he lay awake for a few minutes, waiting for the sound, until he chuckled and decided he was crazy. Then, just as he was about to try to go back to sleep, he heard it again.

He kicked off the covers, climbed out of the bed and pulled on his jeans and a T-shirt. He was staying with Elena in an apartment that apparently belonged to her mother, but Jack was skeptical. He didn't know too many people who kept a fully furnished but otherwise vacant apartment just in case their visiting children needed it. He hadn't argued though – they couldn't stay in a hotel and it sure beat curling up in a Chevy.

He rushed to the master bedroom and shook her firmly. "Elena. Wake up. We need to get moving."

She mumbled something that rhymed with duck.

He shook her again and then turned on the lamp. "Come on, there's fighting in the streets."

"I know." She groaned loudly as she squinted against the light. "A bit early, but yeah. I know. It'll be fine."

He stared at her, waiting for an explanation. None was forthcoming. His synapses were firing on all cylinders, sending a million thoughts rushing through his head. Every single one of them was telling him that he'd been played. He just wasn't sure why. She'd brought him here deliberately and had known there would be conflict. He wasn't sure what she was playing at.

"Elena?" He sat on the edge of her bed. "I've come a long fucking way to be kept in the dark."

"It's not dark. You made sure of that." She snorted. "Spare me. If I hadn't pulled you out of Chicago you'd be in prison right now, or worse."

Furious, he grabbed the covers and pulled as hard as he could. If he'd have thought about it before acting, he'd have considered the possibility of her not wearing very much under them. As it was, he saw plenty of her in her underwear. His cheeks flushed and his anger subsided nearly instantly. She ripped at the covers in his hands, pure rage burning in her eyes.

"What the fuck? Why are you being an asshole?" Her

voice was vicious. "No wonder you got a divorce."

He didn't rise to her bait. "I know machine-gun fire. By my figuring, we should be leaving here right now, in the complete opposite direction."

"No can do." She exhaled long and hard, apparently letting some of her fury subside with it. "I told you we were stopping a few places along the way."

"Why?"

"We've got work to do, though it's a few hours sooner than I'd expected. You should have caught some zees while you had the chance. Turn around."

He turned around and felt movement behind him as she got out of bed. She stood and moved past him, and he shifted his gaze away from her as she gathered up her clothes and started to dress. He'd had more than an eyeful of her, and despite the gravity of the situation and his anger, he felt it was polite to give her at least some privacy.

"We're here to cover the first strike of the resistance. The gunfire is a couple of brigades of the 38th Infantry Division. This is where we start to take the country back."

"You're joking."

"Afraid not. It's happening. There'll be tanks in the streets soon. The underground media and a handful of southern militia aren't really enough to overcome all of this, Jack. We need some big guns. This is the birth of the resistance. The 38th is taking back their city." She paused and gave a long sigh. "Come on, you didn't really think we were just going to New York to have a chat?"

He turned around. She'd put on the same clothes as the day before. "Well, the thought did cross my mind. The State Guard in town—"

"Will surrender." She sat on the edge of the bed and started to slide on her shoes. "They're weekend warriors."

"And if they don't?"

"Why wouldn't they? They're all puffed up and tough in

their black Humvees, but nothing against real army."

"You're mad."

"Maybe, but it doesn't matter. It's happening, we're just here to report it. If it works, and we can get the message out, the whole country will know. Come on."

Without waiting for him to follow, she grabbed her backpack and walked to the front door. He sighed, returned to his own room and grabbed his bag. Postings in a lot of dangerous places had taught him to be ready to go with all possessions of importance at a moment's notice, but he'd never had to, not even in Afghanistan or Syria. He ran out the door and followed her down the hall.

"Keep up!"

"Where the fuck are we going, Elena? New York, I hope."

"Sure." She bolted down the staircase, taking them two at a time. "Eventually."

They burst onto the street through the fire door. The alleyway seemed quiet enough and Jack decided it was time to steal back some of the initiative from her. He rushed to the end of the alleyway, stopping at the brick wall with Elena only a step behind. He held his breath and peered around the corner. His eyes widened. There was something large and squat and tan that made for a very bad day.

"Um, we might want to go back."

"Why?" Elena grabbed his shoulder and started to edge around.

"We both must have slept through the tank rolling into the park!"

"Well, they're ahead of schedule. This is perfect!"

He shook his head, exasperated. As he watched, the tank's turret rotated, but because of the darkness he couldn't see what it was targeting. Less than a second after its cannon boomed, a fireball roared into the air off into the distance. He hid back behind the corner and was horrified to see Elena, phone in hand, filming the whole lot. He glared at her, not quite believing it.

"What?" She spoke without turning around to look at him as she kept filming. "Don't stare."

"What're you doing?"

"My job."

He took a few steps back into the alley. "Remind me again why I'm hiding in the middle of fucking nowhere while tanks roll through the streets?"

She kept filming, but turned and flashed him a smile. "Because you're turned on by adventure?"

"I had plenty of that in Afghanistan...and China...and Syria. I never thought I'd get another dose in downtown Indianapolis!"

When he'd left Syria, Jack had thought he'd seen the last of his time as a conflict reporter. The siege of Homs had been brutal and it had taken a great toll on him, to see both the Syrian government of Bashar Al-Assad and the rebels who opposed him fight with such blatant disregard for civilians. They'd ground whole cities to dust between them. He wondered if the same thing would happen here.

The boom of the tank's cannon drowned out Elena's reply, but he saw her visibly tense.

"What?" He heard a gun shot from nearby, then another.

"The turret's turning."

Jack pushed her deeper into the alley, then looked back around the corner. The tank's cannon was pointed at the building they were hiding behind. From above them came small arms fire, which was being returned by infantry beyond the tank. They were in the middle of a warzone. He started walking away and then turned back to her. She was rooted to the spot.

"Elena, we need to move—"

"I was told we'd be safe here."

"Guess not." Jack glanced back around the corner. The tank turret was now pointed at the base of the building. "*Fuck!* We have to move, *now!*"

He grabbed her hand and broke into a run. He pulled her down the alleyway as fast as he could, but they hadn't made it to the far end when the deafening roar from the Abrams' cannon sounded. The building shook with the impact and he heard the front of the building start to collapse. In the aftermath, he heard the tank's engine rev and the grinding sound of its treads as it moved.

"Come on. This is getting nasty." He increased the pace, away from the tank and deeper into the city.

Elena jogged behind him. "Jack, I'm sorry. I was told—"

"I get it. Apologize later, we need to focus on getting out of this alive."

THE NOISE of the machines filled Callum's ears. His mind was foggy as he tried to open his eyes. Achieving that one thing consumed him.

Beep...Beep...

He managed to flick them open briefly but, unprepared for the assault of the light, he closed them again.

Beep...Beep...

Eventually he managed to keep them open if he squinted. The ceiling was white with harsh fluorescents.

Beep...Beep...

He had no idea where he was. The only clues were the noises of the machine and the white lights.

Beep...Beep...

The last thing he could remember was being shot several times at the distribution center and hitting the ground. His friends had been shot, too.

Beep...Beep...

He lifted his right arm off the bed about an inch, though it felt like he was trying to powerlift 400 lbs. He shifted his head a little. IV drips were hooked to him.

Beep...Beep...

His mind slowly started to unfog. He could barely shuffle an inch to the right, but he did manage to turn his head sideways.

Beep...Beep...

He wasn't sure there were plastic pink drink bottles in the afterlife. Suddenly, getting hold of the bottle from the side table was the only thing he wanted.

Beep...Be—

"Ah, you're finally awake. Good. Good." A nurse appeared in his vision then leaned in with a soft smile.

He tried to speak but didn't recognize his voice. He closed his eyes again and then felt something press against his lips, something moist. Water dribbled into his mouth. It was the best thing he'd ever tasted. He sucked at it fiercely and then coughed heavily as he tried to swallow too much. His eyes felt heavy. He tried to keep them open.

When he woke, some time later, smiling down at him was another nurse with a kind smile. He tried to speak. "Where am—"

"Mr Watkins, you're okay. You're at Mount Sinai Hospital. You're safe and you're going to be okay. The doctor will be around to see you soon."

Callum tried to speak again but she shushed him. She stayed with him for a few minutes, while the cloudy haze of the medication lifted, then left Callum to his thoughts. He began to slowly piece everything together, though it seemed harder than it should have been. He was alive. Somehow. He'd been wounded, but he'd woken up. His team had been shot to hell.

Callum's eyes flew open. Someone was touching his shoulder and shaking him slightly. He must have dozed off again. This time, he managed to keep his eyes open fully, though his head still felt heavy. A doctor in a white coat stared down at him, but lacked the same cheer the nurses had offered. He picked up Callum's chart and studied it.

"How's it looking, doc?" Callum had one million questions, but started with the most obvious.

"It'll take a few more hours for the sedatives to clear your system entirely." The doctor didn't look up from the chart. "Your vitals are good. You'll be fine. You're lucky."

"What happened to me?"

"That I don't know." The doctor paused and looked up. "You came in with three bullet wounds. We asked what happened and got told not to. We patched you up."

The answer was thoroughly unsatisfying, but it wasn't the doctor's fault. "Am I going to be alright?"

The doctor shrugged. "You'll be weak for a bit. You took one in the foot, one in the shoulder and a third in the chest, but it bounced off a rib. You'll have some rehab."

"How long until I'm out of here?"

"It'll take time." The doctor looked back down at the chart. "A week, if we have our way, sooner if the gentleman outside has his. I'll leave you to it."

"What do you mean?"

"There are some journalists who want to speak to you." The doctor smiled sympathetically. "I refused on your behalf, but you've got a friend out there who's insisted."

"You can't make him go away?"

The doctor laughed. "Like the rest of us these days, I serve at the pleasure of FEMA. You'll have to excuse me."

Callum tried to say more, to ask more questions, but the doctor didn't respond and left the room. It was only a few seconds before the door slid open again, admitting an impeccably dressed man in a business suit. He wore glasses and had slightly longer hair than would have been allowed in the military. Bureaucrat, the sort Callum hated.

"Glad you're awake, Callum." The man approached the bed with a slimy smile. "I'm Tim Dobbins."

"Can you tell me what happened at the distribution center?"

"I sure can, but there's more to—"

"I'm not discussing anything until I know what happened to the rest of my unit." Callum turned his head away from the bureaucrat.

Dobbins sighed. "Fine. Everyone in Mobile Three was KIA. Same story for Mobile Four except for you and Todd Bowles, but—"

"Wait a second, Todd is alive?"

Dobbins shook his head slightly. "No, he didn't make it. You very nearly joined him, but your injuries were less critical. You're a lucky man, Sergeant."

"So people keep telling me."

"When our reinforcements arrived they secured the scene and aided the casualties. You were evacuated, but things got a bit hairy after that. The center was blown sky high. Timed explosives. It killed more and has disrupted our supply chain massively."

Callum didn't care about toilet paper and razor blades. Or even about the other dead, if he was being honest. He turned his head away from Dobbins, to hide the tear that streaked down his face. Though he wasn't so clichéd to say he'd rather be dead, he'd known Bowles and Pettine for a long time. He struggled to understand how he could be alive.

Dobbins cleared his throat. "I've been sitting here a long while waiting for you to wake up, you know? You've got an interview to do. As soon as possible."

"Not interested. Thanks for letting me know about what happened, but I'd like to be alone now if you don't mind." Callum closed his eyes.

"I don't, but my superiors would. It's not a request.

You're a uniformed serviceman. You don't have an option here."

Callum sighed and opened his eyes. He'd been fed shit sandwiches by command before, but this one was a double whopper. He knew when he was beaten. The best way to get some peace was to give them a line or two that they could beam out nationally in support of the cause. Then they'd cast him as a hero and pin a medal on his chest.

"Fine." He scooted up the bed, managing to get himself slightly elevated. It felt a bit more dignified than lying on his back.

"I'm glad you've seen the value in what we're trying to do." Dobbins smiled as he pulled out his cell phone and walked back to the door. "You're going to be a star."

"PLEASE, BUDDY." Jack held out his hands, pleading for the other man to listen. "We just found out that my girlfriend is pregnant and our home is rubble."

The man had his hands gripped tightly around the bars of the security gate as if it were a life raft. His eyes narrowed. "What's it worth to you?"

Jack looked back over his shoulder, half expecting to see troops. He dug into his pocket and counted his cash. "Seventy bucks and my watch?"

With a nod, the other man unlocked the security gate, opened it and held out his hand. Jack unclasped his Tissot and handed it over with the cash. Once he had the loot in hand, the man stepped aside and let them past. Jack led the way inside and Elena followed as they took the stairs two at a time, racing for the rooftop. He hoped the position was worth the price of admission, but figured the rooftop of the five-story low-rise was the best view they'd get.

He still couldn't believe he was back in the middle of a

warzone. As soon as they'd escaped the tank at the apartment, he'd demanded answers. She hadn't blanched and had explained how Major General Anthony Stern and the leadership of the 38th Infantry Division had chosen to liberate Indianapolis. Guerrilla Radio was to cover it all and Elena firmly believed that it was the birthing of the resistance. The conflict had been brutally brief as it rolled across the city and they'd filmed some of it.

Jack reached the roof and ran toward the edge. It gave a commanding view of the streets surrounding Indianapolis State House. "This is perfect."

"Brilliant spot, Jack." Elena's breathing was heavy as she stopped beside him. "I reckon you might have done this before?"

"Couple of times, yeah." Jack smiled and looked back to the street. "This is my personal best, though."

The State House held the headquarters and administration hub for FEMA in the city. Elena had wanted to film the minute the last defenders surrendered, to put the final flourish on the footage they'd collected. Jack had agreed and they'd lucked across the guy at the entrance to the building. It was a good thing for two reasons: Jack preferred to be above the action to get better quality footage, and they were less likely to be shot at.

He leaned down and rummaged around in his pack, pulling out his camera. As he looked out from the roof, the final act was drawing to a close. While the result hadn't been in doubt – the 38th had cut through the State Guard like balsawood – the final act still needed to play out. With the conflict confined to isolated skirmishes there hadn't been a mass exodus of civilians from the city and, as far as Jack knew, the only remaining State Guard defensive positions in the city were at the State House.

Now he had a better view of those defenses, he was unimpressed. Sandbags and a few hard points were about as complicated as it got. Jack knew it wouldn't hold up against the attackers and he'd found it hard to understand why they were still fighting, until he'd turned on the radio and heard over the broadcast that the army was executing anyone who surrendered. Jack didn't believe it, but the average guardsman might.

Elena stood and pointed. "Here comes the army, Jack. They're not messing around, are they?"

Jack lifted the binoculars he'd stolen from a camping store from around his neck. Army units were advancing from three directions. "It's a ton of hardware."

Elena nodded and crouched lower behind the safety wall on the roof of the building. "We're safe up here, right?"

Jack laughed, despite the situation. "As safe as it gets in the middle of two groups of combat troo—"

"Fucking hell!" Elena ducked in response to the boom of a tank's cannon less than a mile away.

An explosion flared near the State House. Jack swung the binoculars toward it and could see several State Guard troops scattered and unmoving among their defensive positions. "Don't they know there're civilians inside? That old stone building won't hold up against this kind of pounding."

Elena checked her phone, which she'd been using to patch into some sort of feed of information relating to the attack. "Um. The army doesn't know that. Stern has demanded they surrender, but they've refused. FEMA is saying that 'terrorists' are executing all prisoners."

Jack started to stand. "Keep filming."

Elena looked at him with wide eyes. "Where the hell are you going?"

"To stop a slaughter and prevent a stake through the heart of your rebellion."

"But—"

"You think it's good vision for your friends to flatten an

iconic building full of civilians? Just keep filming! And tell the army to cool their heels!"

He broke into a run toward the edge of the rooftop, not waiting for her response. He started down the fire escape, a stream of thoughts rushing through his head, mostly involving how stupid an idea this was. He didn't even have anything identifying him as a member of the press. As he descended the stairs two at a time, he unzipped his jacket and tore at his T-shirt. It would make a passable white flag.

He reached the street and broke into a sprint across the park, towards the State House. As he drew closer, he took some solace from the fact that the tanks had stopped firing. He didn't know whether the advance had stopped or not, but as he came to the attention of the State Guardsmen behind the sandbags, he was suddenly aware of several weapons pointing in his direction.

"Whoa! Whoa! Fellas!" Jack held up his hands, his voice as loud as he could make it. "I'm neutral."

One of the Guardsman spoke from down his sights. "What do you want, pal? You got a death wish or something? Army is hitting us hard. Go back to your home."

"You guys don't have a chance." Jack stood firm. "There're two brigades gunning for you."

"You don't think we know that?" The same trooper sounded angry now. "We're boxed in and they're not taking prisoners."

Jack thought about arguing, but thought better of it. "If I can negotiate a release, will you consider it?"

They paused and looked at each other. Finally, the leader of the unit shrugged. "You get us a guarantee of safety and we'll withdraw with our civilian staff."

Jack nodded. He doubted the army was interested in killing any more State Guardsman than necessary to take the city, but knew they wouldn't stop until their foes were rooted out and the city was theirs. Jack saw a chance to save lives and also give Guerrilla Radio and the resistance a huge public relations victory. Now he just had to make it happen.

He raised his hands into the air again and walked toward the army forces encircling the State House. He half expected to be met with gunfire, but he inched closer, one foot in front of the other, until finally he reached the forward elements of the army. He was ushered away by soldiers to a Humvee in the rear. Jack kept his arms high as an older officer climbed out of the Humvee.

The officer rubbed his salt and pepper moustache. "Who the fuck are you, son? I see you walking out on your own and I get a message telling me that you're a friendly?"

"I'm Jack Emery." Jack kept deathly still. "The forces guarding the State House want to walk out of the city, but think you'll kill them if they surrender."

"That explains a few things, then." The old soldier removed his hat and ran a hand through his hair. "You're sure they'll budge without me having to kick the door in?"

"Yep." Jack hoped he was right. "Make them an offer and they'll take it. I've got a colleague up on the rooftops ready to film the withdrawal."

The officer considered Jack's words for a moment, nodded and then walked back to the Humvee. Jack swallowed. The air was electric. He thought back to the scared men behind the sandbags. These were two groups of angry and tense men – one stray shot and hot lead would start flying. He wished he could see the State House, but he was too far away.

He just hoped for an outcome that he and Elena could work with.

8

FEMA has announced that all travel in and out of Indianapolis, Indiana, is restricted until further notice following an attack on the city. Elements of the 38th Infantry Division of the US Army appear to be working in concert with terrorists and other agitators. While FEMA and the State Guard respond, those inside the city should stay indoors. FEMA would like to join the President and other authorities in calling for a peaceful surrender by these individuals.

Federal Emergency Management Agency
News Release

"Administrator Hall?"

Richard was instantly alert. He rolled over on the sofa as he rubbed his eyes and reached for his glasses. He felt like he'd been awake for days. There was just too much to do. "What is it?"

Rebecca Bianco smiled down at him sympathetically. His chief liaison with the State Guard looked as fresh as morning dew. "I've received confirmation that all elements are in place and ready."

"What time is it?" He sighed and sat up. He was in a small office on the outskirts of Indianapolis. Since the city had fallen and the remaining State Guard had withdrawn, he'd flown in to take control of the situation personally.

"Early, sir. I'll give you a minute." Bianco turned and walked out of the room.

Richard ran his hands across his face a few times, trying to wake up. As he did, he thought about the situation. The occupation of Indianapolis was the greatest challenge to his authority yet, given the extent to which Guerrilla Radio and the resistance were claiming it as a victory. He wasn't worried by general friction – gun-nut militias in the south and protestors waving placards in Washington – because he'd expected such agitation.

What he hadn't expected was elements of the US military rebelling. Had they no respect for order and stability? Couldn't they see the merit in what he was doing? His entire effort to bring peace to America was based on the removal of some individual rights to the greater benefit of everyone. It also relied on the authorities doing their jobs, no matter what was asked of them, in order to get results. The assault by the 38th contravened both of these. It was a cigarette flicked into dry grass, igniting a wildfire.

He'd called in a huge number of State Guard from all over Indiana and neighboring states to surround the city and, if necessary, retake it. It had left other parts of the country bare, but this situation had to be put down. If the 38th were allowed to dictate terms here, and Guerrilla Radio were able to claim it as a victory against the express will and authority of Richard and FEMA, chaos would break out across the country. But he'd hoped it wouldn't come to this.

He climbed to his feet and walked out of the small office. Bianco was waiting. "They haven't responded to our ultimatum?"

"Not quite, sir." She paused.

"Tell me."

"It came in a few minutes ago." Bianco looked down at her papers. "I'm told that the formal response was 'Tell that little tin Hitler to fuck himself', sir."

Richard laughed. "I thought it might be along those lines. Very well. Issue one final ultimatum: The 38th Infantry Division has thirty minutes to surrender. If they don't, order all drone commands to execute their orders. At that point we'll re-evaluate and decide whether to send in ground troops."

Bianco's sharp intake of breath told him his chance of a nap was lost. "They let our people walk out of the city. You're going to flatten the whole lot?"

Richard stared at her. "I'm giving them one more chance to surrender. That's one more than terrorists deserve. We can't let them hold this city."

"It's the United States Army, Administrator!"

Richard sighed and stared at the wall. He didn't understand why some of his junior staff found it so difficult to comprehend the necessity of action like this. An agenda as ambitious as the one he was pursuing required extreme action. The quicker others fell into line, the quicker life would get back to normal, and the less extreme his measures had to be.

"I don't enjoy doing this, Rebecca. Indianapolis should be safe from unmanned drones raining Hellfire missiles on it. But they've left me no choice!" She didn't looked convinced. Richard didn't care. He started to talk again, but paused briefly. He smiled. "Actually, I've changed my mind."

Her eyes widened, then she exhaled deeply and smiled back at him. "I'm so glad, sir. I think it would have been a mistake to—"

"You misunderstand."

"Wh—"

"No ultimatum. No opportunity for surrender." He talked over her. "Give the go ahead to drone commanders. I want the 38th Infantry Division destroyed."

She seemed to be on the verge of refusing him, but eventually nodded and picked up a radio. "General? This is Rebecca Bianco. The administrator has given the order."

Richard was under no illusion that this would be painless – there would obviously be casualties, but they concerned him less than the public relations issues. The continued success of Guerrilla Radio and its role in the growth of the resistance was becoming a real problem. It concerned him far more than rooting the army out of Indianapolis. It needed to be crushed.

After a few moments, Bianco spoke into the radio again. "Affirmative, General. No final warning. The order is correct."

Richard reached into his pocket and pulled out his tin of breath mints. He popped the lid, shook one into his hand and put it in his mouth. As he started to suck on the mint, he held the container out to Bianco. She shook her head and watched him in silence, with a look he was sure was disgust. But she maintained her professionalism and kept her feelings to herself. He appreciated that and smiled at her gently. She was young. She still had the luxury of a conscience.

He didn't require everyone to believe in what was being done. Though it was preferable, so many government employees had become so used to mediocre leadership that they didn't recognize the decisive, inspired kind when they saw it. FEMA had been the same when he'd taken over, after Katrina. Shellshocked staff had hated him at first, but grown to regard him as a legend. The same would happen across America once he solved this crisis. It would be his legacy.

No, he didn't need everyone to love him. He just needed them to do their jobs.

JACK WAS STANDING at the front of the State House chambers, watching as General Stern and his senior officers held an impromptu staff meeting inside the beautiful rooms. The midday sun was peeking through the windows, causing hell with his attempts to film the meeting. It was a good problem to have, though. Being inside the building meant they'd won the battle. Afterwards it had taken less than an hour for General Stern and his staff to take up residence in the building and begin planning the next phase of their operation: the spread of their area of control to the towns of Anderson, Franklin and Martinsville.

Jack had been allowed inside the chambers with Elena to film the opening few minutes of the meeting. It was nothing but platitudes and backslapping, but it was important to broadcast to America that the adults were back in charge, at least in this small part of the country. It felt like, with the capture of Indianapolis, the first strike had been made in getting things back to normal. He hoped a proper resistance might start to form in place of a few tin-pot militias and Guerrilla Radio. For Jack, it was also the first time he felt part of it all.

He kept filming as Stern looked straight at him and spoke. "Finally, I'd like to say that freedom is our birth right as citizens of this country. We must take it back."

Jack stopped recording. "Thanks, General, that should play well. You've done good work here."

Stern nodded. "We're about to discuss things that aren't fit for public consumption, so we'll need some privacy."

"No problem, General. We might make a nuisance of ourselves talking to some of your troops."

The general looked down at his papers and started talking to his officers. As Jack and Elena packed up and moved toward the exit, Jack reached out and placed a hand on her shoulder. She looked at him and smiled warmly. He was about to open his mouth to say something when a thunderclap filled his ears and a flash of light seared his eyes. He was thrown forward several feet and landed hard on the carpeted floor.

He could see a glow and hear more explosions. *Explosions. Trying to stay low, behind cover. Others not so lucky. Fire.*

He felt heat. *People burning. Screaming.*

He heard someone shout his name. *A child in his mother's arms. Crying.*

He felt someone touch him. *A hand reaches out to help the mother. She falls, limp. The hand catches the child.*

He was being shaken. The shouting was right in his ear. *The hand is his. He turns the child over. He's already dead.*

Jack rolled onto his back and shook his head, finally recognizing what was happening. The explosions weren't in Homs, they were in Indianapolis – the Indianapolis State House. He looked up at Elena, who had a mix of fear and relief painted on her features. She held out a hand. Jack took it, using her help to get up off the ground. His entire body was sore, the numb replaced by a deep ache.

"Thanks."

"We need to go, Jack. We need to go now." She started to jog.

He looked back. Where the general and his staff had been there was now only death and fire. He followed her as quickly as he could, trying to figure out what was happening as the building was rocked by another explosion. Stern had been the most senior military officer in the local rebellion and a chance to become the figurehead of the entire resistance. His success would have led to others taking notice. Asking questions. Now he was dead.

Jack flinched and ducked instinctively as more explosions boomed in the distance, adding to the cacophony now rolling through the city. Whoever was attacking had started with the command and control of Stern's army and was now attacking the secondary targets. He pushed himself to catch up with Elena. She was out of sight, but when he rounded a corner she was standing near the exit.

"They're hitting the city, Jack." Her voice cracked. "Are you okay now? What was all that back there?"

"The result of too many close calls like this." He held her gaze. "Sorry, I'm fine now. We need to go."

He'd thought his flashback days were finished, but Homs had obviously stayed with him. That was a problem for later. For now, they had to get the hell out of Indianapolis, because if the hammer was coming down on the city then the State House was the head of the nail. They'd delayed too long and had nearly paid the ultimate price. He doubted the 38th would be in control of the city for very much longer under this sort of bombardment.

The two soldiers guarding the foyer didn't try to stop them as they ran past and pushed the heavy wooden doors open. Outside, Jack stopped on the steps and stared, mouth agape. The city was ablaze. The missile through the window of the council chambers looked to be the least of their problems, with explosions blooming and smoke rising from three dozen places. A tank in the street ahead burned. He ran, away from the State House and back into the city, with Elena right behind him.

They covered a mile before they were back among the buildings, explosions all around but safe for the time being.

He couldn't hear aircraft, so it was clearly drones doing the damage. He couldn't believe FEMA and the State Guard would attack a city so indiscriminately. After another hundred yards, he slowed then stopped. His breath came in ragged chunks and Elena panted next to him, hands on her knees as she tried to catch her breath.

"Jack." Her voice was strained. "This has all gone to shit. I don't know what to do. Where are we going?"

"To get the car and get out of here. Any troops left in this city will be dead within the day. We don't want to be here when FEMA rolls back into town."

"Okay. Let's do that." She looked up at him, and despite her words he saw doubt on her face.

"This place was a false hope. We're going to New York. It's where we should have gone in the first place."

"THANKS SO MUCH, STEPHANIE." Mariposa handed the sitter a handful of notes. "Same time tomorrow, if that's okay?"

The other woman gave a weary smile and then turned and walked away. Mariposa closed the door behind her and placed her keys in the bowl next to the front door. She sighed as she kicked her shoes off then leaned with her back against the door, feeling as if that was all that was holding her up. She closed her eyes for several seconds, then opened them and walked to Juan's room.

She eased the door open, careful to make sure it didn't screech, then entered the room. In the illumination provided by Juan's nightlight, she scooped up a few toys between the door and the bed and deposited them in the corner. The sitter could worry about them tomorrow – she was here for one reason. She sat on the edge of the bed and smiled, reaching out and running her thumb down her son's cheek.

Juan was asleep, curled up on his side and hugging his teddy. She stroked his cheek again, then his hair. Guilt hit her like a wave and she fought back tears. She felt like she'd missed the last few months of his life, spending eighty hours a week at the office and relying exclusively on a sitter. She told herself it was necessary and that her job was important, but the guilt threatened to overwhelm her.

She made sure he was tucked in, determined that she'd spend breakfast with him before going into the office. She flicked off the nightlight and crept back through the door. Walking to her own bedroom, she emptied her pockets onto the bed. Amid the usual dross of her day – crumpled-up post-its and a few pens – she found a pamphlet she'd been handed on her way to lunch. She opened it.

It was a small A5 brochure with black and white lettering. It had a small map with a circle around Indianapolis, Indiana, with the words liberation starts here across the top, and guerilla radio along the bottom. She screwed it up and went to work unbuttoning her blouse. She wasn't much interested in propaganda. From either side. Nobody had come out of the mess in Indianapolis looking good.

Given Area V took in Indiana, she'd been briefed on the incident in the city. Though Administrator Hall and the State Guard were overseeing the response, she still took an interest. She was patched into the national command network and received reports about issues and setbacks across the whole country. It was a level of information that most people had been starved of since the clampdown.

She removed her skirt. With this new information, she'd seen the whole picture for the first time. Parts of the country were ablaze in conflict. Southern militias were ambushing supply convoys. Army units across the country were agitating. The terrorist attacks had lessened, but not ceased entirely. FEMA responded more harshly every day.

She was about to collapse into bed when her cell phone started to ring. She stared at her purse, willing the whole thing to combust and give her some peace, but the phone kept ringing. One of the struggles of leadership, she'd discovered, was having to always be available. Decision makers were expected to sort problems out, even when they were dead tired and standing in their underwear.

She reached for her purse, dug around inside and answered the phone. "This is Mariposa Esposito."

"Ms Esposito?" The man's voice was unfamiliar to her. "This is Ray Felton calling from headquarters."

She sat on the bed, wishing he'd just go away. "What can I do for you, Ray? I've had a long day."

"I understand." His tone suggested he probably didn't. "Administrator Hall has asked me to brief you on developments in Indiana."

She lay back on the bed and closed her eyes. "I've read the reports on the incident. I don't think I nee—"

"We've retaken the city. But casualties among the rebels and civilians were immense. The administrator oversaw the operation personally and wanted you to be aware. A full report is being sent to your inbox. There'll be a teleconference with all areas at seven tomorrow morning to discuss recovery."

Her mind screamed with fury. "Okay, thanks, Ray. I appreciate the heads up. Have a good night."

She hung up. Not for the first time she considered calling in to resign, crawling under the covers and letting the world pass her by. The violence and the mayhem was not what she'd signed up for. She'd been with FEMA for years, yet she barely recognized the organization or believed in its purpose anymore. It was supposed to protect, to save and to build. Instead, it seemed to be doing little more than destroying and suppressing.

While she didn't doubt the threat that the terrorist

attacks represented, she didn't think it was any more disastrous than a cyclone or wildfire. That FEMA had been given such power irked her more with each passing day, with all that she saw and heard – hell, the more she *ordered*. Things were getting out of hand. Apparently, FEMA could do anything. Even attack a city, bomb an army into submission and slaughter civilians in the crossfire.

She shook her head. As bad as things were – and no matter how terrible they became – she was tied to FEMA. If working too much and being responsible for some morally questionable acts was the cost she had to pay to keep a roof over her child's head, then there was no decision to make. They paid well and working for FEMA meant extra rations for her son. If she couldn't be here for him, she at least could make sure he had a full stomach.

If she was laid off, or quit, her situation would be desperate. She had no savings and hardly any support network in Chicago to speak of. Worse, chances were, given the executive orders, she'd be unable to get work with the companies that now loathed FEMA. Nor would she likely to get any work with other government agencies. She opened her eyes and looked at the clock: 3.00 am. She counted back in her head from the meeting in four hours. She'd have time to read over the briefing and then call the sitter at dawn.

She could shower at the office.

9

Following recent tragic events, FEMA and the State Guard are pleased to announce that Sergeant Callum Watkins, the sole survivor the attack on FEMA Distribution Center Echo, has today been downgraded from critical condition to stable. Sergeant Watkins made a brief statement to the media, in which he thanked the medical professionals who saved his life and expressed huge grief at the loss of his colleagues. In closing, Sergeant Watkins called for unity across America while the threat is dealt with. He will be discharged from hospital today.

Federal Emergency Management Agency
News Release

C allum woke with a scream.

He was covered in sweat and tangled in his bed linen, but he slowly realized the nightmare had been just that. He sat up and rubbed a hand over his face before releasing a growl. Since waking up in hospital, the nights had been full of such moments. The nightmare always began with him stepping out of the Humvee at the distribution center, then flashed forward to the moment he was shot, then ended in darkness. At that point, he woke up.

He shook his head and looked at the clock. 8:30 am. He smiled slightly. He'd actually forgotten to set his alarm, so the timing of the dream was fortunate. He had a meeting in half an hour with a State Guard psychologist. Along with his physical rehabilitation, the psychologist's report was just another step in the long path back to active duty. Or so the theory went. In reality, Callum had a very different purpose in mind for the meeting.

It was just good to be home. He climbed out of bed, showered and dressed while trying not to dwell on the nightmare. He sat at his kitchen table in silence, preparing his mind for the meeting to come. As the clock struck the hour his doorbell rang. The guy was punctual, if nothing else. Callum stood up, walked to the door and opened it. He was immediately forced to revaluate his chances of getting what he wanted when he saw the man waiting outside.

"Sergeant Watkins? I'm Major John Bainbridge." Bainbridge stood as straight as a board. "Illinois State Guard Chief Psychologist."

Callum had hoped he might get someone a bit softer, a bit more open to the case he was about to make, but Major Bainbridge appeared to be the consummate hardass: his uniform was sharp and his features were hard. Once he removed his sunglasses, Callum could see his eyes held little sympathy. He wouldn't back down and would still try to make his case, but it looked more difficult than he'd expected even before he'd started.

"Good morning, Major." Callum saluted and then waited while Bainbridge returned it. He walked inside and gestured toward the table. "Take a seat."

"Thanks, Sergeant." Bainbridge removed his hat and

placed it on the table, appearing to size up Callum while he did. "I appreciate you meeting with me."

"No problem, sir." Callum sat alert, waiting for Bainbridge to begin. "Where do you want to start, Major?"

Bainbridge's smile was thin and without any hint of warmth. "Before you're cleared to return to duty, I need to check there are no lasting ill-effects from the incident."

"The incident?" Callum was immediately incensed. "The *incident?*"

Bainbridge's eyes were hard as diamonds. "You getting shot and—"

"And my team being killed." Callum regretted interrupting the major, but he was that angry. "Sorry, Major, but is that the one you mean?"

Bainbridge's blank expression didn't change. "Yes, that one."

Callum closed his eyes for a second and forced the anger down. It wouldn't help. He sat forward. "My intention is to resign from the State Guard."

This time Bainbridge raised an eyebrow and gave the slightest hint of a smirk. "Is that so, Sergeant?"

"Yes. I'd like to get back to my normal job." Callum knew he was screwed, but he had to try. "I've been involved in two fatal incidents now. I think that's enough."

Bainbridge said nothing. Callum had been through enough therapy following his troubles in Iraq to know that the major was leaving space for him to fill. He was being assessed and analyzed. Bainbridge didn't have a notepad, but Callum knew that he was building a file nonetheless. Callum just had to make sure that the other man was logging the right information.

Callum sighed. "I saw my friends get shot to death, sir. I think I've done my duty for my country overseas and now at home as well. I've had enough."

"Nobody would argue that you haven't, Sergeant."

Bainbridge paused and leaned forward slightly. "Look, Callum, I can't sign off on a discharge. You know that."

Callum scoffed. "I'm a volunteer. I haven't signed any contract binding me to the guard. You can't keep me."

Bainbridge shrugged. "The executive orders granting FEMA authority over the guard also prohibits resignation except in cases approved by the Administrator of FEMA."

Callum felt his dream slipping away, and the nightmare coming back. "Please. I don't want to do this anymore."

Bainbridge was unmoved. "Sergeant, it's time to stop thinking about something that's impossible—"

Callum slammed the table. "It's not impossible."

Bainbridge waited for a second and then continued. "And start thinking about what can be achieved."

Callum looked up at Bainbridge, suddenly sensing that the game had changed. The major was dangling something in front of him, but he couldn't figure out what. Either way, he wasn't well served by his anger. He eased back in his chair, crossed his arms and took a few deep breaths. He kept his eyes locked onto Bainbridge, waiting to see what the other man had to offer.

"Now, you know I can't give you a discharge. Our forces are spread thin and we've taken some losses. But that doesn't necessarily mean you need to go back on patrol."

"Okay, I like the sound of that."

Bainbridge smiled and nodded. "Okay. You're a hero for surviving the distribution center attack and you helped us to tell the world about the atrocities these thugs are committing. More importantly, you showed America that we can survive and endure with the right people in charge."

Callum sighed. He sensed whatever was coming had been cooked up before Bainbridge had even walked in the door. He just wasn't sure what it was. "Okay."

"I'm ordering that you be transferred to a security detail to guard some of the individuals being detained on suspicion of aiding the terrorists." Bainbridge smiled. "It's a hell of a lot better than driving into firefights and getting your ass shot off, don't you think?"

Callum wasn't sure he agreed, but he kept his mouth shut. If he couldn't walk out the door, then he supposed this was a decent compromise. It was hard to imagine a scenario in which guarding a camp would be a problem, but he still wasn't thrilled by the idea. On the other hand, while he'd still have a gun, others wouldn't be trying to shoot at him. The camp was good enough for now, but what if it didn't last?

"You've got yourself a deal, Major."

RICHARD LIFTED the coffee cup to his mouth and took a long sip, savoring the heat that coursed down into his stomach. This was his third coffee for the day and he was well on the way to an all nighter, an all too common occurrence since the activation of the executive orders. He'd never worked so hard in his life, but had no right to complain. He'd wanted this – the chance to lead – and with that came hard work and long hours. Hotspots and flashpoints had stolen his attention, forcing him to focus on putting out fires instead of the direction of the country, but he was intending to change that. He put the cup back on the table, sighed and then went back to work on the smallest mountain of paperwork on his desk – the items his staff considered most critical.

He was glad to be back in Washington. With the issues in Illinois and Indiana sorted, he'd flown back to the capital to get things back on course, take care of paperwork and meet with his senior staff. Though he was still committed to handling the larger spot fires personally, the worst of them were under control. His next problem was dealing with one of the root causes of those spot fires. He picked up another briefing and read the title: *NSA metadata analysis of suspected Guerrilla Radio members.* While crushing the rebellion in Indianapolis would give pause to any further organized armed resistance, it had only dealt with the head of the beast. Its beating heart was the amount of bootleg media that had been allowed to flourish, the so-called Guerrilla Radio.

Though his plan for the administrative takeover of America had included provision for setbacks, he'd not properly considered the strength of an underground media. He'd thought that the media could be handled like any other issue, but he was wrong. The influence and spread of such reporting was growing daily, and was a direct threat to his efforts to bring order and stability to the country. He'd mentally added the crushing of bootleg reporting to his other key priorities: the erosion of personal freedoms that made group cohesion and security difficult, the enforcement of additional control over society, a state controlled media and a strong surveillance state. Combined, these were the only way to ensure no more attacks occurred on home soil.

He flicked through the report, skimming the background information and going straight for the recommendation: that to stop the flouting of the law by Guerrilla Radio and its supporters, all confirmed or suspected members should be detained immediately and indefinitely. Richard tossed the report across the desk with disgust. Whoever was being paid for this analysis had no idea. The problem with journalists was that they were martyrs, the lot of them. Start jailing them and they'd treat it like a badge of honor, meaning the problem would just spread as more reporters became outraged enough to join the cause. More members would lead to more coverage, which would lead to more fires that needed to be put out. Enough of those could cause an inferno he couldn't control.

He picked up his phone and waited for his receptionist to pick up. "Sandra? Get me Rick Sullivan at the NSA."

Despite the hour, he was certain that Sullivan would be available. Finally, the hold music stopped, replaced by a quiet voice. "Hi, Richard."

"Not too late I hope, Rick?" Richard lifted the report again. "I'm looking at the report about Guerrilla Radio that you guys sent over. It's a piece of work."

"Yeah, one of my best guys put it together."

"Hire new guys. It's garbage." There was silence on the other end. Richard exhaled slowly. There was no point in further mocking one of his key allies in government. "Tell me what we know, Rick."

"Given the apparent importance of Guerrilla Radio to the broader resistance, we've used intercepts to establish the network of Guerrilla Radio members. Our working theory is that if we can deal with the communications side of things then we can kill any further armed resistance in utero. But we needed to know who's involved first."

"And do we?"

There was a slight pause. "The list isn't complete and anyone using a VPN or decent encryption will be invisible to us, but it's a decent start. We estimate that scooping up the known suspects will reduce Guerilla Radio membership by sixty-two per cent and degrade their capacity by somewhere in the vicinity of eighty per cent."

Richard was silent for a moment. He'd learned to be suspicious of the intelligence community whenever he had to make a decision based on their analysis. They always painted a complete picture with clear recommendations, but it was a mirage. There was always more to the picture, something untold. He treated their information as one factor in his decision-making. He trusted only his own analysis and his own decisions.

"Richard?"

He took another sip of his coffee. "I'm here. Are we able to track the most common associates of the Guerrilla Radio members? Family, close friends, that kind of thing?"

"Of course." Sullivan sounded confused. "Easy. Our interns could do that."

Richard was surprised. "You have interns?"

"Figure of speech."

Richard didn't laugh. "Okay. I want a list showing me the two most important social links for each member on your initial list. If you're unsure, make your best guess."

"To what end?"

"We're going to send some people to prison."

"It'll be thousands of people." Sullivan scoffed. "How will you detain them?"

"Let me worry about that. You just get me that list. You have six hours."

Richard hung up the phone, stood and stretched his back. He walked over to the floor-to-ceiling window that offered a commanding view of the Mall. When he wavered in his conviction, he just had to stare at it for long enough to know that it was all worth it. Great men had led the country from Washington, and he'd grown tired of waiting for another one to step forward. The country had decayed and chaos had become the norm. He was determined. Order would be brought to America, whatever the cost. It would be his gift to the American people.

But first he had to deal with the problems getting in his way. He was not worried about the resistance, yet, but he was concerned by Guerrilla Radio. They had to be crushed.

While journalists may be martyrs, they were still people. By taking away the ones they loved and giving them an ultimatum, most would fall into line. The ones that didn't could then be dealt with directly. He'd be able to starve the existing members of their motivation and, more importantly, targeting the loved ones of existing members made it far less likely that new recruits would be in a hurry to join. Though he'd authorized a few arrests so far and ordered camps be built to detain people, it was time to scale up.

He'd tried being subtle, but it hadn't worked. It was time to swing a sledgehammer. It was just a shame all the highly paid analysts in the world couldn't come with an idea half as good as his own.

THE CHEVY PULLED to a stop with the screech of well-worn brakes as Jack turned to Elena. "We're here."

She nodded and gestured out the window, toward the house they'd pulled up in front of. "Time to meet your girlfriend."

Jack winced. "She's not my girlfriend."

She winked. "Sure."

Jack groaned as she opened the door and climbed out. They'd left Indianapolis with a stream of other civilian refugees. Luckily, the State Guard hadn't targeted them as overwhelming force was brought to bear on the 38th Infantry Division. The civilian casualties had been immense, as had damage to the city, but Jack and Elena had been lucky enough to make it to New York without further incident.

Now they were at Celeste's house. He sighed and turned off the ignition. Part of him preferred the idea of being in combat to what was to come. He and Celeste hadn't exactly parted on the best of terms. He'd fled his responsibilities and shut her out, along with everyone else, and he was sure their relationship had been damaged. But he'd driven halfway across the country and it was time to front up to her.

He opened the door, climbed out of the car and locked it. As Elena fell in behind him he climbed the steps and knocked on the door. He wondered if Celeste was on the other side, sizing him up through the peephole and deciding whether to let him in. There was a roughly even chance of her opening the door armed with a handgun as there was of her not answering at all. The door opened. Turns out he was wrong.

"Good to see you, Jack." Peter smiled.

Peter Weston had been Ernest McDowell's assistant for a decade, prior to McDowell's death. Now he was the Managing Director of EMCorp, appointed by Ernest's daughter in her stead. The stresses of the new job looked to have aged Peter, but his smile was no less warm than Jack remembered. He'd expected him to be here, but it was still nice to see the other man, if only to have a witness present if Celeste came at him with a cleaver.

"Hi Peter." He held out his arms and gave Peter a quick hug. "Been a rough time trying to get here. Thanks for coming."

"Not a problem." Peter's eyes twinkled in the streetlight. "I thought the reporting from Indianapolis might be your handiwork."

"You saw that?" Jack winked, but didn't confirm anything.

"We still have some connection to the outside world, you know."

Jack bit the bullet. "Celeste around?"

Peter's features hardened. "She's inside."

"Okay." Jack started to walk inside, past Peter, when he felt a hand on his shoulder.

"Take it easy, Jack." Peter's voice was heavy with warning. "She's still upset at you."

"I know. Give me five?"

"Sure." Peter nodded. "I'll keep your friend company."

"Thanks."

He walked down the hall until he reached the open-plan kitchen and living room at the back of the house. He pulled up short when he saw her sitting on the sofa, a glass of wine in her hand and lit only by a lamp. As she stared at him, a wave of emotions hit him: guilt, fear, lust. He hadn't seen her in a long time – this meeting would determine if he got to see her much into the future. Suddenly he realized that he wanted that very much.

"Nice of you to drop in." Her British accent somehow made her sound all the more icy.

"Hi." He walked across the room and moved to sit next to her on the sofa.

She held up a hand, her face a picture of darkness. "You don't get to sit."

He nodded and backed off, feeling awkward. He could feel the waves of pain and anger radiating off her. He couldn't blame her. While he'd hoped that once they were together in the same place again things wouldn't be so bad between them, it looked like a false hope. It was looking unlikely that she'd speak to him, let alone forgive him. He needed to have another shot at explaining the reasons for his absence, though it might not satisfy her.

"I'm sorry, Celeste." He held his hands out, palms facing upward. "No reservations."

She stood, her wine glass still in her hand. He waited and watched as she came closer, then in one quick flick of her wrist sprayed him with the remnants of her drink. He felt the moisture on his face but resisted the urge to reach up and wipe it off. She tossed the glass onto the floor, smashing it on the tiles, then sat back down again. He stood, unmoving, and waited for whatever happened next.

"Now you can explain." Her voice was barely a whisper. "You've got one chance."

He felt the wine slowly drip from his face, but he ignored it. "I needed to heal, Celeste. After we stopped the Foundation and I won the Pulitzer, things—"

She scoffed. "Things started to happen between us. Things you were a willing participant in, Jack. Then, just as I was starting to have feelings for you, you ran."

"I know." He shrugged. "I don't have an answer, not one to fix my mistake or satisfy you. I thought I could heal and stay in New York, but I was wrong. It was too much."

She continued to stare up at him, and he thought he could see a tear in her eye. "You don't think I had healing to do? I was okay being friends but you pressed for more."

"I know."

"Then you ran."

"I know."

She curled her legs underneath her and hugged her knees. "You know what hurt most?"

He braced himself. "Go on."

"After all the shit we went through, you didn't just say 'let's cool it' and go to Florida. You jumped on a flight and crossed the globe. I didn't think I'd ever see you alive again." She closed her eyes for a second, then opened them again. "You cultivated feelings in me, then ran as far away as you could once we started to grow close."

"I know." Jack put his hands in his pocket. "I'm sorry. There's no justification. I felt something for you that I wasn't ready for, so I ran."

He watched as she sized him up. Her eyes narrowed and she stared at him for several long moments. He'd known for months that when this moment came it would be a close call. He could have done more, had more phone conversations with her, but he'd been an idiot. Seeing her in front of him, he was now certain that he wanted her in his life. He just hoped he hadn't screwed it up.

He stepped forward a little. "I want to give this a try, if you'll let me. But I understand the damage I've caused. The crime is mine, the verdict is yours."

"I need to think." She let out a long sigh. "Go and get Peter."

He nodded, stood and went to the front of the house, where Peter and Elena were making small talk. By the time he returned, Celeste had turned some lights on and he could see the kitchen table was already covered with platters of food. When Elena entered the larger room, Jack felt the temperature drop as Celeste summed her up. He wondered if Celeste was getting the wrong message from Elena's presence, so soon after he'd apologized.

For her part, Elena was standing awkwardly in the entrance to the living area, as if some invisible force had stopped her in her tracks. He'd never seen her looking like she lacked confidence, but on the other hand, their time together had been brief. You could never tell how someone would react to being the outsider in a social situation, especially when the insiders had shared as much as Jack, Celeste and Peter had. He had to do something.

Jack waved Elena over. "Celeste? I want you to meet Elena Winston."

Elena lifted a hand up and offered a weak smile. "Hi."

"Nice to meet you." Celeste's voice remained cold. "Come in. Eat if you want."

They sat around the dining table. Peter did his best to lighten the mood as the two women remained reserved. Jack and Peter chatted about the crackdown, the terrorist attacks, the FEMA atrocities and gossip they'd heard about the situation in other places. Jack shared his and Elena's experience in Indianapolis and when it was their turn, Peter and Celeste shared insight into what was happening on the east coast, including the extent and limits of FEMA control. Though both Peter and Celeste were still at EMCorp, they were horribly constrained in what could be reported. Jack sensed frustration, but saw no obvious sign that they'd be in a hurry to join the resistance.

Finally, he decided it was time. "Ah, so guys? Elena is one of the leaders of Guerrilla Radio. I'm working with her to get word of FEMA overreach out."

Elena gave a small laugh, but there was silence from the others. He wondered if he'd gotten it wrong, as Peter's eyes widened and Celeste crossed her arms.

Finally, Peter broke the silence. "Why are you involved, Jack?"

"I wasn't at first. I wanted nothing to do with it."

"What happened?" Peter seemed genuinely interested. "What changed?"

"A friend I owe everything to asked for my help. Elena helped me to help him, and it meant I had to get out of Chicago. We were doing the filming in Indianapolis."

"Indianapolis." Celeste cut in, her voice sharp.

"Yes." He stared straight at her. "Indianapolis."

"She nearly got you killed, Jack." She stared back.

"I did a pretty good job of that myself." He shrugged. "I was actually hoping you guys might be willing to help us out in New York."

Celeste shook her head and stood, bringing the conversation to an abrupt close. She picked up her wine glass and walked to the back door. She slid it open, stepped outside then closed it again. Jack could see her outline, staring out into the night. Every inch of him ached to join her and to comfort her, but there was larger business to complete. Or so he thought.

Peter cleared his throat. "I think we're all tired. A few of us in particular."

Jack smiled. "Sorry, Peter. It's good to see you, anyway."

"Jack, I'm not opposed to helping you. I actually respect what you're trying to do. But you need to get your house in order with Celeste before anything else."

"I know."

"And another thing." Peter frowned. "I want Jo Tokaloka left out of this, whether or not Celeste and I end up helping. His heart won't stand up to it."

Jack nodded. "Okay."

Peter stood. "Why don't I show you to one of the guest bedrooms, Elena?"

"I don't know." Elena looked unsure. "She doesn't seem thrilled that I'm here."

"Good thing I pay her salary." Peter patted Elena on the shoulder.

"Go on." Jack smiled at Elena, trying to reassure her. "It'll be fine."

Elena nodded, but Jack could see the doubt on her face. She stood and followed Peter without further word, leaving Jack sitting at the table with his thoughts. He sipped his own wine, ate a few biscuits and delayed the inevitable until, eventually, he stood. He walked to the back door, slid it open and stepped outside. He closed the door and stood just behind Celeste. She was sobbing quietly.

"It wasn't so long ago you were standing behind me on the *George Washington* when I was upset." His voice was barely a whisper. "A lot has changed."

"You didn't even know about Jo's heart attack! I wanted to tell you, but Peter wouldn't let me. You disappeared." Celeste turned to face him, tears streaming down her face. "You were a fucking coward. Others needed you and you weren't here. That's not Jack Emery. Not the Jack Emery I know, anyway!"

Her words felt like a jab to his stomach. "I'm sorry. I let you down."

She let out a long sigh. "It's a long way back for you."

"I know."

"And I may not be able to forgive you."

"Fair enough."

Her features lightened for the first time. "But I think I'd like to try."

10

FEMA is pleased to announce that increased restrictions on movement in Indianapolis, Indiana, will be lifted. The restrictions, in place since the city was liberated from rebellious elements of the military, were required to ensure the threat to the city was fully dealt with. Administrator Hall has praised the patience of residents in Indianapolis, noting that although their city was violently assaulted things are now back to normal. Administrator Hall also expressed the need to be vigilant against those who wish us harm, noting that some FEMA staff and State Guard troops remain in conflict with terrorists in other parts of the country.

 Federal Emergency Management Agency
 News Release

Jack enjoyed the rhythm. He lay on his back with his hands behind his head, taking in the view with hunger. Celeste's features looked wonderful in the lamplight, moving slowly back and forth as she ran both hands through her mess of shoulder-length red hair.

She offered a cautious smile, which he returned, then continued to allow his gaze to devour her entire body.

They'd talked into the early hours of the morning, agreeing that they still had feelings for each other but the potential for hurt was enormous. Celeste had made no promises, but had asked to go to bed together. She'd told him that, after a delay of over a year, she wanted to be with him, to be held by him. They'd slept like that, but woken up to more.

She writhed on top of him and her breathing became heavier. He felt his own pace quicken and a soft moan escaped from each of them. He felt his hunger turn to desperation and they pressed closer together, until his abdominals tightened. He reached out and gripped her tightly. A second later her quiet, brief moans became more sustained and he had to put his hand over her mouth.

He smiled up at her. "The others might hear."

Her eyes narrowed as she continued to press down onto him. She kissed his palm, then sucked one of his fingers and bit it playfully. Slowly her pleasure seemed to subside and he rolled sideways with her, into an easy embrace. She snuggled in close and they said nothing for several minutes, as their breathing returned to normal.

"I'm glad you're here, Jack." Her voice was a mix of satisfaction and sleepiness. "Don't make me regret this."

He kissed her head and pulled her closer. He started to doze as she roamed his body, stopping occasionally on his scars, examining them then moving on. He knew that her scars weren't visible, and his knowledge of what had happened to her in China – her rape – had made him hesitant. He'd let her take the lead and the result had been spectacular.

"So, what do you need from us out here, Jack?" Celeste's voice was thick with sleep when they stirred, hours later.

"What do you mean?"

"Guerrilla Radio." She pulled away from him and put her head on the pillow, her eyes boring into him. "I want to help. What do you need?"

He thought for a moment, trying to clear his mind from the hazy mix of sex and sleep. "The failure in Indianapolis showed us a few things. We need to develop a proper national network before we let it loose. Once that's done properly we can discuss the growth of the resistance more broadly."

Celeste smiled. "I can start to sound out some EMCorp colleagues. I'm sure there are some who'll help. Peter, for starters."

"Yeah, I spoke to him briefly last night. He's on board."

An enormous bang from the other end of the house interrupted their conversation. Celeste immediately sat bolt upright. "What was that?"

Jack remained still, listening. He wondered if Elena had done something to cause the noise, but couldn't immediately think what. But when he heard a second bang and the sound of cracking timber, he had a fair idea what it was. He rushed out of bed and started to rummage around for his clothing, which was scattered around on the floor.

"What's going on?" Celeste's voice was an higher than usual.

"Trouble."

"What are you doing?" She hugged the covers.

"Getting dressed." He smiled sadly as he pulled on his underwear. "You should too."

She didn't get the chance and he only had his jeans half on when the shouts started. "*NYPD! All occupants need to stay where they are.*"

The door to the bedroom was kicked in a second later and four officers dressed in Kevlar vests poured through, pointing pistols at the two of them. One of them flicked a switch and the quiet solitude of dawn was broken. Jack blinked a few times to help his eyes adjust to the light as Celeste pulled the covers higher. Jack raised his arms as he thought about Elena, who'd been sleeping at the front of the house. They must have scooped her up.

"Get down. Get down now!" An officer shouted as he moved around the bed, keeping the pistol trained on Jack. "On the floor."

Jack complied. He immediately raised his hands and dropped to his knees. "No need to wave the guns around, fellas."

"Keep your mouth shut." The officer pulled Jack's hands together roughly behind his back and cuffed them. "Up."

Jack started to stand, helped by the officer. Another officer had his pistol trained on Jack while the final two were focused on Celeste. He'd been arrested before – once in Australia for taking a drunken swing at someone and a few times overseas for reporting on various stories – but he'd never been assaulted by storm troopers in such a way. He thought this might be Celeste's first experience with police, though not with the authorities.

"Take it easy, guys." He looked down at Celeste, who was cowering in fear, and he thought back to their experiences in China. "This doesn't need to happen like this."

The officers ignored him and one of them stepped toward the bed and addressed Celeste. "I need you to show me your hands, miss, then I'm going to pull back the covers and you're going to climb out of the bed and get dressed. It's important that you make no sudden movements."

Jack started to protest, but was pulled back by the officer holding him. The one with the pistol trained on him stepped forward an inch. "You need to calm down."

He took a breath to compose himself. "You're here for me, fellas. This is stupid."

"Calm down."

Jack watched as Celeste pulled her hands out over the covers, then placed them down slowly. She sobbed. "I'm naked under here, guys, can I have a minute?"

"Negative. I'm going to pull back the covers and you're going to climb out of the bed." The officer repeated himself. "Remember, no sudden movements."

She nodded and bit her lip as the officer held his pistol in one hand and ripped the covers off the bed with the other. Jack felt the anger well inside of him as he watched Celeste start to sob harder. She kept her hands exactly where they'd been, not even daring to cover up, though she did press her legs together. His face burned red at her humiliation, but any protest he made would just make things worse. He kept his mouth shut.

"Okay, get up." The officer reached onto the floor and tossed her a blouse. He then spoke into the radio that was mounted on his shoulder. "All clear. Suspect located and detained."

Jack found his voice again. "What now?"

"Look, pal." The officer holding the pistol on him spoke. "We're not here for you, but if you don't pipe down, you're coming in too. Okay?"

"Who are you here for, then?" Celeste, now dressed, turned to the officer. "Me?"

"You."

To her credit, she sensed that further protest was pointless. "Okay."

Jack had no such sense. "Come on. She's a journalist, not a terrorist."

The only officer who hadn't spoken yet piped in. "I don't care. One more word and you'll be sitting next to her in the van."

Jack started forward, causing the officer with the pistol on him to tense slightly. Celeste locked eyes with him and shook her head very slightly. She was clearly thinking that there was no point both of them being locked up. He rocked back on the balls of his feet and didn't move any further as the officer relaxed and Celeste was led from the room. Only then did they uncuff him and leave.

~

"ONE *THOUSAND* IN ILLINOIS ALONE?" Mariposa looked up from the report that Murray Devereaux had handed her.

Murray chewed on his gum. "Yeah, and they picked up some doozies. Everything from an eighteen-year-old to a ninety-three-year-old. Real threats to security."

"Seems a bit ridiculous, doesn't it?" She shook her head and placed the report on the table.

He shrugged and placed his coffee on top of the document, showing what he thought of its value. It was a hundred pages long, a dossier of every Guerrilla Radio sympathizer who'd been picked up across Illinois by a mix of police and State Guard. She knew the same action had taken place in other states as well, in an attempt by the administrator to clamp down on the activity of Guerrilla Radio and, in turn, stem the growth of the resistance.

She sighed. "Command tells me it's to wrap up the Guerrilla Radio network that's popped up, but it seems like a big show of force and an awful lot of people to detain."

"Fuck command. They've screwed the pooch on this whole episode. Why attack the friends and family?" He snorted, his disdain for what had happened clear on his face. "That's some Stasi-type shit right there. If you know who's breaking the law, take them down, but as far as I can see these folks are innocent."

She nodded and left it at that. He was right. Her new job gave her huge access to information she'd previously been denied and most of it disgusted her. It told her that they were no closer to stopping the attacks around the whole country, that the presence of Guerrilla Radio was growing, and that FEMA's actions were getting increasingly desperate – and violent – to keep order. The detention of thousands of people was the latest attempt.

"I wonder what the story is in other states." He raised an eyebrow.

"Classified."

He rolled his eyes. "Of course."

"Thanks, Murray."

She was glad he took the hint. He picked up his coffee and left her office. She leaned back in her chair and looked at the ceiling. Every negative thought she'd had about FEMA and the path it was on came crashing back. She'd done her best to busy herself with work, trying to hide away her larger concerns, but even that dam was starting to crack and spew out negative thoughts. Her career. Her pay check. Her colleagues. Her safety. Her son. All were reasons to will away the ill-feeling she had about everything that was happening. But it wasn't enough. With each draconian measure she signed off on, the further into the maw of evil she felt herself slipping.

Sooner or later, she knew that the Nuremberg defense wouldn't hold up against her conscience. Doing something that she disagreed with because she was ordered to, even if she spoke out against it occasionally, was not acceptable. She was as culpable as the drone pilots firing on Indianapolis or the SWAT teams who'd kicked in doors and arrested thousands of innocent people around the country. She made her decision. She stood up, walked out of her office and toward the central meeting point where they held the staff briefings. She pressed the button that started the chime, then she waited in silence while the whole staff came together.

"Thanks, everyone." She smiled, wanting to convey as

normal an impression as possible. "We're not doing a briefing, unless anyone has anything critical?"

She looked to each of the managers, who looked to their staff in turn. There were a few confused faces, but mostly a lot of shaking heads. Illinois was buttoned up pretty tight. Incidents like the arrests aside, there wasn't much happening. Her team was doing a great job at what they'd been ordered to do, which broke her heart all the more. It was all wrong. She steeled herself for the path she was about to start down.

"Okay, given everything is under control, I've informed command that I'm sending you all home early for the day." She smiled at the lie, and as faces around the room brightened she caught sight of Murray looking at her carefully. "It's been a long time since any of you spent some real time with your families, so off you go."

"What about our work?" Murray spoke up, asking what everyone else was likely thinking.

She lied again. "Area IV is going to take care of any non-essential overflow for the day and we'll be doing the same for them next week. If anything comes up, you'll be contacted. Enjoy yourselves."

She smiled one last time then returned to her office. She left the door open and sat down, busying herself with paperwork as the staff cleared out quickly – it was as if they thought the bubble might burst or she might change her mind. She kept her head down and tried her best to ward off the doubts that were creeping in. The minute the last staff member walked out, there was no turning back.

She closed the manila folder that held the file she was reading and walked from her office. She needed to make sure everyone had left. Her heart nearly jumped out of her chest when she saw Murray leaning against one of the cubicle partitions right outside her office, blowing bubbles with his gum. She punched him in the arm and he responded with a smile and another bubble.

"What's the story?" His voice was firm. "Sending everyone home for a little R and R? Right after we discussed how much of a joke those arrests were?"

"It's fine, Murray. Really. I just think we're all spread a bit too thinly right now and I wanted to give everyone a break." She wasn't lying, technically. "You should go too."

"Okay, I'll walk out with you?" He crossed his arms and raised an eyebrow when she didn't move. "Didn't think so. I want a piece of whatever you're up to."

She sighed. Now that she'd finally made a decision and put in place the first part of it, the last thing she wanted was to have an argument with Murray. He was her best friend at the office and she didn't want him caught up in what she was about to do. Worse, if he wouldn't budge, not only would he be implicated but she wouldn't achieve what she had to either. He had to go.

"Murray, I want you to go home now. Please." She turned back into her office, and nearly roared with frustration when he followed her.

"Nope." He moved closer to her, standing inches away as she backed up against the desk. "Tell me what you're up to."

She sighed. It was time to fight dirty. "Murray, this is your last chance. We're friends, but now I'm giving you an order as your superior. You need to leave."

"No." He crossed his arms. "Not until I know what you're doing."

"I'm doing my job. But if you keep it up and continue to disobey my instructions, I'm going to issue you with a formal warning. That'd be your third, wouldn't it?"

"You wouldn't!" He backed away, fury in his eyes. "I'd lose my job! You know that!"

She did know that. She kept her voice sharp. "I do. Now I want you to go home."

Her heart broke as he looked at the floor. His fists were balled at his sides and he started to say something, then shook his head. He turned and left the room without saying anything further. She sighed and felt the tension drain out of her, but knew that she'd crossed a much more final precipice than the treason she was about to commit. Her friendship with Murray was damaged, perhaps destroyed.

She dug through the paperwork on her desk, picking out the most important pieces. A few tears splashed against the papers as she gathered them together, but she ignored them. She was no expert in the release of information, but she was going to photocopy and scan the heck out of anything she could find that she considered to be a breach of FEMA's mandate.

If she was successful in distributing the information, she might begin to end the organization's vice-like grip on the country. If nothing else, she was confident she could have some success locally and make life for the residents of Illinois a bit easier. She picked up the stack of hastily gathered paperwork and moved towards the photocopier. It was all about to change.

RICHARD SMILED at the White House staffer as she opened the door leading into the Oval Office. He adjusted his tie absentmindedly and then walked inside. On the other side of the room, President Helen Morris was consumed by paperwork, a feeling he knew all too well. He'd only just reached the bottom of his pile. It surprised him that she had so much to do, considering he was running the country.

She was concentrating and hadn't noticed him enter.

She had her head resting in one hand and a pen in the other. He stopped and coughed quietly. She looked up and her eyes blinked a couple of times, as if he'd pulled her out of a deep trance. She appeared tired and drawn, but a broad smile cracked through the gloom on her face like sun on an overcast day.

"Madam President." Richard stood as tall as he could. "It's wonderful to see you again."

"Hi Richard." She held the smile and gestured him toward the sofa. "Thanks for coming in."

"No problem. I was surprised though." He knew as he sat that he shouldn't have said it, but couldn't resist. What had once been a rarity for him – meeting alone with the President – had become common since the state of emergency was declared. He had a mountain of work and no time for this, but he knew that with power came the need to reassure the person who'd given it to him and who, if pushed, could theoretically take it away again.

"Why?" She winced as she sat heavily on the lounge opposite him, obviously in pain from too many hours at a desk. "I want an update on our efforts to stop the attacks."

Richard caught his sigh before it showed obvious disrespect. He didn't have time for this. "Did you see the latest report?"

She raised an eyebrow, but he held her gaze. "I don't want paperwork, Richard. I gave you the responsibility to end this, and I want to hear it from your mouth."

He wondered why he bothered to have his staff compile enormous reports of FEMA's operations and successes if she was just going to cast them aside. He had a preferred way of working, a *proven* way of working, and by asking for a verbal update she was shitting all over that. This was one of the reasons he'd grown tired of waiting for a great leader to come along, the reason he'd had to take over. Why couldn't she recognize that things were under control and just sit back and watch?

Sitting in front of him was a pale caricature of a President. Morris had been a fierce woman. She'd roared through the Washington establishment like a firestorm following the revelations about the Foundation for a New America. No corner of government had been spared the excision of corruption. All had felt her wrath equally and Richard had gained an enormous respect for the woman's sense of order. That had been the high point.

Now she was a frightened shell. She'd proven to be the same disappointment that most of her predecessors had ended up being. She'd been unable to grapple with the dysfunction, unable to fend off the rent seekers, unable to bend the country to her will and do what was needed to save it. The attacks had overwhelmed her ability to lead, and she'd looked for someone – anyone – to save her. Richard would provide that salvation. It would be his legacy.

"I see." He kept his voice level. "In short, the number of major terrorist attacks has fallen significantly since the commencement of the special arrangements. We're not out of the woods yet, but the steps we've taken are working."

Morris looked over her glasses, then sighed and removed them. "Don't play me for the fool, Richard. Indianapolis. The agitation in the south. Though they were dealt with, all were serious."

"Different matters." He shrugged. "Those were the work of traitors and rebellious elements who don't want to toe the line, not terrorists. They're reacting to our movements to end the bigger threat."

"What's the difference?" Morris looked unconvinced. "An attack is an attack."

Richard frowned. "I disagree. Terrorism is an attempt to instill chaos. These attacks are quite different – they're a response to order, a rebellion against the effort we're making to stabilize our country."

She seemed to consider his words carefully. "Okay, assuming I accept your proposition, what're we doing about it?"

He smiled. "The worst of the rebellious activity is being fuelled by the underground media. I've countered it."

"Will it be enough?"

"I think so." He was counting on it.

"Fine. I'm not thrilled though. I hate seeing us kill civilians and members of the military like in Indianapolis – rebellious or not." She rubbed a hand over her face. "Beyond that, if the attacks have stopped – the real attacks – then we can look to pull the plug on the state of emergency and the executive orders."

"That would be a mistake, I'm afraid." He'd seen this coming – she was so predictable. He rattled off his rehearsed lines. "Even though the attacks have stopped, it's more because of the increased security than anything else. We haven't yet apprehended any of those responsible for the attacks."

"Sorry, Richard. You said it yourself, the attacks have slowed. It's time to end the emergency measures and get things back to normal. The rest will melt away."

He kept his features even. "I'm not certain that's true. If we revoke the state of emergency, we're likely to see more attacks and carnage."

"More deaths." She sighed and paused, apparently deep in thought. "So what do you need to smoke out those responsible for the attacks and to defeat this rebellion? I'm of a mind to mobilize the military to end this thing once and for all. Maybe the Joint Chiefs were right all along."

He leaned forward, resting his elbows on his knees but with his hands held out. "I can assure you that things are under control, Madam President. FEMA and the State

Guard are preventing many attacks, and those that do occur are being contained and cleaned up as best as we can."

"Okay, and finding those responsible? Dealing with the resistance?"

"I'm in the process of taking care of the resistance and our efforts to find the original attackers continue. Our operations haven't been perfect, but close to it. My strong advice is to stay the course as planned." He knew she'd go with it. To revoke his powers and risk reigniting the worst of the attacks seen months ago was a chance she wouldn't take.

She sat back in the chair with her arms crossed, stared at him for a few long moments, then exhaled deeply. "Look, Richard, I'm going to be blunt. The reason I turned to you is that you're a lot more effective than the rest of the blowhards. I'm not entirely satisfied, but you've made a good start. But I want no more civilian casualties from FEMA operations."

He nodded, though he had no intention of complying. "I'll continue to get results."

11

FEMA, the State Guard and police across the country have arrested a large number of individuals on terror-related charges. The operation was the result of much hard work and investigation, aimed at disrupting the propaganda machine and communications networks of the perpetrators of recent terror attacks. Administrator Hall praised the work of all involved.

> *Federal Emergency Management Agency*
> *News Release*

C allum hocked and spat over the safety rail. He watched it sail toward the ground and then began the short lap of the guard tower for what felt like the thousandth time. Down below, a few of the inmates in the yard looked up briefly then down again. They tended to stay away from the tower and the fenced off walkways at ground level that let the security staff move through the camp securely. They knew better than to tempt bored guards, even if Callum wasn't the sort to bust chops just for the fun of it.

Following his meeting with Bainbridge, he'd received a letter posting him to the security detail at a subversive internment camp near Effingham, Illinois. The facility housed around two thousand, with the capacity for more. He was still resentful that he hadn't received his discharge, but if there was an easier posting in America right now, he wasn't sure where. The major had been good to his word: Callum had stayed in the State Guard and in return he'd been posted as far away as possible from places where he was likely to be shot at.

Callum approached one of the other guards stationed in the tower, Staff Sergeant Micah Hill, who was busy reading a magazine. "Good to see you working hard."

The large black man smiled as he looked up from his magazine, something with cars and tits on it. "You're too stupid for sarcasm, Callum."

"That's fair." Callum laughed. "Doubt we'll be putting down any riots though. This lot can barely look sideways without pissing their pants."

Hill's smile vanished. "Fine by me. I had buddies in Indianapolis. We got the golden ticket right here. Don't jinx it."

Callum grunted in response. Dusk was starting to settle and as he looked out over the yard he reflected again on the size of the camp. Twelve pre-fabricated sheds dominated most of the space, though there was also a central recreation area and a well-guarded sub-complex along the western side of the facility which housed the hospital and administration wing. It was all divided by razor wire–topped cyclone fences and walkways for the guards. The prison was testament to how much could be built quickly if you put your mind to it.

"Hey, Micah?" He turned his head to Hill. "Just heading downstairs for a walk around and to make sure they all get to dinner. On the radio if you need."

"No problem, Cal." Hill didn't look up from his titty magazine. "Make sure you leave the rifle behind though."

Callum nodded and racked his rifle. Leaving it behind was a small price to pay for some freedom from the tower. Besides, he still had his pistol and Taser. He walked to the circular staircase. Lately he'd found himself taking these leisurely walks at least once a day, just to break up the drudgery of guarding people who posed no threat to anyone at all. Hell, most of them still seemed in shock that they were here at all. He appreciated that – they moved, ate and slept when told to, and were unlikely to try to shiv him or steal his weapon.

He reached the ground and swiped his access card on the reader. The gate unlocked with a clunk and he pushed it open and walked into the yard, protected on either side by the fence. He walked twenty feet before he was among the first inmates. They was a mix of gender, race and age. The only thing they appeared to have in common was loving the wrong person. That wasn't the official line, of course, but it was whispered enough among the inmates for him to believe. Most or all of them were guilty of no crime.

When he was halfway between the tower and the first pre-fab building, a bell started to blare over the PA system. Dinner time. The inmates around him started to walk toward the dining hall, except for one woman who moved towards him instead. He caressed his pistol, but the fact that she was alone made the threat tolerable. As she drew closer he could see her eyes were puffy and red from too much crying. Despite that, she was very beautiful, with pretty features and nice curves.

"Slow it down, inmate." He turned to face her straight on and called out. "I need you to think a bit harder about what you're doing and stay away from the fence."

"What the *fuck* do you think I'm doing?" She was visibly

shaking as she approached. "I'm in jail for having a journalist for a husband. I need to get home to my children."

He lifted one hand, palm facing outward and trying to calm her down. "This isn't the way to do it. Don't come any closer to this fence."

"What is the way to do it then?" As she walked, she removed the top of her orange prison garb, exposing a tan-colored bra and a flat stomach. "Like what you see?"

Callum struggled to look away as he drew his pistol. "Inmate, stop where you are and put your clothes back on."

He got one out of two. The woman stopped in her tracks, then started lowering her shapeless orange pants. He mused darkly that this was the issue with having the yard segregated from the paths the guards walked – he couldn't quickly end this. Once her pants hit the grass, she reached behind her back and unclasped her bra. She didn't immediately let it fall, however, but held her hands over the front as she took a few more steps forward. He wasn't going to shoot her, but this mischief had to end.

"Last warning before you find yourself in isolation." He leaned in to the radio mounted on his shoulder in a deliberate enough warning.

She laughed. "Isolation? What do you call being stuck in prison for doing nothing, away from my family and without knowing a single soul in here?"

He pressed the button down on the radio. "Hey, Micah? Can you send a team down to me, I've—"

She raised her hands in mock surrender. The bra fell. "Look, all I want to do is get out of here. I'll do whatever you and your buddies need doing, if that's what it takes."

"Callum, you okay?" The radio crackled. Micah's voice had a slight hint of concern. "View looks good from here."

"Not interested." He looked away from the woman then

leaned back in to the radio. "Micah, send someone to collect the naked princess for a day in isolation."

He turned and kept walking. Once he'd walked a few yards down the path he glanced back to see the half-naked woman slumped on her knees on the lawn. She'd gathered her orange clothing and now hugged it to herself, her sobs audible even over the dinner chime. He shook his head. It wasn't his job to question the decision to imprison these people. But he did wonder how long it would be until someone *was* trying to shiv him, rather than offering her body in return for freedom. He let out a long, slow sigh.

Being in combat might be dangerous, but Callum understood it a hell of a lot more than here.

RICHARD FELT ONLY a slight bump as the helicopter touched down softly on the rooftop, and he wasted no time sliding the door open and climbing out. He was here for one reason – this was one conversation he couldn't have by phone or email – and the helicopter's engine would barely have time to cool before he was in the air again. He glanced at the pilot, who stared ahead minding his own business. Good. He crossed the rooftop, entered the stairwell, walked down several flights and then placed his hand on the door handle. He took a deep breath, turned it and walked through.

The floor was vacant and painted a sterile white that wouldn't have been out of place in a hospital. Plastic sheeting covered the cubicles and other assorted furniture that might one day house federal employees. But for now the entire building was empty, except for one table. She sat there with her back to him, her blond curls flowing down just past her shoulders. It was odd. For someone so deadly, she clearly trusted him not to stick a knife in her back. Or, more likely, her men were close enough to prevent that.

He could sense the anger radiating off her. She'd told him that the distribution center attack would be her last, that her team had taken on enough high profile jobs for him. She'd wanted to bank the enormous amount of money she'd earned and sit on a beach in South America for a few years, while the heat died down. But Richard couldn't have that. He'd cultivated her for too long to lose her as an asset. He'd twisted her arm to accept one last job, to make one last attack, to help keep Morris convinced of the need for the state of emergency.

She'd attacked Times Square and the attack had gone well, but at a cost.

They'd lost one commando. *Her* commando.

He stopped five yards from her. If she was feeling violent, a little distance wouldn't hurt. Not that he could do anything to stop her anyway. He was a bureaucrat. A skilled one, with a great deal of power, but still a bureaucrat. His power was in bringing the sledgehammer of government to bear. She wielded a more surgical type of power. Both were vital to his plans. She hadn't been behind all of the attacks, but she'd been behind many. She'd helped whip the country into such hysteria about terorrism that Morris had declared a state of emergency and put Richard in charge.

Now he had to soothe her. "I'm sorry about M—"

"Names." The fury rolled off her in waves and her voice was barbed.

"Oh, don't be so paranoid. The building is safe."

"Remember who you're talking to." Her voice had pure menace as she stood and turned. "I told you I wanted to take a break. I told you Times Square was too hot."

"It was." Richard started to say more, bit his tongue, then continued. "I'm sorry."

"I lost a man."

"I know, and—"

"I don't care." Her hands were balled into fists. "I'd worked with him for a long time."

"I know." Richard was growing tired of this, but he needed to humour her.

"This is it. I'm out. I don't work for you any more and neither does my team."

He laughed, despite the fact that he was slightly afraid of her. One was not a woman to be mocked lightly. Even if her team wasn't present, of which there could be no guarantee, she could kill him with her bare hands. On the other hand, the whole reason he knew her, and the whole reason she was willing to work for him, was the past they shared. Richard had saved One from a terrible situation. They didn't talk about it anymore, but they both knew about it. He held the whip hand and, despite her bravado, she knew it.

"You don't get that choice." He kept his voice even. "You're out when I say you are."

She snarled and her eyes narrowed. "I've repaid my debt."

"We'll have to agree to disagree." Richard smiled. "But you have earned a break."

Her eyes narrowed. "Go on."

He brushed some imaginary lint off his suit jacket. "I don't believe it will be necessary to stage any further attacks. You've done enough."

Richard smiled at her look of surprise. While it was true that more attacks would make it easier to keep the pressure on Morris and keep the state of emergency in place, he'd known this moment would come sooner or later. At some point, FEMA's control would inevitably reach its zenith. At that point, it was imperative that the attacks began to slow. While this might be occuring a little earlier than he'd hoped, the risk of having One pissed off was too great. The attacks to date would have to be enough.

She nodded. He knew that his words had been accepted. She probably didn't trust him to keep his word, but she didn't have a choice. If push came to shove, he had the leverage to get her to do whatever needed doing. In the meantime, she'd be quiet and away from the eyes of authorities, and he could start making the case that he had brought peace to America. Or at least the start of it. He knew this might be the last time he saw her, or needed her.

But probably not.

JACK PULLED the baseball cap a bit lower, to hide as much of his face as possible from the State Guard troopers walking on the other side of the street. He stared straight ahead as he walked, but kept the patrol in his peripheral vision. He had no reason to think they were after him, but he didn't know what to expect from FEMA and their minions since Celeste and the others had been taken. Yet this lot didn't even look at him, too busy talking among themselves and strolling along.

Once he was out of their sight, he leaned against the side of a building and composed himself. New York had been saturated with uniforms for the past few days as FEMA, the State Guard and the NYPD made noise about the detention of terrorists, supporters and sympathizers. Now the point had been made and with their targets in custody, he hoped that the tide would start to recede. Only then could they count the cost.

Since Celeste had been taken he'd kept a low profile, trying to decipher where she was, who else had been taken, and what was left of his support network. It was bleak. None of his old sources in New York had been any help:

most had vanished, others claimed to know nothing and some refused to talk. Only Peter remained free. As for Guerrilla Radio, he'd had no word from Elena and he had to assume the resistance was stillborn.

Best he could figure, Celeste must have been sent to one of the camps that FEMA had erected, though he had no way of finding out which one. Worse still, the detentions had everyone on the edge of a razorblade. Nobody knew if they'd be arrested and detained for talking to the wrong person, or even who those people were. It meant people kept their mouths shut and their ears closed. It was exactly what FEMA wanted.

He took a left off 51st Street and onto 8th Avenue. He had to find something to eat and get back to Celeste's house by curfew. He had no idea what to do or where to go, so he focused on nothing but living. He kicked at a loose piece of pavement, then watched it skid down the street and nearly hit a woman who was standing against a stop sign in a trench and boots. He squinted, then his eyes widened in realization. Elena.

He balled his fists by his side and huffed as he walked closer, ready to confront her, but he never got the chance. As he drew closer, she pushed herself off the pole. She'd clearly been waiting for him and there were tears in her eyes. While he'd lost Celeste, he hadn't yet discovered what Elena had lost. She probably knew dozens of others scooped up in the raids. His anger subsided just a bit, but he still wanted answers.

"Hi Jack. It's good to see you." Her voice was soft, weak.

"How did you get out of the house?" His fingernails dug into the his palms. "You were in the front room. Where did you go?"

"What?" She wiped at her face, which contained tears mixed with a look of confusion. "I was out front. They rolled up in a SWAT van so I stayed where I was."

Jack was speechless. He'd like to think that if he was in a similar situation he'd try to intervene, to help his friends or at the least make sure there were enough witnesses to keep the cops honest. The fact that she'd stood back and watched it happen – watched Celeste be taken – shocked him. It drove home the fact that he barely knew her at all, despite all that they'd shared in Chicago and Indianapolis and at the kitchen table in Celeste's house in New York.

"Look, Jack, cool your jets, okay?" The conviction in her voice increased. "A lot of people important to me have been locked up too, just like Celeste."

Jack huffed. "But—"

"No Jack." She held up her hand. "You've lost one person, I've lost everything. While you were inside the house dealing with Celeste's arrest, my phone was lighting up. A lot of people got picked up all over the country. A lot of colleagues, friends and allies – and their families – got locked up or killed."

He tried to hold his anger, but it dissipated. She had a point. He let out a long breath. "Okay."

Her face crumpled. "They arrested Brad as well."

"Your fiancé?" Jack stepped closer and hugged her. "Why? Where—"

"It doesn't matter!" Her voice was a little louder than she'd probably intended.

He backed away from the hug. "We'll get them back."

Her eyes were squeezed shut and her hands balled into fists. "It's not just family and friends, Jack. We've lost people as well. Matt Barker got shot dead trying to protect his sister. The south-east was hardest hit. We've lost good people there. They know we're not toeing the line, so they've targeted our loved ones."

"I know." Jack shrugged. "We can go back to Chicago if you—"

"No." She opened her eyes and her eyes locked onto his. "That's what they want."

"What do you mean?"

"If they wanted me, or you, they could have scooped us up. But doing that would only embolden more of us, right?"

He wasn't convinced. "Maybe."

"They want to twist our arms. For each of us that gives in there'll be one less voice speaking out and trying to recruit for our cause."

"I understand." Jack reached out and grabbed her hand. He gave it a squeeze then let go again. "I just wondered where you'd been."

"Catching up with an old friend. I needed to figure out how they tracked down all our supporters." She stopped in front of a café and opened the door. "After you."

Confused, he walked inside. The café was tiny, with only four small tables along the left side and a breakfast bar with eight stools. Only one table was occupied, by a man with his back to the door. Jack turned to Elena. She had a broad smile on her face, a strange contrast to her tears. Given the news she'd just shared, he couldn't understand why. She gestured toward the seated man. He turned around and saw a face he could nearly kiss.

"Jack! Mate!"

The hug was high impact. Jack and Simon Hickens wrapped their arms around each other and slapped each other's back hard. Though he hadn't seen the surly IT pro from Chelsea for over a year, it was like they'd never been separated. More importantly, if he was standing here then there was at least one person who hadn't been scooped up by FEMA. Simon had a habit of helping Jack out of binds, so it felt good to have him here.

"Sorry to hear about Celeste, mate." Hickens backed away and gestured them over to his table. "She's being held in Illinois by FEMA, but I can't get an exact location."

Jack didn't even ask how he knew. Knowing which state she was in didn't change much. "Doesn't matter, we can't get her out of a prison camp."

"No." Hickens shrugged then dug into his pocket. He placed a couple of small flip phones on the table. "Take these."

Jack sat and looked down at the phone, then something clicked into place in his mind. He looked back up at Hickens. "NSA?"

Hickens nodded. "They tracked all of your mates down. All of everyone's mates. Celeste included, given I'm sure you couldn't resist calling to kiss her goodnight."

Jack could kick himself. It was so obvious. While Guerrilla Radio might have been growing in influence, with that influence came an increase in membership, communication and activity. Like a spider's web, the further out from the center the network spread, the less it could be watched and protected by the core membership. FEMA, through the NSA, had taken advantage of that, scooping up the details of any known Guerrilla Radio member and the people important to them.

"The mass detentions were designed to shut Guerrilla Radio down." Jack shook his head, then turned to Elena. "Detain supporters, scare off the less committed."

"Then isolate and attack the core." Her features were grim. "In sum, stem the growth of the resistance."

"That's where these come in." Hickens smiled and pushed the phones toward them. "Think of that phone like the rubber that protects your giant cock when it's doing the dirty work. Most of the time, you're fine, but when you need it you'll be glad you've got it."

"This will hide us?" Jack raised an eyebrow.

Hickens shrugged. "They know who you are, but they won't be able to find you using electronic means if you're careful with these."

"Thanks." Jack hefted the phone. It was heavy and square. It felt like a trip back to the mid-'90s. "Vintage."

"Pre-PRISM, with a few of my personal modifications." Hickens shrugged. "They can't be tracked or listened in on. Don't let them out of your sight."

Jack stared. "Simon, I could kiss you."

"Nah, mate, but thanks." Simon winked. "Save it until we end these bastards."

Jack smiled. He was glad to have Hickens on board. More importantly, he now had an idea about what was happening, where Celeste was and how to fight back. His network of friends and allies was shrinking and he was fighting the government he'd worked so hard to protect, but it was a start. The hopelessness and desperation of an hour before had been replaced by a seething, angry determination. He was back among friends.

"We need to make a move." Jack pocketed the phone, his gaze shifting between Hickens and Elena. "They think they've won, that we'll just sit on our hands in fear."

"Most people will, mate. Don't kid yourself." Hickens shrugged. "You lock up someone's friends or spouse, they'll shut up well enough."

Jack slammed his fist down on the table. "There's enough shit going on around the country that people will act, if they're given the confidence and support they need."

Elena put a hand on his fist. "What're you up to?"

"I'm going to talk to some old friends." He smiled. "I'd love you to meet them. I'm taking charge of this shit. We're not just getting information out now."

Elena and Simon spoke in unison. "What then?"

"We're forming the goddamn resistance ourselves."

12

Together we remain committed to staying the course against the threats that plague our country, whether the original terrorist threat or the new threat of those dissenting and taking actions against the common good. A number of internment camps have been established to house those suspected of such crimes, to remove this cancer from our society faster than our legal system can. These camps, and all other extraordinary measures, will remain in place for however long they are necessary and until the attacks and the dissent cease. As always, good and law-abiding citizens have nothing to fear.

President Morris and Administrator Hall
Joint statement

Mariposa pressed the button on the Xerox and waited as the yellow light ran across the gap. Once the light went out she lifted the lid and removed the document, as the machine whirred and spat out the copy. As she grabbed the pile of papers out of the hopper she wished again that her office had a faster machine, but it would have to do. She looked around, satisfied that the office was still empty.

This was the best material she'd been able to get her hands on yet – evidence showing that the orders for attacks on Guerrilla Radio members in the south-east had originated from this office, when Richard Hall had been in town. She'd copied documents showing the attackers had been given orders to kill any journalists not willing to identify the leadership of the organization. Along with the information about the attacks, she had information about the immunity granted to State Guard troopers charged with crimes. The charges ranged from petty theft and assault, right through to rape and a murder. None of the charges had proceeded, nor had there been any coverage in the media.

FEMA's involvement with the atrocities was a serious matter needing air and sunlight to disinfect. She had no idea how to get the information out, but she'd compiled a dossier large enough to sink FEMA – thousands of pages of classified documents. She'd figure out a way to get it out, but first she needed to get through the day. She stifled a yawn. The doubt that had clouded her thinking had dissipated. She'd also started to feel better about her role in the administration of the executive orders, the crackdowns and, if she had to admit it, the brutalities. She wasn't innocent, but she was doing her best to make amends. She smiled at the thought and hummed a tune as she walked to her office.

A squeal caught in her throat and she stopped dead in her tracks. Two men in suits were waiting for her. The larger and younger of the two was perched against her desk, staring at his cell phone. The older man, forty or so, simply stood with his arms crossed. She felt a flutter of fear, but forced it down. She wanted to run, but if she acted guilty she was doomed. She gripped the documents tightly.

"Who're you?" She raised her voice and mustered all the outrage she could bring to bear. "You've no right to be in this office unsupervised."

"Ms Esposito." The older man raised an eyebrow and ignored her bluster. "May I ask that you sit down?"

"You may not. I'm the supervisor in this office and I've got work to do. My staff will be here soon, including my secretary. You're welcome to make an appointment."

The younger man laughed, pushed himself off the desk and stepped forward inside her comfort zone. "We don't make appointments."

Mariposa felt a chill down her spine as the younger man's blue eyes stared at her from his expressionless face. He was apparently waiting for her to act. She felt trapped in her own office with a pair of large predators stalking her. Though she didn't know what they wanted, she could guess. The door was at her back and she could try to run, but doing so would only confirm everything they were here to accuse her of.

"Very well." She crossed her arms. "What can I do for you?"

"We need you to come with us." The older man shrugged. "Voluntarily."

"You're joking?" She stepped back. "I'm not going anywhere. Who are you?"

"Classified."

She took another step back and started to turn. She didn't get the chance. The older man lunged at her, grabbed an arm and held it tightly. She pulled her arm. "Let go!"

The younger man spoke. "This is your last chance, Ms Esposito. Voluntarily or in cuffs. Your decision."

"Go fuck yourself!" She screamed as loudly as she could as the older man grabbed her other arm. She struggled but failed to escape his tight grip. "*Help!*"

The younger man smiled. With her arms held she spat at him and did her best to kick out at him as he drew closer, but it was difficult in heels. He laughed as he pulled a hood from his jacket, dodged her blows and placed it over her head. She kept screaming as the blackness descended and breathing became harder. With each shout she sucked in a breath, but the hood prevented much air from entering her lungs. She needed to get it off her.

"Let me *go!*" She gritted her teeth against the pain. The hood was suffocating. Her heart pounded in her chest. "Let me *go!*"

"Stop struggling and you won't be hurt." The older man's voice was strained. "You need to recognize the situation and look after yourself here. Think about your son."

"Okay. Okay." She stopped struggling. "I'll come with you."

"Wasn't that easy? Give us the answers we need. You'll see your boy soon."

She nodded and did her best to breathe. She let them lead her out of the office, through the cubicle farm and out of the building. She hoped that one of her staff members would arrive and take issue with her abduction, but they'd probably thought of that. She was marched down steps, bundled into a car and driven for about fifteen minutes. As they drove, neither of her captors said a thing. It added to her worry. She tried her best to calm herself and concentrate on breathing.

Then the process reversed. Out of the car, into a building, onto a seat, hands cuffed in front of her. All the while she tried to quash her fears and prepare for the questions. Light pierced the darkness like a supernova as the hood was lifted off her head. She squeezed her eyes shut then blinked repeatedly, waiting for them to adjust to the brightness. When they did, she saw the older man seated across from her, hands steepled in front of him. There was a manila folder on the table.

"Please." Mariposa leaned forward. "There's been a huge mistake. I—"

He stopped her by holding up his hand, then tapped the folder in front of him with his index finger. "I don't care. I just need you to admit that you're responsible for the illegal copying of 11 734 hard copy and electronic documents belonging to the Federal Emergency Management Agency."

"I—"

He didn't let her interrupt. "Some of these documents are classified and have the potential to cause great harm and embarrassment to the organization. If they were made public, they'd severely endanger public confidence in the organization and our current mission to fight terrorism."

Mariposa was fucked. She could think of no way to stop them. She'd done her very best to trawl as much information as possible, but hadn't released a single page. If she had it might have gained her some public profile and protection. As it was, they knew what she'd done but nobody else did. She'd been careless. In her rush to stop the atrocities, she'd given little thought to the consequences or her own safety.

Somebody had clearly noticed and informed the authorities. She regretted now that she hadn't taken more precautions and also started the release. She'd wanted to have a complete dossier before taking that step, but maybe she'd delayed because she was afraid. Now she had a mountain of information that had been wasted. She was on her way to prison and the information would never be seen. She'd failed.

"I've nothing to hide." She started to sob and a tear rolled down her face. She was terrified, but all she could do was deny. "I want my lawyer."

The man smiled. A second later she heard a whoosh of air from behind her. She started to turn her head toward it when her vision exploded with stars. She screamed, fell forward off the chair and hit her head on the table and the ground on the way down. She instinctively grabbed at her head, but it was made difficult by the handcuffs. She heard laughter.

"You don't get a lawyer here."

Mariposa inhaled deeply, coughing as she tried to catch her breath. She crawled to her hands and knees then spat out the blood that was pooling in her mouth, leaving a metallic tang. She'd bitten her tongue on the way down. She ran her swollen, split tongue along the front of her teeth, probing. Several of the teeth on the left side were gone. But worse than the pain was the fear.

"Get up, Ms Esposito."

She spat again and shook her head, trying to clear the fog. She rolled onto her side. She had no chance of getting up while cuffed, but did her best. The guard who'd hit her in the head stepped into her view. It was the younger man, with a jet black baton held limp by his side. He'd hit her and also been at her to get up off the floor. She'd never been more afraid of someone in her life.

"Had your fill?" He hit the baton against his open palm several times. "Ready to admit what you've done and get on with it?"

She coughed and spat again. "Okay."

"This is your last chance. If you don't give us what we want I'll need to interrogate you." He lifted her from under her arms. "Do you understand?"

She nodded. "I think so."

He frowned. "You'd better, or social workers will take young Juan. If you cooperate we'll hose your blood down the drain and you'll be back with him tonight."

The mention of her son hit her harder than the baton

had. She nodded. The game was up. She had to think about Juan now. The younger man helped her back to her seat with a tenderness that confused her, given the violence. After that, the questions came thick and fast. Mariposa answered each honestly. It took hours, but by the end of it they had everything.

"So you confirm that you copied the documents and built an enormous cache of classified material that you intended to release?" The older man slid a piece of paper and a pen toward her, hours later.

"Yes."

"Sign this declaration and we're done here, Ms Esposito. You'll be able to go home."

Mariposa picked up the pen and signed the document.

"We're done here." The older man stood.

She stared up at him, exhausted and terrified. "What now?"

"You'll be detained. I thank you for your honesty."

Mariposa flared with rage. "You promised I'd be able to go home to my son."

"I lied." He shrugged. "I appreciate the cooperation you've given us, but you need to get used to the idea that you're never going to see your son again. It's only because of your service to FEMA and your cooperation that you're making it out of this room at all. If you're free before you're ninety, you can consider yourself lucky."

She started to stand, but the younger man pressed the baton down on her shoulder. She kept trying to rise, but the pressure increased. The message was clear: give it up. She wanted more than anything to keep pushing, but she'd had enough. She sat back down in the seat and fought back sobs. The tears rushed out of her, a torrent of regret. Her moans became deep and long.

～

JACK LOOKED down the table and felt the memories come flooding back. Though the building was different and so was the boardroom, it was the first time he'd been around a corporate table in a long while. Sitting at its head, he felt both excited and exhausted at what was to come. Some of the most prominent figures on the east coast were in the room, all looking to him for answers. They were captains of industry, senior bureaucrats, emergency services chiefs and even a few military men and women. Half had been selected by Peter Weston, one of the few people in the world Jack felt he could still trust.

The rest had been chosen by Bill McGhinnist. The former Director of the FBI had been a casualty of Richard Hall's takeover, a lone voice of reason around the National Security Council table. Jack had reached out to him, they'd met, and discussed what he was planning to do. McGhinnist was dubious it would work, but was pleased to contribute. They'd worked together to end the threat of Michelle Dominique and the Foundation for a New America, only to find themselves back in another fight for America's future less than two years later.

Jack hoped that everyone in the room would form the nucleus of the organized resistance, if they could be persuaded to join. To get them all here without attracting the attention of FEMA had been an enormous challenge. If they were true to their word, there wasn't a cell phone or electronic device in the room, they'd all swapped modes of transport at least three times before making their way to the building and told none of their staff, family or friends about the meeting. The precautions weren't foolproof, but were the best that could be done at short notice.

Jack took a deep breath. He wasn't really sure how to start. It wasn't every day you asked people you barely knew to commit treason. "Thanks for coming in, everyone. You've all placed yourselves in incredible danger coming here."

"No shit. So why don't you get on with it, son?" Cormac Thomas was the gray-haired, ten gallon hat-wearing chief of the largest broker on Wall Street, about the only sector untouched by the executive order. He had been dragged here by Peter Weston.

"Okay, let's skip the niceties, then." Jack nodded. "You're all aware of the draconian regime we're currently living under. It started bad and it's getting worse, and you wouldn't be here unless you agreed that something needed to be done."

"You bet my granddaddy wouldn't have stood by while the government fucked everyone up the ass and told them to smile." Thomas pounded the table. "But I'm going to need some convincing before I put my nuts on the chopping block for you."

The comment drew a few smirks and nods, but Jack could still see a lot of skeptical faces at the table. A degree of concern about the situation and the influence of others had brought most of them here, but he knew that wasn't enough to keep them involved or to compel them to act. He'd made a career out of telling powerful stories. Now he had to do it again, to the most influential audience he'd ever had. He'd had precious little time to prepare, and it looked as if this group was going to need every last ounce of convincing. He hoped he was up to it.

"Look." He scratched his head. "Elena and I were involved with a group that was trying to get the word out, but it's been decimated. FEMA has rounded up the loved ones of just about every member and flat out killed a bunch of us.

"We tried our best, but FEMA is too entrenched and has too much power. Our only chance is to get active: smarter with how we communicate, stronger in the action we take to resist, faster in how we respond to attempts to shut us down."

Jane Fulton, head of public affairs at the New York Police Department, held up her hand. "You're asking us to risk our positions. Our lives. Our loved ones. Who are you to make such a demand of me? I've got kids."

Jack shrugged. "You're right, I'm no one. I'm not even American. But I don't like what's happening, and I also don't think the President and legislature would either if they knew. *Really* knew."

"But if we just get the word out, we—"

Jack held up a hand. "No, sorry. Publicity isn't enough. Leaflets aren't enough. We need real influencers to start turning the tables. That's why you're all here. I need your help to get this country back."

Elena coughed. "*We* need your help."

Jack nodded. "The short of it is that there's a whole lot of shit that's gone on since FEMA's watch started. With your help, we'll find the evidence and get ready to act."

"Resist." Elena smiled.

Fulton leaned back in her chair with a shake of her head and her arms crossed. She clearly wasn't convinced. Jack didn't know where to go next, until Bill McGhinnist cleared his throat. The room fell silent as he locked his gaze on Fulton. She held it, then flicked a look nervously toward Jack, then looked down at her fingernails. Jack was aware of the molten fury that was about to spew from McGhinnist's core.

"Jack Emery has done more for this country than any person seated in this room." McGhinnist's voice was like rolling thunder. "Even though he's not a citizen, he took on the greatest threat we've seen since the collapse of the Twin Towers."

Fulton finally nodded. "I don't mean to cause any—"

McGhinnist smiled. "Good. Because Jack is asking you, asking us, for our help. He's asking us to join together to resist an authority that is stealing our basic freedoms and imprisoning innocent people. That is not the America I stand for. You might hide in your jobs or under your beds, but none of it is going away. Unless people of influence and power unite to fight this thing, the America we know will ebb away to nothing and we'll be picked off one by one."

Jack felt a tingle down his spine at McGhinnist's words. He held his arms out. "Bill has nailed it. If we don't stand up, despite the risk, then who will? If we cower, then the average Joe has no chance and no choice."

"Well I do." Fulton cut into the end of Jack's speech, causing everyone to stare at her. "I'm not going to risk everything in my life for a half-baked plan by a journalist playing hero one time too many. Sorry."

Jack's heart pounded as Fulton stood and moved towards the door. None of them had been forced to attend, and they were free to go. He sighed as a few of the others stood and followed her out without speaking. He should have expected it, really, but it was still hard to see so many people walk away from what he was trying to achieve.

"Fucking cowards." McGhinnist's voice was pure poison. "We're better without them."

"Okay, anyone else?" Jack looked at everyone left in turn. "To be clear, I don't want to do this. None of us does. I'm terrified and you should be too. But they've already locked up the one woman in America who I love. I've got nothing to lose."

"Okay, son." Thomas's guffaw cut through the tension in the room like a knife. "Want to get to the point?"

Jack laughed, feeling the pressure on his shoulders ease slightly. He'd hoped to convince some of them, to begin to form a nucleus, and it looked like he had. "I'm asking you all to risk your freedom, if not your life. Once you're in, there's no turning back. Who's in?"

His heart was pounding. He knew that to set up this sort of network across the entire country would be a massive effort. But if he couldn't achieve it in New York, where many of his most influential friends were, then it would be an impossible task. His heart nearly leaped from his chest when he saw nods up and down the table. He also received a few affirmations and more than a few pledges of support.

He looked over to Elena, who was taking notes on a pad. She looked up and gave him a warm smile. He knew she was still fragile following the arrest of her fiancé, the detention of her friends and the death of colleagues. He wondered where she found the energy reserves to keep going. It was inspiring. He hoped he could mirror her effort and, together, spoil FEMA's agenda and free their loved ones. Free Celeste.

He turned back to the others. "Okay. You all need to convince others. You all need to be ready to speak out and act strongly when the time is right."

"Fuckin' A." Thomas's voice boomed. "Try and stop me."

Jack smiled as cheers rang out down the table. Already they were discussing ideas, ways to resist and people to recruit. Jack looked over at Simon Hickens, nodded and then watched as Hickens stood and started to hand out cell phones up and down the table. Hickens explained the phones and what exactly was safe to do. Nobody seemed opposed to having technology the NSA couldn't hit.

Jack leaned forward. "Okay, first we build the network. Then, when we're ready, we act."

CALLUM WINCED as the horn from the yellow school bus gave a long blast. The sound reverberated through his skull and gave his already tortured brain hell. He held his shotgun in his left hand as he lifted his right and flipped the bird. That earned him another short honk and a grin from the bus driver, who obviously had no respect for camp guards with a hangover. The convoy kept rolling.

Callum shook his head as the buses drove inside the gates, like they had every hour for the past few days. It was incredible. The hastily engineered dirt and gravel road had been turned mostly to mud and a detail of detainees had to constantly cover the road with more gravel to stop the vehicles from getting bogged. FEMA hadn't thought of everything when constructing these camps, it seemed.

"Record number of buses today." Micah Hill scoffed as he walked up next to Callum, his eyes hidden behind Aviators and a toothpick protruding from his lips.

"It's crazy." Callum turned to face Hill. "How's the head after last night?"

"Fine, man." Hill smiled slightly and looked down at Callum. "Yours?"

"Fuck you."

Callum ignored Hill's deep laugh and turned back to the busses. A State Guard trooper positioned at the door of each bus held up a hand and, in unison, the doors on the yellow school buses squealed open. A police officer stepped off each bus, followed by a steady stream of fresh meat for the camp. Men and women, old and young, a broad mix of race and class – all in cuffs and looking terrified.

The process ran like clockwork. The human tide flowed from the buses and was forced into a straight line parallel to their bus. The doors closed, the buses drove off, the new detainees had instructions shouted at them and then were marched toward the camp one group at a time. The design of the fencing forced the groups to walk in single file, with cover provided by the escorts, guard towers and the few State Guard troops not assigned to a group, like Callum and Hill. The process ran smoothly for the first couple of groups, but as the numbers going through the gate grew, there were delays. It had been like this every day, a giant case of administrative constipation as the staff struggled to get all the new inmates inside and processed before the next lot arrived.

Callum frowned. "This group doesn't even have Guerrilla Radio sympathizers. Not entirely, anyway."

Hill shrugged. "Whatever, man. FEMA has its panties in a twist about all sorts of people. Why question it?"

Callum sighed as he watched a man the size of a line-backer push past two women who were chatting and waiting patiently for the line to advance. One of the women moved aside willingly, but the other turned around and fronted up to him. It was a comical sight, really, a thin red head blazing anger at a brick of a man who was a foot taller and covered with tattoos. He knew trouble when he saw it.

"Come on." Callum started to walk toward the disruption, which was barely thirty yards away. Hill followed.

The woman gave the large man a shove to the chest, but without the force required to move him. "Who the fuck do you think you are, asshole? You don't talk to her like that."

He laughed. "If they're going to let women inside with us, you'd better get used to a few unkind words. Or worse. I might protect you, if you keep me warm at night."

As Callum walked closer, the woman hissed and charged forward. Her hands were cuffed in front of her and she used them as a club to wail on the man's torso. He was cuffed behind, so couldn't strike back, but he didn't seem interested in that anyway. He laughed as she flailed madly – until she hit him in the balls. At that point he roared and threw a kick that put her on her rear, then slumped over in pain.

"Detainees! Enough!" Callum shouted as loudly as he could, just as the woman was regaining her feet. He raised the shotgun and pointed it at the man. "Micah, got the lady?"

"Sure do. Not sure about the lady bit, though."

Callum snorted and inched toward the man. He really was a beast, even with cuffs on and after a nut shot. He was a big dude with a shaved head and neck tattoos. "Take it easy."

"What the fuck do you want?" The man spat at Callum's feet. "I fought for this country, now they're locking me up on no charge."

"So did I." Callum was deadpan. "Here's what's going to happen. You'll take five steps back, slowly, with no sudden moves. You'll re-join the line. Behind the ladies."

"Fuck you." The man clearly didn't want to budge.

Callum pressed the shotgun into his chest. "Move."

The man snarled, but took one step backward, then another. He seemed less keen to tangle with a 12-gauge than a woman who'd weigh hardly anything soaking wet. When Callum had him back in the line, under the watchful eye of some other State Guard colleagues, he lowered the shotgun and left the giant with a smile and a wave. Only then did he turn to Hill, who had the woman quiet ten yards away.

"All good, Cal?" Hill asked, as Callum approached. "Can we let little miss back in the queue yet?"

"Why not?" Callum smiled, and turned to the woman. She had an impressive mop of red hair that had been messed up in the scuffle. "You okay?"

"No, I'm not okay." She was puffed and clearly still angry. "I don't understand why I'm being detained on no charge. Or why I was moved from the other camp."

"That's not my business. Your safety is. I'd advise you against trying to pick fights with men three times your size." Callum shrugged. "What was that all about?"

"He pushed past a dozen people, shoved me, shoved her

over there." She gestured toward the other woman. "Then he called us both whores."

Callum sighed. "Okay. Cool down. And get back in the line."

She nodded and walked back to her position in the line. Callum doubted she'd be much more of a problem, she'd just been standing up for herself. Like the rest of them, she was here on no charge. He admired her spunk and doubted he'd be willing to go toe to toe with the guy like she had. As she re-joined the line, he exhaled slowly and held the shotgun casually by his side.

"That sure was fun." Hill laughed. "I thought you'd have to shoot the dickhead."

"Me too. Not sure one shell would have done the job."

"Yeah." Hill laughed and then flicked his chin toward the female detainees. "She's alright, isn't she? Her friend is too. Looks like she's been roughed up a bit. Might be fun."

Callum frowned but said nothing.

13

FEMA Administrator Richard Hall today announced the first relaxation of the emergency measures since their enactment nearly six months ago. Speaking to the assembled media, Administrator Hall thanked Americans for their patience and for their forbearance, and noted that gatherings larger than six would now be permitted, with the new cap on non-family gatherings set at ten. He cited this as a sign of progress in returning the country to normal.

    Federal Emergency Management Agency
    News Release

Mariposa closed her eyes and raised her face to the showerhead. The near scalding water felt amazing as it ran over her skin, still black and blue from the beating she'd taken at the hands of her interrogators. It took her mind off her situation and off her son, just for a moment. She was finding it hard to adjust to being away from Juan. She tried not to think about him too much because it just made her cry, but the idea of him living with some random family organized by a social worker terrified her. She reached up and wiped away a tear, then gave a hollow laugh when she realized the water would take care of it. She was tired, both physically and mentally.

After a few minutes of just standing there, letting the water soak over her, she looked to her left. Celeste was looking straight at her, concern in her eyes. She'd been Mariposa's saving grace since helping her in the line outside the camp gates. She'd stood up for the both of them when the tattooed giant had tried to push in. Mariposa would have let him past, but Celeste had confronted him and the guards had intervened. Mariposa wasn't sure why she had, but she was thankful. Since then, they'd become fast friends. They'd shared meals and gossip as they tried to cling to some amount of normalcy. She smiled at the other woman.

"How're you holding up?" Celeste reached out and touched her on the shoulder gently, the concern clear in her eyes. "You were a million miles away."

"I just miss my son." Mariposa gave a sad smile, feeling self-conscious. She wasn't the only person missing loved ones. "You worry too much. You know that?"

The concern in Celeste's eyes was replaced by a frown. "Sorry. Force of habit when I'm locked up. It's happened all too often lately."

Mariposa started to say something, then stopped, as a dark look crossed the other woman's face. The previous night Celeste had shared a fraction of her Chinese prison experience, speaking until she'd ended up in tears. She'd explained that this was a cakewalk in comparison, but it also showed why she was so determined to stand up for herself and for others. She'd no right to ask Celeste to dwell on it further.

"Let's get dressed and get something to eat." Mariposa jerked her head towards the benches outside the shower.

Celeste nodded and they both stepped out from under the water. They walked over to their towels and bright orange clothing. Mariposa had just slipped on her underwear when there was a series of fast taps against the tiles. She looked at the door, where a large, black guard was standing in the way. He was smiling like a hyena as he watched the women, his baton beating softly against the wall to draw their attention.

"Detainees!" His smile was replaced by a frown. "Out!"

Mariposa felt a tinge of fear. He was one of the guards who'd intervened to help in the line outside the camp. But her gratitude toward him had been misplaced and the other women had warned her about Micah Hill. They'd warned everyone about him. He liked to catch an eyeful in the shower block. Harmless, apparently, unless you spoke back to him. They'd told her that it was best to just keep your eyes down and ignore it.

She suppressed her revulsion as best she could as she pulled her towel up to cover herself. She looked over at Celeste, who already had her bright orange pants on and made no attempt to cover up, despite wearing nothing else but a bra. Mariposa jerked her head toward the door and they joined the other women in various states of undress shuffling out of the shower room. The guard inspected each of them as they passed.

Mariposa was near the exit when the guard held out his nightstick, blocking the path. She stopped in her tracks and the guard gestured to the wall. His intent was clear. Mariposa dropped her head and stepped to the side. Once she was against the wall the guard dropped his arm and the exit was clear again. Mariposa looked up. Celeste was standing there, free to exit but as still as if she was cemented to the floor.

"Go, Celeste." Her voice cracked as she spoke. "I don't want you in trouble. It'll be okay. I'm sure."

Celeste shook her head and stayed rooted in place, with her fists balled at her side. Mariposa was ashamed that, again, she was unable to help as Celeste protected her. She watched, standing helpless against the wall, as the guard took a step forward with his palm facing outward and the baton raised to strike. Celeste gave ground, backed away and found herself against the wall alongside Mariposa.

"You an idiot?" The guard's voice was laced with menace. "You nearly got your skull caved in the other day and now I'm noticing you again. I don't like noticing people."

"Let us walk out of here then." Celeste's voice started to waiver. "I'm not after any trouble. *We're* not after any trouble. I'm sure you've got better things to do than harass us."

"Oh, you'd be surprised." He patted the baton against his hand hard enough to produce a clapping sound. He took a few steps straight at Mariposa.

She sunk against the wall as the man reached out to touch her face. His hand brushed against her cheek and kept moving upward to her hair. She wanted to fight back, to be worthy of Celeste's defense of her, but she was frozen with fear. If anything happened to her, if she resisted, she'd be in here longer and there would be far less chance of getting Juan out of state care. She had to take what was coming.

She shrieked as he gripped her hair and pulled her up harshly. She reached up for his hand and screamed again as her towel fell away. "Let me go!"

"I knew I liked you." He reached out with the nightstick and pressed it firmly into her exposed breast. "We're going to have some fun."

Mariposa tried to ease the pain, reaching her tiptoes, but the more she compensated the higher he pulled her. It was excruciating. She clawed at his hands but it was no good. She closed her eyes and cleared her thoughts of everything but Juan. If she complied, it would be over sooner. He kept hold of her hair as he separated her legs roughly and reached up inside of her. She winced at the pain but kept her mouth shut, squeezing her eyes tightly.

She felt his breath against her neck. His mouth was an inch from her ear. "I knew you'd be up for it, once you gave me a chance."

A whisper escaped her lips. "Please don't."

"This is *not* going to happen here, you fuck!" Celeste voice was shrill as she jumped on the guard's back.

Mariposa cried out in pain as the guard fell to the tiles, yanking her hair on the way down. As she hit the ground beside him, she struck his hands as hard as she could with her fists, trying to break his grip. It was no good. After that, she did her best to push the guard away. She kept her left palm over his face while punching out at every part of him with her right hand. It was pointless. He was twice her size and as strong as an ox.

At some point in the rolling melee he let go, distancing himself from Mariposa and Celeste, who'd been wailing on him from behind. He scampered away on the tiles then stood up, panting and heaving. His hat was on the tiles and he was glistening with sweat. His eyes were menacing and his mouth twisted with rage as he reached down for the nightstick. Celeste was already standing as Mariposa struggled to her feet.

"Stay away from us!" Mariposa didn't recognize her own voice, hoarse and guttural. "Leave us alone."

"You can lock us up, but you can't rape us, you fucking asshole." Celeste was panting, her sweat-soaked red hair matted over her face.

Mariposa did her best to stay brave as he advanced on her again. Celeste stepped between them. Her fists were at her side but her knuckles were white. The guard smiled darkly. Blood covered his teeth, the legacy of some blow or another. He advanced further and raised the baton. Celeste gave an ear-curdling scream as the baton connected with the side of her knee. She crumpled to the wet tiles.

As if snapped out of her paralysis, Mariposa shuffled forward to help, her heart torn in half as the younger woman shrieked in pain and held her knee. Mariposa placed a hand on her head and stroked her hair. She looked up at the guard, waiting for him to strike her. The blow didn't come. Whichever emotion had driven him to rape and violence was apparently satiated for now. He took a step back.

"Cock teases, the fucking lot of you." He shook his head and then spat at them, the fury draining from his eyes. "You're both in here for a long time. Your life just got harder."

As the guard turned away, Mariposa cradled Celeste's head in her lap and watched as blood, tears and the guard's spittle mixed with the water on the tiles.

JACK HELD his arms out as the Secret Service agent ran a metal detecting wand along his arms, down his torso and his legs. Though the device made an occasional squealing noise, none were apparently large enough to cause any concern. The metal detector completed the trifecta after they'd patted him down and scanned him for bomb residue. He was glad he'd left his Swiss army knife at home.

The agent stepped back and gestured Jack forward. "Follow me, sir. Please stay close and display your tag at all times."

Jack felt for his temporary security pass, hanging by a lanyard around his neck, and did his best not to be overawed by the West Wing of the White House. While he walked, he reflected on the events that had carried him here. He'd thought he was done with all of this, the politics, the intrigue, the danger. He wanted nothing more than to opt out and wait for it all to blow over, but he had too much skin in the game to do that now.

He'd made a start on leading the resistance: the first cells had been established, resourced and equipped. Hickens had come through with the technology, Cormac Thomas had come through with the dollars, McGhinnist had helped Jack to configure the ever expanding operation in a way that was less likely to be exposed, and everyone had helped with contacts, friends and influencers in government, media, law enforcement, the military – anyone fed up with things. Elena had been the star. She was recruiting all over the place.

The Secret Service stopped and held out his hand towards a sofa. "We're here."

Jack nodded. "Okay, thanks. What now?"

The agent smiled. "You sit just over there until the President is ready to see you, then you say 'Hello, Madam President' and go from there."

Jack took a seat and settled in. He knew that it could be a while, and thought again that he shouldn't even be here. The others had advised against it, but he had to try. He had the celebrity and the credits in the bank to get an audience with a grateful President. He had to know if the belief in what FEMA was doing went all the way to the top. He owed it to everyone he was asking to risk their life to try the direct route. Before he flicked the switch on open rebellion, he needed to be sure that the takeover couldn't be reversed by negotiation between reasonable people. It was a risk, but one he needed to take. He gently drummed his knuckles on the armrest of the sofa, until the President's secretary approached and invited him inside the Oval Office.

"Mr Emery." President Helen Morris stood and rounded

her desk to greet him just inside the door. She held out her hand. "It's a pleasure."

Jack shook her hand. "Thanks for meeting with me, Madam President."

"Come and sit." She smiled as they walked over to the couches.

Jack was a little surprised by the warm reception. "Thanks."

She sat opposite him, leaned forward and rested her elbows on her knees. "Now, what can I do for you? I was surprised to see you in my diary."

Even though she'd largely been sidelined by FEMA, Morris was still the President. He needed to make each word count, because he wasn't likely to get many. "Madam President, I've come here to implore you to revoke the executive order granting FEMA extensive control over the country. The consequences have been enormous."

Morris considered him for a few moments. "Mr Emery, while I respect your impressive career and the help you've provided this country, I disagree."

"But—"

Morris held up a hand, frowning. "We've taken the actions necessary to safeguard the country and the measures are working, more or less."

Jack shook his head. Though he'd considered the chances of changing Morris's mind to be remote, he'd been entirely unprepared for the strength of her convictions. She seemed confident in the decisions she'd taken and that the response was proportional to the threat. It defied belief. She apparently had no problem with the abuses taking place. Or she didn't know about them. The leadership of the country had been bubble wrapped by FEMA.

"Madam President. You need to get outside the Oval Office more often. Your country is burning around you."

Morris laughed softly. Her continued smile didn't hide

the frostiness in her eyes. "Don't mistake me welcoming you here as an invitation to flippancy, Mr Emery. Let me be clear. Administrator Hall has my complete support. Your past service was exceptional, indeed, exemplary, but you don't know what you're talking about."

Jack nodded, even though he didn't agree. The conversation was over. He stood. "Madam President, thank you for your time."

She nodded, but stayed seated. "I hope you'll think carefully about your next move. America needs patriots, not more loose cannons."

Jack nodded and turned to leave the office. He'd tried staying out of the situation, then been dragged in. He'd tried resisting with information, and his friends had suffered. He'd tried to directly question those in power, then been threatened. Deep down, he knew there was only one course of action left open to him, one he was prepared for but loath to commence. He saw no other way.

It was time to go to war.

"I SEE. Thanks for letting me know." Richard frowned, trying to process the information being fed down the phone line. Then he made a decision. "Pick him up. I want a chat."

He hung up and tossed his cell phone onto the desk, where it found a place among the mountains of paperwork. He leaned back in his chair and looked up at the ceiling. The call had been from his mole in the Secret Service, who'd escorted journalist Jack Emery through the West Wing to meet with the President. His man couldn't tell him what they'd discussed, only that the meeting had been brief. While Richard doubted anything Emery could say would impact too heavily upon his efforts, to have another bird chirping in Morris's ear was not something he needed. When that particular bird was Jack Emery, it was all the worse.

Emery's successes in exposing the corruption in Washington by Michelle Dominique and the Foundation for a New America were legend. Dominique had been an egotistical sociopath who'd caused havoc throughout the world in an attempt to control the political agenda in the United States and stack Congress. She'd also been an idiot, trying to influence events from outside of halls of power, thrashing madly to control those inside and trying to join them as equals. It had brought her unstuck. Richard knew that true power, true influence, was wielded from the inside. Anonymous. Sudden. Final. He'd been glad to see her go.

Jack Emery wasn't his enemy, or shouldn't be. He should be a natural ally in bringing peace and stability to America, yet somehow he doubted Emery had met with the President to express faith in the administration. With Emery circling, there was no telling what was coming next. On top of that, there were rumors that a more organized resistance was being established, which made him furious. He'd wanted the dismantling of the journalist network to be the end of it, but they clearly couldn't take a hint. It was possible that a new, more dangerous beast could rise from the ashes of Guerrilla Radio like a phoenix. He was going to have a chat with Jack Emery.

He let out a long sigh and was about to start back on his pile of paperwork when the phone rang again. He answered. "Hello?"

"Good morning, Administrator, this is Ashley Madigan at the Effingham Detention Center. We've had an incident with Mariposa Esposito. You asked to be notified in such a case."

"Yes." Richard closed his eyes. "What is it?"

There was a pause on the other end. "She was assaulted by one of our guards. Another detainee was hospitalized."

"I see." He reached for a file and flicked through it. It had Mariposa's photo clipped to a series of copied pages. "Tell me what happened."

As the news filled his ear, he only partially listened. With the rest of his attention he flicked through Mariposa's file, trying to answer a question that had plagued his mind for several days. Though she'd betrayed him badly and been detained, she was still one of his people. Where possible, he looked after staff at FEMA. They were his foot soldiers in the war to achieve stability. That's why he'd been so hurt by her betrayal. The young woman he'd entrusted with FEMA's Area V command had copied classified documents with the intention of leaking them. She'd been interrogated, out of necessity, but he hoped that she could be rehabilitated once the crisis was over.

He searched through the file, his eyes scanning the pages. He wanted badly to find a reason to let her out of detention, but her crimes were serious. If she was smart, she'd keep her head down and stay out of trouble, despite the issue with the guards. But he was concerned by her apparent lack of remorse. He could free her, under the right circumstances, but he wasn't able to abide the risk of her spreading more information, telling more secrets, riling up more dissent. There was no telling what she still knew, gleaned from her time spent in his inner sanctum. If she was to ever see the light of day, she had to repent and he had to be convinced that it was safe to release her.

He was about to close the file, his decision deferred for now, when his eyes grew wider. He stared at the sheet for several moments, the voice in his ear becoming so much noise as his mind worked frantically to understand the ramifications. He cursed himself for not looking more closely earlier. Richard pounded the table with his fist. "*Fuck!*"

"Excuse me, Administrator?"

He was surprised that the woman was still on the phone. He ignored her, enraged that he hadn't put two and two together. For someone in such immense command of his organization, his people and most of America, he'd missed a critical detail. Mariposa Esposito had documents linking FEMA to supplies that had been provided to One and her team. It had all occurred through back channels, of course, but with enough analysis the documents could be used to prove his link to One. A list of documents she'd copied – many damning – had been inside the folder on his desk for days. But he'd delayed looking at it, wanting to find a way to free her. He'd been careless.

"I want her dealt with." He pressed the button to terminate the call.

He hadn't wanted to keep her detained, but by trying to find a way to free her he'd exposed himself. No more. She'd be dead within twenty-four hours.

14

As arrests continue across the country and the first of the detainees start to face justice, FEMA can announce the resumption of some private internet service to approved families. Households with no criminal convictions and with no web history of searching for prohibited topics will be provided with a login to the FEMA administered gateway, which allows access to a large number of websites.

Federal Emergency Management Agency
News Release

J ack felt his stomach rise to somewhere near his throat as the helicopter started to descend. He mumbled a curse under his breath and gripped the overhead rail so tightly that his knuckles went white. It was irrational, given he was seated and strapped in, but the last time he'd been aboard a helicopter he'd thought safe it had crashed into the South China Sea. His heart was pounding when the helicopter touched down with a light bump. He waited. When there was no hint of fiery explosion, he opened his eyes. He realized he'd been holding his breath and exhaled slowly. It had taken a lot of convincing and coercion to get him aboard. He'd never make the mistake again. He was done with helicopters.

"Mr Emery? You can let go of the rail now, sir. We don't want you to damage it." The pilot's mocking in Jack's headset was made worse by his southern drawl. "We're here."

Jack looked up. The pilot and co-pilot both had their necks craned to watch him, doing their best to conceal their smiles. He gave them a thumbs-up and removed the headset as one of the ground staff slid the door open and gestured for him to exit. He unbuckled and climbed out, keeping his head ducked low as he walked to the waiting convoy of vehicles. Or golf carts, anyway.

He approached a crowd of men and women surrounding one older man, who appeared to be sipping iced tea. This man was the whole reason he'd ventured onto the helicopter – despite his better judgment – and agreed to be flown right to the tee of the third hole at the East Potomac Golf Course. He was hardly able to refuse the invitation of FEMA in the current climate.

After his meeting with the President he'd checked in to a Washington hotel, given it had been too late to fly. He'd slept soundly and woken early, only to find Hall's people waiting for him the minute he reached the lobby. They'd obviously known about his meeting with the President. They'd asked him to join them for a helicopter flight to meet with Richard Hall. He'd hardly had a choice.

As he reached Hall and his entourage, he lifted a hand in a lazy greeting. "Good morning for it."

Richard Hall took one last sip of his iced tea, handed the glass to an assistant then pushed himself off the golf cart he'd been leaning on. "Good to meet you, Jack."

"Likewise." Jack kept his expression neutral, but was unable to resist the chance for a jab. "Didn't think a man of your stature would have to work so hard to make friends, though."

Hall's lips thinned in what Jack gathered was a smile. "You've become a person of interest. I wanted to meet before you disappeared down your hole again."

Jack doubted Hall would have any trouble finding him down any hole and suspected the timing of their meeting had been calculated for maximum impact. Though Hall might know he'd been involved in Guerrilla Radio and that he'd met with the President, Jack felt for sure that Hall was trying to work him out and intimidate him. Jack nearly laughed at the thought. Hall may have a lot of power, but he was an elderly career bureaucrat. He was hardly tough as nails.

Hall reached out and placed a hand on Jack's back, directing him gently toward the tee. "Walk with me, Jack. I need to have a discussion with you."

"Okay."

"I need you to understand the bind I'm in." Hall looked pained as he reached the tee. "Against every fiber of my being, I've given you a degree of special treatment already."

"You have?"

"Yes, I have." Hall sighed and selected a driver from the bag of clubs that was waiting next to the tee. "What's your handicap, Jack?"

"My swing." Jack gave a small laugh. "I'm not much of a golfer, Administrator. I tend to whack and pray."

Hall smiled, a twinkle in his eye. "I respect a man who appreciates his own limitations enough to make light of them."

Jack watched as Hall reached down and placed the ball on the tee then stood up straight. He seemed transfixed on the ball. He lined his shot up, drew the club back high and gave it his full swing. It was an exceptional shot. Hall held the club still as he watched the ball sail straight and true down the fairway. Jack doubted he could do better in a hundred tries. Hell, even a thousand tries.

"As I mentioned, I've given you a degree of special favor already." Hall turned back to him, his face a picture of seriousness. "My bind, Jack, is that I know your agenda."

Jack showed no emotion, though he did inch closer towards the golf bag. If this was an ambush it might help to have some iron in his hands. "I have no agenda, Administrator."

Hall sighed. "Can we be honest? I know of your involvement in Guerrilla Radio. I know you were helping to stir up events in Indianapolis. I know you met with the President. I also know you're not the kind of man to be easily dissuaded, but I need to try anyway. I owe you that much, out of respect for your achievements."

Jack's eyes narrowed, as his mind struggled to find Hall's angle. Then, it hit him like a brick. He nearly laughed. "My achievement against the Foundation? That was a long time ago. And you'd be surprised by the number of times I heard that right before people tell me something I don't want to hear."

"I'd like to hear your side of it first." Hall placed his club back in the bag and faced Jack front on. "Then I'll give you mine."

Jack shrugged. He had nothing to lose. "Look, cards on the table, I don't agree with the executive orders and I have huge concerns about what you and FEMA are doing. It stinks."

Hall frowned. "You seem to deny me the respect I'm affording you. I think I'm being incredibly reasonable here, Jack. The President has made a number of decisions in the interests of protecting the country and I'm responsible for implementing those decisions. I'm doing my job. Surely you can respect that."

"You've got a job to do, sure." Jack wasn't buying the

tortured bureaucrat act. Hall knew what he was doing and the impact of his actions. Jack chose his words carefully, being sure not to mention Celeste. "But the same justification has been used by tyrants for centuries. I'm struggling to see the difference."

"Sorry, I—"

Jack held up his hand, feeling the anger well up inside of him. "I was in Indianapolis. You've locked innocent people up. You've killed civilians. You may have a job to do, but I don't think I like where things are heading or where it all ends. So forgive me if I don't buy the shit you're selling, Administrator."

Hall's eyes narrowed, his face flushed red and his mouth opened and closed a few times, in a way that reminded Jack of a floundering fish. Jack wondered if he'd pushed the administrator too far. He'd definitely lost his cool, if nothing else. He wondered if he'd soon be joining Celeste in one of the camps. He took another step closer to the golf bag, now just a few feet away. A nine-iron might just hit the smug off Hall.

Finally, Hall began to speak. "Very well. I was hoping I'd be able to convince you to keep your head down while the trouble passes, but you've made your position clear. I won't waste your time or my breath. You're a hero, Jack, and I regret that it's come to this, but your special treatment is at an end. You've been warned."

"I understand." Jack's voice was barely a whisper and he was surprised by the menace in his voice.

Hall gave a short, sharp laugh. "I don't think you do. The next time you slip up, the next time you pop up on my radar, your precious Celeste will begin to feel pain."

Jack flared. He took a single, final step towards the golf bag and grabbed a club. He flicked it up into his hand and held it, with both hands, ready to strike Hall. "Do not threaten her!"

Jack heard a commotion and shouts from behind him, but he kept his eyes locked on the administrator. Hall, surprisingly, didn't move. He stared at Jack as he might a stray cat that had strolled into his yard. Jack gripped the club tighter, wanting to swing it and cave in Hall's head, decapitating FEMA at the same time. But he knew that doing so would sign Celeste's death warrant.

"Freeze!" A voice behind Jack shouted with authority. "Drop the club or we shoot."

Jack flicked a glance behind him. Several suited men were pointing pistols at him. Every fiber in his being wanted to take the shot, to swing the thing at Hall's head, to end this.

Hall coughed. "Done? If you were going to swing that thing, you'd have done it by now."

Jack closed his eyes as his grip on the club slackened. He knew that the only way forward was organized resistance. He lowered the club and tossed it on the ground. "Fuck you."

Hall gave the same laugh. "I don't want to hurt you, Jack, or your girlfriend. As I said, I respect you. You achieved a great deal for our country. My reaction will be directly proportional to your action. There's no simpler way for me to say it and you'll need to decide what comes next."

Jack seethed. "I'd like to go back now."

Hall's features lightened and he cracked a smile. "Sure you wouldn't like to join us for a game? The sixth is a killer."

Jack balled his fists by his side. "I'd like to go back."

Hall shrugged. "Okay, it was nice to meet you and I hope that you'll consider my words. My helicopter will take you back."

Hall picked up the club Jack had tossed and replaced it in the bag. Without looking at Jack, he turned and started off down the fairway. Jack fumed, fists clenched, for several long moments as the other man walked away. He tried to calm down, but was struggling. He'd expected Hall to be a tyrant, a maniac. He'd expected threats of violence and bribes to get Jack to stop doing what he was doing.

Instead, Jack had met a normal man, a bureaucrat who believed in what he was doing and would squeeze Jack – and Celeste – as hard as needed to get the desired result. To Hall, this wasn't personal. It was just another problem faced by a man who was used to dealing with them. His position was crystal clear: back off, or Celeste will start to become mightily uncomfortable in FEMA custody.

Jack was more committed than ever to ending him.

CALLUM CLOSED his eyes for the first time in sixteen hours. It wasn't quite as good as having his head on a pillow, but a comfortable chair and his feet on the desk was the best he could manage for the moment. He was on duty for another half-hour and for once there was nothing happening that required his attention. He hoped his luck would hold. He'd been on desk duty for the past few days, as part of a rotating shift involving all of the guards. Everyone took a turn on the towers, in the yard and in the administration. The latter was the most boring slot on the duty roster. It also had the longest shifts.

He hated himself for thinking it, but he wondered whether it would be a better idea to return to active duty. He hated the politics of the camp: management to guard, guard to guard, guard to prisoner, prisoner to prisoner. With the politics came the issues: maintenance, overcrowding, complaints. The thought of being back in a unit of soldiers, all working toward the same goal, suddenly seemed very appealing, if not for the carnage and violence it risked. He couldn't deal with that. Not yet.

There was a soft knock on the door. His eyes shot open and he nearly fell off the chair, but he managed to grab the desk before he made a fool of himself. "Come in."

The door opened and one of the few civilian staff in the detention center entered. Callum couldn't remember her name, but she flashed him a shy smile. "Hi, sorry to bother you."

"No problem." He waved her inside. She walked towards his desk and placed a single sheet of paper on it. He looked at it, then up at her. "What's that? Can't wait until next shift?"

"I don't think so, Sergeant. It's a, um—"

"It's okay." He smiled at her and held up a hand. "I'll take a look."

Relief spread like a rash across her face. Whatever the document was, it was something she was uncomfortable with. She nodded and backed toward the door. He shook his head, amazed that they'd recruited such a wilting flower to work in a place like this. He glanced at the sheet of paper, hoping he'd be able to palm it off on the next person to warm the chair, then sighed. It had the FEMA and State Guard logos side by side at the top. That made it important. He removed his feet from the desk and started to read the document.

He had to read it through four times before he processed and believed what was on the piece of paper. It was astonishing, to the point where he suspected fraud or some sort of practical joke. Except that this was no laughing matter. He flipped through the papers on his desk until he found a post-it with the number he was looking for. He picked up the phone, but paused before dialing. He looked once more at the newly arrived sheet of paper then dialed with a shake of his head.

The call was picked up quickly. "Operations, Nancy speaking."

"Hi Nancy, it's Callum Watkins out at Effingham."

"Hi Callum, how can I help?"

Callum leaned in to look at the sheet. "Can you confirm that correspondence Alpha-Hotel-Four-One-Five is legitimate?"

"Just give me a minute." He heard the sound of fast typing in the background. "Looks like it's legit. It has all the requisite approvals."

Callum's eyes widened as she spoke. "Okay. Thanks."

He hung up the phone and stared at the sheet for a few long moments. A detainee was to be executed for treason. The order was clear. Now it was confirmed as well. There was nothing else to do but act. He climbed to his feet and grabbed his shotgun from the rack on the wall. He checked the load and made sure the safety was on. If he was to detain a woman for execution, it meant separation from the other detainees. It could mean trouble.

He'd nearly reached the door when Micah Hill appeared on the other side. Callum winced, then regretted it – the other man had seen. He'd tried to avoid Micah since the incident in the shower block with the female detainees. Callum would prefer not to be associated with Hill's lack of professionalism and borderline criminal behavior, if he could, but they worked so closely together that it was hard to avoid the other man entirely.

Callum forced a smile. "How's it going, Micah?"

The other man ignored his greeting and glanced down at the shotgun. "Where you going, Cal? Your shift doesn't end for another twenty minutes."

Callum bit his tongue. He had to be careful. Despite his issues, Hill was still a superior. Callum waved the paper. "Orders."

"Oh yeah?" Hill reached out and grabbed the piece of paper.

Callum didn't resist or speak up as the other man read

it. His eyes flicked back and forth rapidly, as a grin grew slowly on his face. When he finished reading, he resembled a wolf that had just been handed the key to the chicken coop. "You've checked it out? It's legit? Damn."

"Yep." Callum shrugged. "It checks out."

"Well I guess that little bitch is going to get what's coming to her." The grin turned cold. "I'll take care of this one, Cal. You take it easy."

"But—"

"Don't worry about it." Hill's tone was sharp. "You take the next one."

Even though Callum doubted there would be a next one, and the other man made his skin crawl, he could hardly resist the order. In truth, Callum was glad to avoid the job. He needed, and wanted, to keep his hands clean – that was the deal with Bainbridge. If Callum could hand this over to someone else, he had to take the chance. Hill would handle the prep for the execution. If he fucked up, it was on him.

He nodded. "Okay."

"Later, man." Hill turned and stalked after his prey.

Callum shook his head as he closed the door. He placed the shotgun back on its rack and then walked back to the desk. Before he closed his eyes, he glanced at the clock. Another thirteen minutes and he was in the clear. He did all he could to avoid thinking about the unfortunate woman, whatever her crime. But no matter how hard he thought about other things, the order haunted him.

And she would haunt his dreams.

MARIPOSA WINCED as she watched Celeste struggle to shift her position in the bed slightly. Though she offered a brave smile, the woman was clearly in a lot of pain. It was hardly surprising. The guard's nightstick had shattered her kneecap and she'd also done some damage to the ligaments in the knee when she'd fallen. It was a combination of injuries that would take a while to heal.

Mariposa looked around. There was only one other patient in the small detention center hospital. She'd heard that the guards were quite hesitant to permit a trip to the hospital for most people, but they could hardly argue a shattered kneecap. It was more surprising that she'd been allowed to keep Celeste company, though. They'd spent the time chatting, getting to know each other more.

"Can I get you anything?"

"A frozen Margarita?" Celeste's smile was contagious.

"No, unfortunately." Mariposa laughed softly. "But I could get you—"

"Seriously, I'm fine." Celeste reached out and gripped Mariposa's hand. "Stop worrying. I'm just glad I've got someone to talk to."

Mariposa felt her face flush. She felt like she owed Celeste so much. Twice now she'd saved her, this time at great personal cost. "Do you have a boyfriend?"

"No." Celeste gave a tired looking frown. "Well, maybe. I don't know. It's complicated. Absurdly so."

"What do you mean?"

"It's a really long story." She shook her head in near disbelief. "I hadn't seen him for a long time, then our first night together was the night I was arrested."

Mariposa didn't know what to say. "What happens if you get out of here?"

"I don't know. Hopefully a hug and a smile. But I'm not sure. This is the second time we've spent a lot of time apart in less than eighteen months. It might be too late."

Mariposa nodded and Celeste went quiet. They sat in silence until she noticed Celeste blinking a few times, as if trying to ward off sleep. Mariposa reached out and gave her hand a squeeze. As if she'd pressed a button, Celeste's eyes closed and before long she'd started to breathe heavily. Mariposa could have left, but she kept holding the other woman's hand.

Mariposa woke when she heard a noise behind her, shocked by the noise as much as the by the fact she'd fallen asleep. She turned around and felt her heart jump into her throat as she saw him – the black man who'd assaulted them in the bathroom. There was no doubt who he was here for. Mariposa let go of Celeste's hand and held her hands up slightly, showing him she was no threat.

He approached the bed, shotgun held casually. "On your feet."

Mariposa kept her voice to a whisper. "Please be quiet. She's only just gone to sleep."

"Detainee, on your feet. I've got orders to take you to a different wing."

"What wing? My friend—"

"I'm not asking." He yanked her back, away from the bed.

She squealed but didn't resist. She'd had her fill of fighting authority, it had done nothing but lead her here. She was going to be assaulted by the man, but she couldn't ask Celeste for help this time, even if the other woman was capable of providing it. She would fight, for all that she was worth, but she'd do it away from Celeste Adams.

"Please let me say a few words?" Mariposa looked him straight in the eyes. "Then I'll come with you."

"You better." His eyes narrowed and something in his voice seemed very final as he backed away. "You've got two minutes."

Mariposa nodded and walked over to Celeste. She wasn't thinking clearly, but she didn't have time to fix that. She shook the woman's arm. Celeste stirred and mumbled something. Mariposa shook her some more, and Celeste's eyes flickered open. She looked up at Mariposa, confused. Celeste winced in pain as she tried to move.

"What's up?" Celeste blinked a few more times. "I just need to sleep, Mari."

"I know." Mariposa smiled sadly as she squeezed Celeste's hand. "I have to talk to you."

"Okay." Celeste's eyes started to close again.

Mariposa pinched Celeste's chin and shook her head slightly. "Celeste, you need to stay awake. Just a few more minutes."

"Okay."

"If you ever get out of here and something has happened to me, I want you to go to my home. Just look it up."

"Okay. I'll say hi to your son."

"Good." Mariposa smiled sadly. "There's a spare key under the ceramic cat out the back. I want you to go inside and find my mother."

Celeste fell silent and started to snore softly again. Mariposa cursed under her breath and tried to shake her. She was about to try harder when the guard grabbed her again and pulled her away from the bed. She'd clearly had all the time she was going to get. She let herself be led outside, hoping her final words to Celeste had registered.

As they walked along the path, surrounded on either side by a high chain-link fence, she started to get a sinking feeling. In an overcrowded camp where there was no privacy or free space, she was amazed by the lack of people around. The lack of witnesses. She walked for another dozen steps and then turned around.

She looked him straight in the eye. He stared back. There was nothing in his eyes, no spark, no warmth. She tried her luck. "Where are we going?"

He raised an eyebrow and gripped his weapon tighter.

"I like that you think you have a right to question me, detainee."

"Please." Mariposa fought back tears. "I know you're going to rape me, but please. I have a son. You don't have to do this."

"That's where you're wrong." He shrugged. "You're not going to be raped. But you should start praying to whichever god is your thing."

"No!" Her eyes widened. Ten minutes ago she'd been talking to her friend, now she was facing her end. She fell to her knees, prostrating herself before him as tears flowed down her face.

He sighed. "Get up."

"I have a son! I don't want to die, you bastard! There's no reason for this. I have a son!"

She'd lost it all. Her job, her freedom. Her son. The thought of Juan growing up without her was devastating. She collapsed into the dirt and couldn't stop the sobs. She struggled to breathe. Her chest hurt. She wanted to talk, but no words came. She gripped the small crushed rocks on the pathway, grabbed a handful and threw it at him.

It didn't help. She knew this was a one way trip.

ACT III

15

At a morning tea with State Guard troops wounded in the line of duty, President Morris, Administrator Hall and a number of cabinet secretaries celebrated three full months without a terrorist attack on American soil. President Morris presented each of the wounded men and women with a newly struck medal, the Peace Cross, noting that America has pushed through the darker clouds and that rays of sunshine were ahead. Administrator Hall was unavailable for comment.

Federal Emergency Management Agency
News Release

C allum squinted and shook his head as he looked down from the guard tower with his binoculars. He could see Micah Hill walking alongside a detainee, down the same path he walked every day at about this time. This detainee looked young, a scrawny twenty-something with a shaved head. Hill gripped his shotgun casually by his side. He was headed for the motor pool, where the prisoner would be hauled into a van and off to his death.

Callum lowered the binoculars and ran a hand through his hair as he exhaled slowly. He'd watched the same thing dozens of times over the past few months, and knew there'd been about one per day. Mariposa Esposito had been the first, shot by Hill against protocol. Hill had claimed she'd resisted on the way to the motorpool. Since then orders had come in for more. The only thing that prevented the prisoners from rioting was secrecy. They were told they'd been transferred.

Callum had refused to participate, citing Bainbridge's psychological report as sufficient reason why. When a guard officer had called Bainbridge to take issue, the psychologist had given the officer an earful. Though Callum had been spared the need to take part in the executions, he'd still had to stand and watch as more and more detainees were led to their death. He didn't know if the same situation was taking place in other camps, but figured it must have.

But today the order had come in that he'd feared. It was the first time that there'd been two executions ordered on the one day and his name had been put down to transport one of them. Apparently not even Bainbridge had the pull to get Callum out of the duty, or else he'd changed his mind. Callum wasn't sure. But whatever had happened, the order was clear and he had a job to do. He was posted in the guard tower until the time came to drive the young woman to her death.

As if on cue, the camp's PA system gave a loud squeal and then Callum heard the words he dreaded. "Detainee Celeste Adams, please report to the B wing courtyard immediately."

He sighed loudly, gripped the shotgun and patted his holster to make sure his pistol was in place. As ready as he could ever be, he descended the stairs from the guard tower. It was a short walk through the compound to where the motor pool was located. As he walked, he tried to deal with the conflicting thoughts racing around his head.

"Reporting as ordered, sir." Celeste Adams was already waiting for him.

Callum jerked a thumb towards the nearby van. "I need to head into Effingham and I'm hung over. You're going to drive."

Her lips pursed and he thought she might mouth off, but after a moment she nodded and walked toward the van. He watched as she opened the door and climbed in. This all seemed so pointless, orders be damned. He'd read her file. She was the detainee he'd helped in the intake line. Her knee had only just recovered from being shattered by Hill's baton months ago in the shower block. She'd certainly had an eventful stay. He climbed into the van.

She started the engine, keeping her eyes ahead. "There's no need for this charade. If you're going to do it, just do it."

"Just drive the vehicle, detainee."

She kept quiet as he entered the address of the town into the GPS and hit start. He cradled the shotgun between his legs and eased back into the chair. The van picked up pace, until they reached the guardhouse to the only gate out of the camp. Adams pulled the vehicle up next to it and wound the window down when prompted by a guard, who strolled out of the guardhouse and over to their vehicle with a clipboard in hand.

"Hey, Callum." The gate guard leaned his head inside the van with a smile. "Where y'all heading?"

"Hi Andy. Just have to head to Effingham. Too hung over to drive, so thought I'd take fuck up over here."

"Not a bad fuck up, if you're going to take one, if you catch my drift." Andy Ward gave a long laugh, as if Adams wasn't even there. "Okay. Enjoy your drive."

Callum forced a laugh as Adams wound up the window

and they started to move again. They drove in silence for nearly an hour. He'd usually listen to the radio, but he needed time to think and process what he was about to do: drop a woman off for execution. It violated every inch of his moral code. He gripped the shotgun tighter and wished there was some other way. As they drove further, the sun disappeared behind a large, dark cloud. It seemed like fitting symbolism.

He looked over at her. "Pull over."

She glanced at him, indicated and pulled over to the side of the road. He sat in silence as he thought hard. She wasn't stupid. He could sense her looking at the shotgun in between his legs, probably weighing up whether she could grab for it, escape or do something else before the hammer came down. He let out a breath, lifted the gun and opened the door. He climbed out of the van.

She looked at him quizzically. "What are you doing?"

"Go." He slammed the door shut and held the shotgun casually at his side.

The electric window on his side wound down and when he looked inside she was staring at him. "What the fuck?"

He took a step back from the vehicle. When she made no move to depart, he raised an eyebrow. "Go. That's an order."

"Um, no?" She took her hands off the wheel and crossed her arm. "You're suggesting a sure-fire way to end up dead or in a real prison."

Callum glared. "You may end up in prison, yes. But I've been ordered to drop you off to be executed. Even if you eventually end up dead, you break even. This is your chance. Go!"

She looked at him for a moment or two and then nodded. She started the van, wound up the window and glanced at him again. It was as if she expected him to change his mind, but he'd never been surer about anything in his whole life. She placed her hands on the wheel and inched the van forward. He laughed when she thought to indicate as she pulled away, kicking up a small plume of dust.

He hadn't known which way his mind would take him, which choice he'd make. It was against every fiber of his being to help execute a civilian, despite whatever puffed-up crime they'd been accused of. On the other hand, carrying out those orders would have been easier than what faced him now his decision was made. He waited until the van was a speck in the distance. Whatever. He'd done the right thing. Damn Hill, Bainbridge or anyone else who tried to bust him for it.

He stretched his neck, rotating it left and right, and then sighed as he unsafed the shotgun. He raised it to his shoulder, pointed it in the air and squeezed the trigger. The gun roared and kicked into his shoulder. He lowered it, pumped it and then repeated the action. Done, he safed the weapon and threw it onto the ground. Now there were a couple of spent shells to prove he'd tried to stop her. He pulled his cell phone from his pocket, dialed and waited for an answer.

"This is Major Bainbridge."

"Major? It's Sergeant Callum Watkins. There's been an incident. I need some help."

Jack glanced up at the four-story heritage building with some pride. In the heart of Chicago's Old Town, it was far enough from downtown to avoid FEMA saturation, but in a convenient enough location to suit his needs. It was discreet and low key – absolutely perfect. He'd been surprised when Elena had revealed that she'd arranged for the resistance to use the building as its headquarters.

It had been a busy couple of months. Since he'd met with the initial members of the resistance in New York, the movement had grown at great pace. They hadn't commenced operations, but had been busy gathering information and readying themselves to agitate and resist when the time came. After his meetings with Morris and Hall, Jack had wanted to make sure they were ready before acting. The time was now.

He'd traveled to Chicago with Peter Weston the previous day. It was risky to move so far across the country, but Jack had seen no alternative. New York was too close to Washington, and there was a strong cell established there now. He had to trust others to maintain the operations there while he prepared to kick off their activity. Though he'd half expected to be detained a dozen times on the road, he'd made it.

"Just the trick, I'd say." Peter patted him on the shoulder and looked up at the building. "Looks good, doesn't it?"

"Sure does. Elena has done a great job." Jack smiled and jerked his head toward the door. "Let's go in and check it out?"

They rode the elevator to the top floor. It opened with a chime and a pair of burly-looking men met them at the door. He shouldn't have been surprised that Elena had organized some security to protect the inner sanctum of the resistance from prying eyes. She'd apparently thought of everything. One of the guards stepped forward, a clipboard in hand, while the other maintained a watchful distance.

Jack smiled. He was certain they'd know who he was, given he was the nominal leader of the resistance. "Good to see you, fellas."

"Need to get your names, gentlemen." There was no

warmth from clipboard man. "Please also keep your movements slow and your hands where we can see them."

"Not a problem." Jack sighed and tapped his leg. "I'm Jack Emery and this is Peter Weston. Elena Winston is expecting both of us. Can we make this quick?"

"It'll take as long as it takes, sir." Clipboard man looked down at his list.

Jack crossed his arms and turned to Peter. He kept his voice low. "Can you believe this?"

Peter gave a pained look. "Bunch of little dictators, aren't they?"

Clipboard man looked up at them. "Okay, you're alright to head on through."

Jack didn't give them another second of his time. He walked down the corridor, which opened up into a large, open-plan space with some desks and meeting spaces, but only a single office at the back of the room. There was a handful of people scattered about, but for the most part the room was empty. Jack didn't know any of them except for one – Elena. She was leaning against a doorframe, a broad smile on her face.

Jack smiled and crossed the distance quickly, as the others in the cubicle farm stared at him strangely. He didn't care. Elena was one of the few people who understood what was happening, what he was going through and what he was trying to do. When he reached her, they hugged tightly. The friendship they shared still surprised him a little, but they'd become allies under fire.

"I'm glad you're okay, Jack." Her voice wavered slightly. "I was worried you wouldn't make it. It's really good to see you."

He backed away from her. "I've kept my streak going. I think FEMA likes having me around."

"Is that so?" She smirked. "Meeting the President, golf

with Hall, months underground – shame you couldn't get them to change their mind, with all that popularity."

"It would make all this unnecessary." Peter gestured around the office.

Elena jerked a thumb behind her. "Come inside."

Jack nodded and the three of them stepped inside the office. He used the spare moment to gather his thoughts. Something felt wrong. It was odd that Elena had mentioned the meetings with Morris and Hall from months ago. They'd been the final straw for Jack, proof that the balance of power in America had shifted massively. It had been his last attempt to use reason and argument to free the country from FEMA's web.

In the preceding months, a network of influential Americans had sprung up using the technology Hickens had provided to block electronic eavesdropping. Jack had been in hiding, along with most of the leadership, waiting patiently as their power grew. Though there had been setbacks, for the first time there were people in place across nearly the whole country. The resistance was ready to move.

"This is perfect, Elena." Jack smiled as he closed the door, then walked over to sit on one of the chairs. "Your office, I presume?"

"No, nothing of the sort." She shook her head. "It hasn't been assigned yet. I want to know what comes next, Jack. The network is ready."

"Guerrilla Radio was all about information." Jack patted her shoulder. "Now we've spent months building something a little bit more potent than that."

"And what're we doing?" Elena stared at him, a strange look in her eyes. "I want to know, Jack. I've earned that."

"We're taking the country back. They have control of civilian government and a paramilitary force to back them up. We've gathered a bunch of influential people around us to speak out, act out, advocate, resist, provide finance and sustenance. Thousands. All we need to do is tip the scales and the people will follow. They have to."

"But—"

Peter stepped forward. "I know you're worried, but we've evolved, Elena. They think they've shut us down, Hall included, but there'll be eyes on us waiting for us to do something wrong. We just have to be careful and hope Hickens' technology keeps us off their radar for long enough to do what needs doing."

"Don't worry just yet, Elena." Jack walked over to her and placed his hands on her shoulders. "You've got a role to play, just like everybody else."

She sighed and squirmed away from his touch. "Jack, I really need to speak with you in private about something."

He shook his head and smiled. "Can it wait? I've got to call Bill McGhinnist. He only has a small window. Catch you later?"

"No." She was jittery. "It's important. It really can't—"

He was surprised by how on edge she seemed. He'd never seen her act like this before, not even at their most desperate, in Indianapolis. Perhaps she was just nervous that things were close to kicking off, given how poorly that had gone with Guerrilla Radio. But he couldn't indulge her now. He thought about how much work he had to do – a dozen calls to make and so much to organize.

"Please, Elena. Peter. I just need a few minutes." He didn't wait for them to leave the room, but turned away and started to dial. He lifted the phone to his ear.

He had to speak to McGhinnist and check in on efforts on the east coast. After that, he had to check in on the other cells. One of the problems of a tight cell structure and a small leadership was the amount of work each member had to do. It was critical to limit information to those in the inner sanctum, to reduce the risk of exposure and protect those close to him, but it took a heavy toll.

He turned around as McGhinnist picked up, just as the door closed behind Peter and Elena. He let out a deep breath. It was time to unleash the beast.

THE BIRD IS *in the nest.*

Richard smiled like a hyena as he read the text message, taking a moment to enjoy the words. He looked up from his phone. His was the only occupied table at the 1789 Restaurant, which had been cleared by his security detail prior. He picked up his glass and drained the last of the pinot. He sloshed the wine around in his mouth, savoring the taste, before swallowing. Along with pleasure came relief. It had been months since Jack Emery had been spotted, but since their meeting at the golf course Richard had kept an eye on him. He'd received intelligence that Emery had been central to the revitalization of the resistance. He'd miscalculated often when dealing with these individuals, but he was determined to get it right this time. He was glad he'd have the chance.

He'd first tried to smash the resistance by making an example out of the agitators in Indianapolis. But in hindsight he'd been too heavy handed. In trying to dampen down one crisis, all he'd done was make martyrs out of the dead and imprisoned. It had vindicated the resistance against FEMA control in the eyes of the neutral observer and emboldened the fanatics. His next miscalculation had been detention of loved ones and surgical strikes. Those hadn't worked either. Neither the journalists or other members of the resistance had been dissuaded, instead all he'd been left with was thousands of people to detain at enormous cost to the taxpayer. It hadn't gone down well with Morris. Finally, he'd hoped an appeal to the resistance's nominal leader, Jack Emery, would work. It hadn't.

At every step he'd miscalculated. He'd secured the country, but failed to eradicate the termites nibbling away at the base of that control. They'd gorged themselves, grown stronger and smarter, and now posed a greater threat to his agenda. But against all temptation to strike again, Richard had waited. He'd learned that not everything could be planned on a corkboard. He'd backed his gut, halted all offensive operations against the resistance and waited for Emery to emerge from hiding. As he did, he'd gradually begun to relinquish some minor elements of control, to show the public that with cooperation came increased freedoms.

Letting the resistance grow had been a huge risk, but he knew that if he couldn't get Emery, he couldn't truly end the resistance. If he'd waited much longer, the resistance would have been in a position to pose a serious threat. But the gamble had paid off. Richard now knew where Jack Emery was. On the eve of the commencement of resistance operations, he was in a position to smash them once and for all. Not only Emery, but a large number of prominent and affluent Americans. It would be a coup de grâce in every possible sense.

He let out a long sigh of relief and stood to stretch his muscles, then picked up his briefcase and walked to the entrance of the restaurant, all thoughts of dinner forgotten. A few of the staff looked at him with confusion, but didn't speak. They were probably appalled that Washington DC's most well regarded restaurant had been cleared out for the evening so he could eat there, and he hadn't even stayed for his second course. He didn't care. He had work to do and his people would fix up the bill. He left the restaurant and climbed into the car that was waiting.

He leaned forward to speak to the driver. "Take me to FEMA headquarters, please."

"Yes, Administrator." The driver fired the engine. "Everything okay with dinner, sir?"

"Lost my appetite." Richard sat back, making it clear he didn't want any more small talk.

As the car inched forward and the lights of the police escort started to flash, he picked up the phone and looked back at the original message. He keyed a response and let his finger hover over the phone for a moment, as his mind processed the situation one more time, looking for any holes in his plan. With a smile and a shake of his head, he hit send. Once she read it, the woman he'd come to rely on would terminate the threat of Jack Emery, bringing a giant hammer down on his resistance. The endgame had arrived. He dialed Rebecca Bianco.

After a moment Bianco answered. "Hello, sir."

"Good evening, Rebecca. Proceed with Operation Barghest."

There was a pause. "Are you sure, Administrator? The cost will be enormous and once the order is given it will be difficult to recall."

He sighed. His underlings continued to disappoint. He was astounded that Bianco had to ask if he was sure, after her hesitation in the face of his orders in Indianapolis. Though the pinot had been fantastic, it was as if she thought he'd made the decision to green light the most ambitious law enforcement operation on American soil in history after a few too many red wines. The weight of the whole country rested on his shoulders, yet stupid questions were still asked and answered. He let it go. She'd been a good operator for the most part. He had precious few of those.

"Yes, I'm sure." His voice was unintentionally sharp.

"I'm on my way to headquarters, I expect you to be there when I arrive."

"That only gives me—"

"Sixteen minutes." Richard terminated the call.

He put the phone beside him on the seat and closed his eyes. He'd underestimated Jack Emery and the resistance from the beginning. It was time to act, to cut off the head of the resistance and crush its membership into dust. Eyes still closed, he allowed himself a small smile. Tomorrow was going to be a good day.

16

In line with the raising of the Homeland Security Advisory System threat level to Severe (Red), FEMA has announced that all emergency measures that have previously been loosened will immediately be reinstated to their original status. All citizens will have a 24-hour grace period to adjust to these measures, after which penalties for breaches will apply. FEMA echoes the calls from President Morris and Administrator Hall for everyone to remain calm.

Federal Emergency Management Agency
News Release

J ack smiled as he looked around the table at the result of months of work. He'd returned to the Old Town office to meet with the team handpicked by Elena to handle all day-to-day coordination of the resistance. Alongside Elena and Peter were about a dozen others united in the same cause. The small group would be responsible for a tectonic shift in American politics, as the resistance began a concerted push against FEMA control across the whole country.

He'd been on the phone until the early hours of the morning, checking in with every cell leader. The people were in place and Jack was as happy as he could be with the preparations. This was their best chance to disrupt FEMA, expose their atrocities, influence neutral decision makers and take back the streets. It mightn't work, but it wouldn't be for lack of trying. Jack considered this network to be his masterpiece, an achievement far beyond what he thought possible.

"Last of all, I just wanted to thank each and every one of you for the risk you're taking by being here and doing this work." He glanced at Elena, then at Peter. "It's all too easy for us, individually, to turn away when we're faced with a situation like this. Hell, I nearly did. But an extraordinary person got me involved. Elena."

Elena flashed beet red. "Jack, I..."

"You're modest." Jack smiled, held out a hand toward her, then started to clap. The others joined him in applause for a moment or two. "You've all built this. It's important we acknowledge the work everyone has put in, but tomorrow the real work starts. We light the first sparks in what'll become a roaring bonfire. Thanks."

Jack nodded and walked away from the table. He could hear Elena telling the staff to go home, take a day for themselves, get some sleep and stay safe. That had been her idea, and he'd taken some convincing, but he'd swallowed his reservations. While he didn't like the idea of a day of inertia, she was right. Everything was in place and it was important his people were rested before they hit the switch.

He moved to the office, closed the door and collapsed into the chair. He was exhausted. For all the talk of letting the team have a break, he hadn't slept properly in a week. He closed his eyes and felt himself start to drift off, despite his mind protesting that he had work to do. His eyes shot back open when the door opened and Elena and Peter walked in chatting. He must have fallen asleep for a moment. They stopped in their tracks.

"Jack, sorry." Peter held up a hand in apology. "Thought you could use a coffee. The others have all gone home."

"Should have grabbed me a double shot." Jack smiled as Peter placed the tray of coffees down on the desk. He stood and took one of them. "Thanks."

Peter patted him on the back then looked to Elena. "And for madam, a soy—"

"Jack, I'm sorry." Elena's voice was pained.

Jack was confused by the shift in conversation. He looked over at her, the coffee cup still held to his mouth. Elena had a pistol trained on Peter. A tear streaked down her face. Jack's cup fell to the carpet and his mouth fell open. A thousand thoughts and a million questions battled for primacy in his head, but they were overwhelmed by far too many memories of being held at gunpoint. One thing won out.

"Help!" Jack's voice pierced the silence.

Elena didn't move. She kept the gun trained on Peter as a single sob added to her tears. Jack held out his hands and tried to talk her down, to get her to lower the weapon, but she just shook her head vigorously. To his credit, Peter didn't move an inch, merely held his hands up. He couldn't comprehend what was happening, but Elena's tears and hesitation gave hope for a peaceful resolution.

The two security goons ran into the office. Jack sighed with relief. The man who'd checked his name off the clipboard on his first visit scanned the room, his hand squeezing a revolver tightly, as his similarly armed colleague used his bulk to block the door. Elena looked over her shoulder at the men, sighed deeply and lowered her weapon. Jack relaxed a little, satisfied that the immediate danger had passed.

"Thanks, fellas." Jack sighed with relief. "Elena, what the fuck?"

"Fucking hell, Jack." Peter's eyes were wide. Jack followed his gaze to clipboard man, whose knuckles were white from squeezing the pistol tightly. "This whole thing is a setu—"

In the small office, the boom sounded like planets colliding. Peter fell to the floor, his blood spraying all over the wall. Jack screamed, fell to his knees and scrambled toward his friend, lifeless and face down on the ground. He cradled the head of the man he'd been to hell and back with. There was no point. There was a hole the size of a small fist in the back of Peter's skull, which oozed blood.

He turned and looked up at Elena. Multiple weapons were trained on him. "Why?"

"This was the only way." Her voice cracked. "They've got my fiancé."

"They've had him for months!" Jack's scream was full of anguish and anger, but she didn't react beyond another small sob. "Why now?"

"These guys are going to have a chat with you." She looked down at the ground. "I'm sorry, Jack."

"Fuck you." He snarled as his head ached, trying to process this. "I assume this means the rest of the resistance is being fucked in the same way right now?"

"Yes." She stared at the ground. "I'm sorry."

Jack climbed slowly to his feet. His legs were wobbly. He spat in Elena's face, his spittle mixing with her tears, then turned to clipboard man. "Let's get this over with."

A voice squawked in Callum's earpiece. "All teams stand by."

Callum nearly laughed at the absurdity of a command

staffer having to warn them that the stroke of the hour was approaching. Every man and woman in his small unit had their eyes glued to their watches. He supposed it was good to let some commanding officer, somewhere, prove that he could tell the time at least as well as the people under his command. On the other hand, his operation was part of a countrywide effort, so maybe there was some logic in having an inane countdown.

Callum had no idea where the other targets were located, but he hadn't been part of an operation of this scale since he'd been in Iraq. More than 120 guard troops had been mobilized to assault a single hotel. It was excessive force, but it would be effective. Shock and awe. He doubted the resistance posed enough of a threat to warrant such a hammering, but not much had been normal lately.

He checked his shotgun once more. There was no need, but he did it out of habit. It felt strange conducting an offensive again, but the weapon felt comfortable in his hand – more comfortable than his presence on the mission, anyway. He'd thought he was done with this business, now he was back in charge of a squad of State Guard troopers about to assault a resistance stronghold in the middle of downtown Chicago. He'd gone from one extreme to the other and then back again.

He let out a sigh. After he'd let Celeste Adams drive off, there had been a brief investigation. Callum doubted that the commanding officer of the detention center had wanted to be associated with an escapee *and* the guard who'd let it happen, so the incident had been brushed under the carpet. He'd been quietly reassigned to one of the active guard battalions. His call to Bainbridge had probably helped with that and, though he hated active duty, he'd hated being a prison guard even more.

That was how he found himself leaning against a concrete wall outside the Club Quarters Hotel in downtown Chicago. Much of the hotel had been booked for months in the name of an influential businessman and State Guard command suspected that much of the hotel was being used as a front for the resistance. Now, Callum's squad had been assigned the task of assaulting the third floor while other squads hit other floors.

"Show time guys." Callum pushed himself off the concrete wall. "Let's go."

His team moved in single file into the hotel lobby. The teams that had been assigned to the upper floors were already moving up the stairs. Once it was their turn, Callum led his team up the stairs and they exited on the third floor, taking up covering positions along either side of the corridor. After a few moments, a buzz sounded in his earpiece. It was time to make some noise. He gave his team thumbs up.

His team started moving in pairs to the door of each room on the floor they'd been ordered to hit. Callum was paired with Paddy Carlisle, a quiet kid from Boston he'd known for less than a day. He took up position on the left side of the door, while Carlisle took up his spot on the right. When his team was in place, Callum shouted for them to go and watched as Carlisle stepped forward with a ram. The soldier didn't hesitate, smashing into the door once, then again. It gave a loud, tortured cracking sound as its timbers protested then gave way.

Carlisle dropped the ram and moved inside with his pistol drawn, followed by Callum with the heavy artillery. Callum scanned the room. There were no targets and only two possible hiding places: behind the bed on the far side of the wall or the bathroom. He gestured for Carlisle to take the bed, while Callum checked the bathroom. He edged forward, until he heard the tell-tale pop of a small caliber handgun. He turned around. A gunman had shot Carlisle from behind the bed, the exact spot Callum had been worried about.

"Freeze!" Callum raised the weapon as Carlisle fell to the ground. "Don't do anything stupid!"

The gunman swung the pistol around. Callum reacted instantly. The shotgun barked and a dozen crimson stains appeared on the man's white T-shirt as he fell. Callum moved over to where Paddy Carlisle lay motionless. The pistol round had hit him in the head. Callum checked his pulse. Nothing. He'd probably been dead before he'd hit the floor. Callum slammed a fist into the ground. With a growl of frustration he ripped the quilt off the bed, threw it over Carlisle's body and then walked out to the corridor. Within two minutes, his entire unit had finished its work. Some prisoners had been taken, and some had fought back.

Callum gathered a detailed picture before he radioed in. "Command, this is Watkins. Third floor is secure. One Guard KIA. Three suspects killed and seventeen in custody. All clear."

He ignored the confirmation from command as he returned to the room he'd cleared, placed his back against the wall and slid down until he was seated on the carpet. He let out a long breath and rested his head in his hands. He couldn't believe he was back here, doing this work again, watching more young men go to their graves. He thought of Celeste Adams. He'd saved her life, but the price may very well have been his own. He wondered if he'd crack and have to have Bainbridge testify on his behalf at some trial or another. He didn't get the chance to finish the thought, as heard a noise and looked up.

"You okay, Sarge?" One of his men was peering in with a strange look on his face.

"Fine, Private. Just a long day." Callum climbed to his feet again. "Let's move out."

The private nodded. "I'll gather the guys."

Callum sighed. He wondered how many more people – Americans – had died today.

JACK'S HEAD THROBBED. He could barely open his left eye, it was that badly swollen. Every time he moved, his chest screamed in pain. He had cuts and lacerations all over body and his blood stained the carpet, mixed with the dried mess of Peter's final moment. He kept his eyes closed as he felt around his body and inspected the damage further. He'd chipped a tooth on a leather boot and was pretty sure he had a broken rib. He wondered if the swollen left eye might have some permanent damage.

He rolled onto his side with a groan. They'd beaten him in the hours since Elena's betrayal. But if there was one saving grace to having the shit kicked out of you by relative amateurs instead of the Chinese military, it was the fact that he'd managed to get some sleep in the early evening when they took a break. It was a small victory, but he'd take it. On the other hand, their lack of finesse also meant they lacked the skill necessary to extract maximum information for minimum damage

He pushed himself up with both hands and an enormous groan. His head spun and a wave of nausea hit him. He forced it down and shook his head, trying to clear the haze. He wondered if he had a concussion on top of the other injures. He did his best to squeeze his eyes open and looked over to where Peter had been shot dead. If nothing else, he was pleased that they'd dragged the body out at some point, though Peter's blood had left a wide red stain on the carpet. He missed his friend already.

He sighed as he leaned forward and hugged his knees, wincing in pain. More painful was the knowledge that he'd fucked everything up and probably gotten everyone killed. He'd been so stupid, blinded by his trust toward Elena and oblivious to the signs of treachery. She'd been absent when Celeste's home was raided. She'd probably betrayed the location of the Guerrilla Radio leadership. She'd leaked other information for god knew how long. She'd caused Peter's death. Worse, she'd probably ended any chance of defeating FEMA.

He didn't know the extent of the damage, but it had to be immense. She'd been at the heart of both Guerrilla Radio and the rebooted resistance effort. If she'd set up an attack in Chicago, chances were good that the other resistance cells had been hit as well. Jack didn't know if anyone was left alive, but from what he'd seen in Indianapolis, Richard Hall would strike hard and aim at the head. Once that was done, the FEMA administrator would grind the body of the movement to a pulp. He wouldn't chance another rebirth.

A small cough behind him startled him, and he growled in frustration at the pain in his ribs. He did his best to turn, but the movement was nearly comical. It was Elena, seated on an office chair with her elbows resting on her knees and her chin cupped in her hands. Make up stained her face and made her look like a panda. Her hair fell across her shoulders in a mess. What surprised him was the satisfaction he felt at the fact that she looked like shit. Fury rumbled in the pit of his stomach, despite the condition he was in.

"Jack." Her voice was soft, full of sadness.

He roared as he tried to push himself forward onto his hands and knees. "I'll kill—"

He heard a pistol cock. She was pointing it at him. "Don't."

Jack paused. He was enraged, but he had no desire to

die. He rested back on his knees and laughed darkly. "I never thought in a million years that this would happen."

"Me either." She held the pistol on him for a second longer and then lowered it, apparently satisfied that he wasn't going to charge her. "We need to talk."

"No, we don't." Jack held his hands out wide. "Fucking hell, Elena. Was all of this worth it, you fucking Judas? I hope you enjoy the thirty pieces of silver."

She stood and took a step toward him, then paused. He saw the pain in her eyes and the tears streaking down her face. They fed his anger. "Jack, I—"

"No!" He shook his head and pointed a finger at her. "You brought the hammer down on me. On *us*. How many of us did you betray? Everyone?"

She staggered back as if he'd struck her. One step, then another, then she caught herself on the edge of a desk. She stared at her feet "Hall said he'd kill my fiancé if I didn't help."

"I just don't want to fucking hear it, Elena. They're going to kill me. I—"

"Nice little love-in we've got here."

He saw Elena look up at the door and followed her gaze to see clipboard man standing in the doorway. He had a broad smile on his face and his offsider leaned against the door frame. They both had pistols drawn. Jack looked back at Elena, who had her weapon held loosely by her side. She dropped it when instructed to. If nothing else, it looked like she mightn't survive her treachery either.

"Looks like you might have changed your mind, young lady." Clipboard man's voice was loaded with sarcasm. "Can't say I'm surprised."

The offsider laughed. "Hey, Mike? After we kill him, I'd like a piece of her. Nothing in the orders said we couldn't have a little fun with her once the job is done."

Clipboard man turned and let out a long laugh. "Sure. It might be fun, even though she looks a bit like a clown."

Jack snarled. His ribs screamed at him as he lunged at clipboard man, who heard the noise and started to turn just as Jack reached him. Jack lowered his shoulder and the force of the tackle pushed the two of them through the office window. The pistol boom mixed with the sound of the glass shattering to form a terrible crescendo. Jack landed heavily on top of the larger man as glass crashed down on top of them.

Clipboard man wasn't idle. He bucked and did his best to dislodge Jack as he pounded his fist into the other man's face. At the same time, clipboard man reached for the pistol that had slipped from his grip. Jack couldn't let that happen. He brought down his clasped hands on clipboard man's arm. He heard a crack and the other man screamed. Jack swung punches wildly as clipboard man changed tactics and started to aim blows at Jack.

Jack winced in pain as he took one glancing hit to the head, then a second to his nose. Stars exploded in his vision and he fell backward. His face felt like it was on fire. He blindly swung another punch as he fell, but hit air. He grunted and heard a crunch as he landed on his back, but didn't have time to consider the glass he'd landed on because the other man threw himself on top of him.

"I was going kill you quickly." Clipboard man wrapped his hands around Jack's neck. "Now I'm going to crush your fucking throat."

Jack struggled to breathe and to dislodge the other man. He clawed at the hands gripping his neck, then attempted to buck the other man off. But it was no good. Clipboard man had fifty pounds on him and the strength of an ox. He started to black out. His vision narrowed. His body screamed in agony. His muscles burned. He lost the strength to struggle against the man, who had his thumbs dug into Jack's throat.

He closed his fingers into a fist and used the last of his strength to swing his hand toward clipboard man's throat. He heard a gurgle and the pressure on his own throat was immediately gone. Jack wheezed and coughed, sucking at air but struggling to breathe even as a torrent of blood sprayed over him. Clipboard man fell off him, clutching his throat, trying to stem the bleeding from his severed artery. Jack rolled over, gripped the piece of glass in his hand tighter and stabbed it into the man's face several times.

Jack kept sucking in air and, as his peripheral vision started to return, he saw the other man struggling with Elena. He must have left clipboard man to finish off Jack and moved in to claim his prize. Her top was ripped and he raised a fist to strike her. Jack dropped the glass and propped himself up onto an elbow. He was surrounded by glass, covered in blood and struggling to stay conscious. He looked at his hands. They were bloody and cut open from the glass. Then he saw the revolver.

He reached out. It was so close, yet the effort required to grab it seemed superhuman. When his hands wrapped around the grip, he pointed the barrel to the floor and used it to push himself off the ground. He coughed hard as he struggled to his feet. He staggered forward, bracing himself on the frame of the door as he raised the revolver unsteadily and fired. Miss. As the other man started to swing around Jack accounted for the recoil and fired again. The second shot hit true. He fell to one knee and dropped the revolver.

He steadied himself then looked up as Elena walked toward him, a step or two away from the body of her attacker. Jack wasn't the best shot, but it was hard to miss from six feet away. The dead man had never seen it coming. She fell to her knees and wrapped Jack in a hug. His mind screamed in protest, despite the battering he'd taken. He pushed her away and struggled to his feet. It took an eternity, but he made it. He said nothing else as he started to walk to the elevator.

"I'm sorry, Jack!" She was crying. "I'm going to fix this."

He didn't look back.

17

Terrorist cells in more than forty cities have been disrupted or destroyed in simultaneous operations by the State Guard and other federal and local authorities. Administrator Hall called it the most significant development since the onset of the crisis, and also released details of the group's leader: Mr Jack Emery. Mr Emery is wanted on a range of terrorism-related charges, which center on a conspiracy to disrupt and degrade the capacity of FEMA and the United States Government. Anyone with information should contact the National Security Hotline.

> *Federal Emergency Management Agency*
> *News Release*

Richard approached the President, who held her arms wide and sported a broad smile on her face. Though he usually didn't like physical contact, he moved in closer and hugged her. She slapped him on the back a few times and then backed away. Richard took a moment to compose himself, then sat in the chair she was gesturing toward. It was probably worth more than he earned in a week on his government salary.

"Richard, hell of a job." She beamed as she took a seat on the sofa opposite him. "Sorry for calling you in, but I read your briefing and couldn't quite believe it."

He'd never been to Camp David before and, as he looked around the President's office, he felt a wave of relief wash over him. The patience to get the resistance in exactly the right spot hadn't been without risk, but it had paid off handsomely. Clearly Morris felt the same way. Usually she was reserved, critical and very sparing in her praise, but from the moment he'd walked in the mood had felt festive.

He sat a little bit taller. "Not a problem, Madam President. The operation was without setback and was a complete success."

She frowned. "As simple as that?"

"As simple as that." He smiled again, so widely his cheeks hurt. "This is the coup we've been waiting for. The resistance has been annihilated. It's over."

"Run me through it."

"Okay." He tried not to show his displeasure – it had all been in the report. "Under FEMA direction, the State Guard and local police forces undertook operations across forty cities in thirty-one states. All known locations of resistance activity were assaulted and the perpetrators arrested or killed. It's as complete a decapitation as possible."

It was true. With Elena Winston's information and the combined resources of the Federal Government, he'd managed to locate nearly the entire network of the resistance: Jack Emery and the leadership, the influencers, the cell leaders and the foot soldiers. His forces had crushed them all. His only mistake had been trusting Winston and the two agents he'd assigned to kill Emery. They'd failed.

"If it's not a complete lopping off of the head, to use your parlance, then what's left hanging from the neck, Richard? I've been burned by your assurances before. If I'm going to close the book on this, I want to know that I'm at the end of the story, and not just starting another chapter."

Richard sighed. He'd hoped to avoid this. "Jack Emery, their leader, is alive. But he's now irrelevant. He has no power base and he's on the run. We'll catch Emery and mop up the remains of his mess in the next few days. There's nothing else left to worry about regarding the resistance in its current form."

"Excellent. Thanks for coming in, Richard." Morris smiled as she got to her feet and extended her hand. "I'm going to ask my chief of staff to prepare for the rescinding of the executive orders. Our regular structure can sort things from here. I can't thank you enough for all you've done. You've been a great help to this administration. Stay the night."

Richard frowned and remained seated as alarm bells rang in his head. He'd waited for the right leader and been disappointed each time. Now he'd taken matters into his own hands, he'd grown accustomed to the power and the ability to shape the country. The last thing he'd expected was for Morris to attempt to seize back the initiative moments after his greatest success. He needed time to secure his legacy before handing back the reins.

"Richard?" Morris raised an eyebrow, the smile still on her face. "Is something wrong?"

Richard shook his head. "Madam President, that would be a mistake."

She hesitated and her smile vanished. "I'm sorry?"

"Rescinding the orders would be a mistake. The state of emergency isn't over."

She sighed and shook her head. "Richard, I know you might have come to like some of this extra power, but the work is done. There hasn't been an attack for a while now, the resistance is smashed – you said so yourself – and order has been restored. I can't ask the American people to continue to live restricted lives. I won't."

Richard had never felt this way about a meeting with the President before. She'd resisted at times, had concerns at others, but for the most part she'd been malleable. He'd come to expect her to swallow her pride and let him do what was necessary to stabilize the country. Morris asserting herself was a new development. An unwelcome one. He laughed. Long and slow and cruel.

"Something funny?" She crossed her arms, displeasure clear on her face.

"With respect. I'm honestly shocked by your lack of understanding."

Her eyes became glaciers and the temperature in the room dropped as she leaned forward, towering over him. "You're staring down the barrel, Richard."

"I understand that." He stood, removing her height advantage. "I've given everything for this country during the crisis, yet you're ready to discard me before my work is complete."

"No. Things need to return to normal and—"

"Normal?" He hissed the words. "The only reason there's order is because of the control FEMA has managed to exert. And the minute we have a comprehensive success you want to give up all of our hard won gains. I'm not convinced that this is over, not by a long shot. I want to continue to have the tools to protect our society for a while longer yet."

"It's over, Richard." She shook her head. "There's no reason to keep a superagency that crushes the liberty of America and its people for no good reason?"

"No good reason? Safety. Order. Those are the reasons, Madam President." Richard scoffed and started to walk toward the door. He paused and turned, feeling the anger surge inside of him. "I came here to report on our greatest success and you propose to pull the rug out. You should hang for treason."

Her face flushed red as her iciness was replaced by rage and fury. She pointed her index finger at him and started to talk, but he didn't want to hear it. She'd made up her mind, and he was wasting his breath and his time. She'd been a patsy, sure, but now she was dangerous. An enemy. If she wasn't prepared to let him do what was needed, she was of no use to him. Or anyone.

He took no notice as she continued to vomit words at him. If the air had been festive a moment ago, it had now become flammable. Morris's stupidity had created a conflagration that would consume everything if it was allowed to. He turned and walked to the door, in no doubt that under her leadership the orders would be revoked and he'd be out of a job within a day.

JACK WOKE with a start and winced at the shot of pain from the sudden movement. His eyes opened in time to see the pigeon that had been resting on top of him take flight. He sat up and rubbed his eyes, then hugged his torso to try to warm up a little. He wasn't surprised to discover that sleeping on a metal park bench was not good for the retention of body heat. It was the best he'd been able to manage.

He sighed and placed his head in his hands. Everything had gone to shit. On his way out of the Old Town office building he'd grabbed his phone and his wallet and then stumbled as far away as he could, given the pain and his exhaustion. He'd thought about a hospital, but that was the first place FEMA would look. He'd tried to think of somewhere smart to hide, but in the end, exhausted and needing sleep, he'd settled on a park bench.

He thought hard, trying to forge some sort of plan, but his mind had abandoned him. He'd lost a friend, been betrayed by another and, to the best of his knowledge, the resistance had been crushed. Losing had been a possibility, but not this way. Of all the scenarios he'd imagined might befall the resistance, this hadn't been one of them. It was over. No smart plan or twist of fate could undo the strategic Armageddon that faced him.

But he needed to know how bad it was. He swung his legs to the ground, stood unsteadily and started to walk. He shuffled, in great pain, to where a mother and young son had their backs turned and were having a picnic. He nearly laughed at the sight of two people so carefree, eating sandwiches on a rug despite the disaster that had played out in the last 24 hours. They weren't to know though.

He kept some distance away from them and cleared his throat. "Excuse me."

The mother turned. She was a cute blond with bright eyes, but her kindness and warm smile evaporated when she looked up at him. Her eyes widened as she reached for her son and her purse simultaneously. She gripped both with the ferocity of a lioness. "Please just leave us alone."

Jack held up his hands. She obviously thought he was a beggar or some kind of creep. "No, you don't—"

"Just *go*." Her voice was cold, far beyond what Jack would have expected. He must look worse than he thought. "I know who you are. Please go."

He rubbed his face and ran a hand through his hair. He was confused by the woman's reaction. He'd only wanted to ask her about the media coverage of the resistance, but she wanted no piece of it. He complied and walked away, determined to check the news the old fashioned way. Since Hickens had expressly told him not to check the news on his phone, he rummaged through a trash can and found a newspaper.

It was bleak. Though the coverage was heavily influenced by FEMA, it was reporting that a large number of operations had been conducted against terrorists all over the country. It reported that casualties were high and that the threat had been obliterated. Jack winced at the next line. Though the majority of the threat had been dealt with, it said, terrorist leader Jack Emery was still at large. His photo was splashed everywhere and there was a reward.

He cursed. That explained the behavior of the woman. It also told him everything he needed to know about his chance of survival and the future of the resistance. He threw the phone onto the grass, collapsed to his knees and then fell to his side. Months of effort and conflict had finally caught up with him. He was spent and on the run, with no resources and no support. The woman might have called and FEMA could already be on their way. He struggled to care.

He wasn't sure how long he laid there, eyes closed and despondent, before his cell phone started to ring. He opened his eyes and stared at it, confused. Everyone who had the number to the phone should be dead or detained by FEMA. Every part of him wanted to let it ring out, but he owed it to the people who'd been smashed because of his carelessness to answer. If just one of them was alive, he'd help them with everything he had left in his body.

He answered. "Hello?"

"Jack? Fucking hell. Jack?"

"Hi Celeste." His head felt light at the sound of her voice, and a few moments passed before he could comprehend what she was saying. He'd never expected to hear her voice again, either because she was dead or he soon would be. An overload of emotion coursed through his body.

"I thought you were dead, Jack." She laughed and he heard her sniff and choke back tears. "I thought I'd escaped only for you to be taken away."

"Afraid not. May as well be, though. It's all gone." He rolled onto his back and looked up at the sky. "I'm glad you're out, though, Celeste. How? And how did you get this number?"

"A guard let me escape." There was a pause. "As for the number, I saw the news and that you were alive, so I called Hickens."

Jack smiled. "Simon is alive?"

"Sure is. He's a broken man, though. I don't know what you guys were cooking, but he tells me most of the rest are dead or in custody, Jack."

"I know. Well, I'm glad he's alive. We need to stay separate, Celeste. They're after me. I'll be lucky to last a day now I'm all over the news."

"No way." Her voice was pure, cold fury. "I didn't get out of there, thinking you're dead then finding out you're alive, only to be told to stay away. I want to help."

"But—"

"You are not sidelining me again, Jack. You are not cutting me off."

He laughed despite the seriousness of the situation. She'd been furious at him for going to Taiwan to confront Chen Shubian and get what he needed to expose the Foundation. She'd been even madder when he'd retreated to Syria to escape from his life. He'd been forgiven, they'd made love and he thought he'd lost her for good. Now, staring into oblivion, he was faced with a choice: to let her in or lose her.

"Jack, I'm a fugitive as well." She was persistent, that was for sure. "If they capture me on the road or hiding or with you it's the same result."

"Okay, Celeste." He shook his head, not quite believing what he was doing. "But being with me is dange—"

"I know." Her voice was sharp.

"I mean it, Celeste. I—"

"Jack, I know."

He wasn't sure that their reunion was a good idea, given the likelihood he'd be dead or in cuffs by the end of the day, but he was done trying to protect Celeste by pushing her away. All that did was enrage her and undermine the feelings they shared. It might end poorly, but it'd end together. His heart thumped, his head screamed, his veins burned with energy and his muscles twitched for him to get up. To see her. To act.

"Plus you really want to see me, right? Pick up where we left off?" Her voice was a little playful, clearly trying to break the awkward silence.

"Okay." He smiled as he pictured her naked body on top of him, despite everything else that was at stake. "I look forward to it."

She laughed. "I bet. But we've got some business to take care of too. You're not going to believe what I've found."

He got to his feet. "What do you mean?"

"I'll explain when I see you, but it's dynamite. I've linked FEMA to the attacks. All of them."

He was confused. "Just how long have you been out, Celeste?"

There was a pause. "Oh, three months or so."

"And you're only just getting in touch now? And you say *I* drop out of contact!"

"I needed to get to the bottom of it, Jack." Her voice had an edge. "I owed it to someone."

He couldn't hold it against her, given his past. "Okay."

"I'll text you an address, meet me there tomorrow. I love you, Jack."

The call ended and Jack looked around. He'd thought

she was dead and that all hope was lost. Now, Celeste was alive and was sitting on something that might give him one last chance. The phone beeped. He looked down at it. He didn't recognize the address, but it wasn't far away. He'd go there, reunite with Celeste and see what she'd got her hands on. He'd never been much of a gambler, preferring his vice in liquid form, but he had played poker and could recognize when it was time to play his final hand.

He was all in. He was done running.

ONE KEPT the night-vision binoculars steady on the road, as she had for the last hour. Not a single vehicle had passed in that time. Her mind had started to wander and, inevitably, question what she was doing. It had been months since she'd spoken to Richard Hall, but he'd called her unexpectedly and offered her a job. She should have declined. She'd enjoyed the break and thought herself done with him, but the challenge had sold her. If she could pull this one off she could do anything.

He'd given her only a moment to accept the job. She'd agreed on the spot. It had been a struggle to get her team together in time, chopper them out and get them into position, but they'd successfully inserted without raising the ire of the authorities. Now all she needed was for the target to appear. If she was honest, it was a strange mission and a strange target, but she was the axe, not the wielder. Whatever reason Hall had for green-lighting the mission was his own. Her job was to pull it off.

The first Chevy Suburban came into sight, rounding the bend with headlights beaming and engine roaring. She waited, breathing deeply as the second, third and final vehicles followed barely ten yards apart. Hall had been as good as his word. Intelligence of a clear and present

danger to the President had flushed Morris from Camp
David. Though she'd usually fly, the weather did not
permit it, so the Secret Service had bundled her into the
car. All according to the book. All very predictable. All very
A to B.

One lowered the binoculars and put her night-vision
goggles into place, then nodded at Two. A second later Two
fired his RPG. It whooshed and the rocket covered the
distance between the tree line and the lead vehicle in a
moment. As the other members of her team fired their
rockets, the first hit the lead Chevy squarely on the engine
grille. An explosion flashed and a fireball blossomed,
followed by a secondary explosion as the fuel tank blew.
The devastated vehicle came to a halt, alight and oozing
smoke.

She took her eyes off the lead vehicle and looked down
the line of the motorcade, where two of the other vehicles
had been dealt with in a similar way. Only the third vehicle
was still intact, and it picked up speed as it swerved around
the destroyed vehicles. The Secret Service driver had to
have veins of ice, given his colleagues had just been
annihilated, but he had no answer for the rifle that roared
and destroyed the vehicle's engine block with a high
caliber, armor piercing round. The car slowed and then
stopped.

"Go!" One lifted her carbine and started to move
through the trees, closer to the road but still concealed. She
closed in on the President's vehicle with single-minded
purpose.

She was within twenty yards of the President's vehicle,
weapon raised, when an agent appeared. She tried to get a
shot off but the gunman dropped suddenly. A millisecond
later she heard the telltale report of one of Five or Six's
rifles. They were on overwatch and taking care of stragglers
while the rest of the team stalked larger game. One kept

moving, around the trunk of the car. The agent was lying dead on the road.

She smiled like a wolf at the door of a hen house at the vehicle in front of her, the only one untouched by the RPGs. The President's vehicle was designed to withstand all sorts of attack. But it was still just a car, not a tank. It had vulnerabilities against a well-equipped foe. That was why the President usually had a dozen Secret Service agents on hand to protect her. When they fell, however, she was vulnerable.

She turned to Two. "You got it?"

"Yep." Two nodded, reached into his combat vest and pulled out a piece of paper.

One took the sheet, unfolded it and walked up to the window of the presidential vehicle as Two, Three and Four took up covering positions. In addition, she knew that Five and Six were also covering her, now that any last Secret Service survivors had been dealt with. She placed the note against the window and waited. She waited a minute or so, but there was no huge hurry. Though reinforcements were on the way, they wouldn't arrive in time.

After a moment, the cell phone in her pocket started to vibrate. She pulled it out and answered. "Good evening, Madam President."

"Who are you?"

"That doesn't matter." One kept her weapon down. If any of the Secret Service agents tried anything, her team would sort it. "We're short on time. I'm glad you see sense."

"I see inevitability. I've called the House Speaker and Senate President and transferred executive power to the Vice President."

"Wonderful." One didn't care. "You have ten seconds to step out of your vehicle. The agents stay inside."

Morris sighed on the other end of the line. "And my daughter will be spared? You give me your word?"

"Yes. And the other agents. Nobody else needs to die."

The phone call ended and the rear door of the vehicle opened. One stood in place, relaxed, even as she saw the Secret Service agents inside gripping their weapons. They wouldn't like it, but with executive power transferred the agents had no further interest in the former President if she ordered otherwise. One was pleased that Morris wasn't stupid. She took a step back as Morris climbed out of the car.

One smiled once Morris was finally out and standing on the road with her hands by her side. "Thanks for being sensible, Madam President."

"It's just Helen, now. And fuck you." Morris scowled. "My car might be tough, but it can't stop an RPG. I shouldn't trust your word, but I have to hope you'll spare my daughter."

"Of course."

"I also hope you know that this is a waste of time. There's nothing you can extort out of me. It's clear to me there's no coincidence between my meeting with Richard Hall and the circumstances I now find myself in. Unusually for Richard, he's fucked this one up in a big way."

"I couldn't comment." One raised her weapon. "Now, I just need you to sign something and we can get this over with."

"This will never be over with. I've made the gravest mistake of my life trusting that man, to the detriment of us all and our country." She slammed a fist against the car door. "I should have seen it. It was all too neat. But I was caught up in the narrative. Just do me a favor and tell Richard I'll keep a seat warm in hell for him."

One said nothing as she held a second piece of paper in front of the former President, along with a pen. Morris looked at her with disgust clear on her face and then snatched at the pen and paper. She read it over briefly in the dim light and her eyes widened. She looked like she might refuse, until she glanced back at the car. She sighed, signed the paperwork and then handed it to Two, who had his hand outstretched.

One fired a single round into the President's head, then turned and started to walk back to the tree line. She heard the whoosh of an RPG round, followed by an explosion. Though she felt the heat of the flames, she didn't look back. She'd wanted to help Morris's daughter, but orders were orders: not a single person was allowed to walk away from the Presidential motorcade.

18

Following the assassination of President Helen Morris and the murder of her daughter and security detail, President Newbold has reiterated his support for the emergency measures. He noted that the attack on the Presidential motorcade signals a new and dark chapter in the country's fight against extremists, and that he would not shirk from doing whatever was necessary to find those responsible. Administrator Hall will speak this morning in Chicago.

Federal Emergency Management Agency
News Release

C allum looked down from the nosebleed seats of Soldier Field. He was standing with his carbine, waiting for Richard Hall to take to the stage that had been hastily erected in the south end zone prior to the Bears game. The stadium was nearly at capacity and Callum was one of the State Guard troops assigned to security.

He scanned the crowd from behind sunglasses, looking for any suspicious movements or overt threats. Nothing jumped out at him, but it was tough to keep tabs on such a large crowd. He was up high, but there were others scattered around the stadium, each looking for the same thing he was. Video cameras all around the stadium would be using facial recognition technology to try to find any problems before they became deadly, while a couple of FEMA helicopters hovered up high. His earpiece was silent as well.

Since the assault on the President's motorcade less than twenty-four hours ago, the whole city had felt on a knife edge. Callum doubted it was different anywhere else. For his own part, he'd felt like someone had punched him in the chest. After everything he'd gone through, he'd thought his latest mission was also his last. But clearly whatever success FEMA and the State Guard had achieved against the terrorists was not complete.

"Sector 37, report." The voice in his earpiece was all business.

Callum took one hand off his carbine and pressed a button on his headset. "37, all clear."

"Confirmed." The voice paused for a second. "All sectors report clear. Proceeding."

Callum chuckled at the charade of it all. With a crowd of around 50 000, spotting a threat before it manifested would be difficult at the best of times. In an angry, frightened nation full of guns, the day after the President has been shot, it would be next to impossible. If the Secret Service couldn't stop a determined attack, Callum doubted a handful of State Guard could.

He watched as Hall approached the stage, climbed the stairs and stopped at the podium. He was probably the only prominent person to visit and be announced at Soldier Field in history to be met by silence. Then a low murmur began, until Hall held out his hands toward the crowd. The gesture was lost from this distance, but the giant scoreboard screens magnified it.

"I'll not take much of your time." Hall smiled. "I understand there's an age-old score to settle today."

"Get this clown off!" The crack from a man near Callum earned a few laughs from those near him. Callum's grip tightened on the carbine but the guy sat down.

Hall ignored the catcalls and booing he was being subjected to. "I, like the rest of the country, was shocked to learn that President Morris's motorcade had been attacked and that she'd been murdered, along with her entire security detail and her daughter. While we're still piecing things together, the attack is unquestionably an escalation by the terrorists who've rocked America for a year."

Callum tuned out as Hall gave all the usual platitudes. The President's death was a huge loss for America and so on. He'd heard it all so many times, usually for friends and fellow soldiers, that it had lost its meaning. He focused on the crowd, but it was a waste of time – there was more danger of spectators falling asleep and hurting themselves than one having a shot at the administrator. Then something Hall said grabbed Callum's attention.

"FEMA is determined that these attacks won't disrupt our operations, or divert us from the correct path." Hall paused. "It's important to remember that."

Callum's eyes narrowed. Hall had used the exact same words when discussing the attack on the distribution center in public. It was a rehearsed line, completely out of place for a man supposedly in shock and dealing with the President's assassination, in unison with the rest of the country. Was the attack a surprise to Hall at all? Callum started to pay close attention to the speech again. Close attention to Hall.

"Though we've had some success against these terrorists, there have been setbacks. To combat this, I met with President Morris yesterday, hours before the attack on her motorcade. She was resolute in her commitment to the path we're traveling." Hall looked straight down the camera. "My staff at FEMA are doing a wonderful job of keeping our society functioning, and their State Guard colleagues are keeping us safe.

"But it hasn't been enough. I came to an agreement with President Morris along these lines." Hall held up a piece of paper. "This document is an executive order authorizing FEMA to take command of elements of the United States Military on home soil. It doesn't apply to overseas forces, or our strategic assets, but it's a necessary next step to help us combat the ongoing threat."

There was a murmur among the crowd. Callum looked around. The civilians were restless in their seats and it felt like the mood in the stadium had switched from mourning to suspicion. Callum's mood was shifting too. For the first time, he felt that Richard Hall was one of the things wrong in America. But he still had a job to do. He scanned the crowd but there was no obvious threat. He looked back to Hall.

Hall placed the sheet of paper down. "I've already spoken to President Newbold. He's as committed as his predecessor was to doing what's necessary to combat this scourge. He's re-affirmed all executive orders that the former President signed. The country will endure, despite these most testing of circumstances."

Callum clenched his jaw. He considered raising his weapon and aiming at Hall. He'd stare down the iron sights as he breathed, in and out, in and out, and prepared himself for the shot. Though the range would be extreme, he wondered if it was worth a try. He shook his head. It was a shot he'd never take. While he regretted some of the things he'd done in Iraq and on his home soil, he wasn't a murderer. He let out a long sigh.

"I want to be clear." Hall's voice was filled with aggression. "The ability of the terrorists to hit the presidential motorcade is unacceptable. With these new powers, we will make our streets and people safe. We will bring order to America. God help anyone in our way. God bless America."

JACK WOULD HAVE LAUGHED if not for the seriousness of the situation. The house was a cliché: white picket fence in front of a red brick home. He looked down at the phone again, then up at the house. He repeated the process a couple of times to be sure the address was right and then opened the gate.

As he approached, he thought for the millionth time that this story all felt a little bit too convenient: Celeste getting out, then calling him months later and begging to meet. He was running to her like a puppy and he knew there was a chance that Celeste was being used to capture him. It was possible. Probable. But he had little left to lose by giving it a shot. He reached the door and knocked twice. There was no answer. He frowned. She had said she'd be here. He tried to peer in the window next to the door, but the curtains were drawn. He knocked again. He could wait a few more moments, on the chance she was in the shower or something, but he felt exposed on the porch.

As he waited, his enthusiasm faded and then evaporated into despair. Since the call, he'd thought of a reunion with Celeste as a second chance, but it was a dead end. He'd never see her again. She was dead or in prison and this was some sort of ruse. He started to turn around, ready to leave the house, when someone's arms encircled his waist. He stiffened and recoiled at the touch, then relaxed as the feminine arms completed their movement and pulled him as tight as a boa constrictor. He felt lightning pass between them as Celeste pulled him closer. He raised his hands and placed them over the top of hers as a broad smile crossed his face.

"Hey." Her voice was a whisper in his ear. "Got you."

He wriggled in her grip, turned around and wrapped her in his arms. He pulled her close and they kissed deeply, fuelled by their relief at the most unlikely of reunions. He should have been concerned that they'd be spotted, two of the most wanted fugitives in America, but all he wanted was to hold her and expunge months of loneliness and guilt and worry. They kissed for nearly a minute until she pulled away. She smiled and he mirrored it.

"We should get inside." He jerked his head toward the door. "I assume you have the key? You had me worried."

"Sorry." Her cunning smile matched the playful gleam in her eye. "I had to make you sweat a little."

Jack smiled as they broke their embrace and she unlocked the door. They stepped inside and Jack was shocked by the broken furniture and stained floors. "Who pissed FEMA off?"

"The owner."

He gave a small laugh, but when he saw the look on her face he changed the topic. "I couldn't believe it when the phone rang and it was you."

"I never thought I'd get out of there." She shrugged and placed a hand on his shoulder. "It's good to see you, Jack. What happened?"

He barely knew where to start. They walked into the dark living room and sat on the sofa, lights off and curtains drawn. He explained everything in as much detail as he could, from the moment they'd been separated in New York. She knew about much of it: the new attacks, the scale of detentions, the atrocities. She gasped and squeezed his hand at key points in his story. She cried when he told her about Peter.

"How the hell did it happen, Jack?" Her voice cracked.

"Elena betrayed us." He gripped her hand, which was trembling. Peter and Celeste had grown close while he was in Syria. He explained the story, fury radiating off him in waves.

Finally, she spoke. "They had her fiancé, Jack. I can't comprehend the damage she's caused, but I understand why she did it."

"That doesn't excuse—"

"No, it doesn't. But I might have done the same. She saw the light in the end."

He shook his head. "But—"

"She let you go." Her voice was firm as she leaned in to kiss him. "I've got you back. You've had your turn, now it's mine."

"What do you mean?"

"Come with me." She stood. "I have to show you. You're not going to believe it."

He didn't think it could be as good as she was claiming. He didn't really care what it was, but he wanted nothing more than to be close to her so he followed. He figured it must be good if she'd sat on it for months and then called him here at great risk to both of them. They walked down the hallway and down the steps to the basement. She turned on the lights and he was amazed by the piles of documents around the room.

She smiled and held her hand out like a game show host presenting a prize. "It's all we need. It's all we've ever needed."

His eyes narrowed, not wanting to believe she'd found a treasure trove. "Is any of it any good?"

"It's better than good." She wrapped an arm around him and ushered him downstairs. "Take a look."

He chose a random pile, picking up a piece of paper concerning the attack on the Hoover Dam. It was a supply manifest of weaponry sent to a warehouse near the Hoover Dam on the eve of the attack. He replaced it and moved to another pile and picked a document. This pile was all about an attack in Phoenix. He whistled. Someone had gone to a lot of trouble and had an awfully high level of access. No wonder it had taken Celeste months.

"Where did this all come from?" Jack turned to her, his eyes wide. "If we can get this out, it's over."

Her features hardened. "Mariposa, a friend inside the camp. She used to be a senior employee at FEMA. She gathered it all. They imprisoned and killed her because of it."

Jack moved closer to her and hugged her again. They embraced for a couple of moments, then she seemed to gather herself. "She never released any of it?"

"Never got the chance. This is why I've stayed off the grid all this time, Jack. It took some effort to get through it all. You should see how many printer cartridges I went through."

"I can imagine." He laughed and looked around again. "Why the hell didn't FEMA find all of this when they arrested her?"

"Looks like they found the hard copies she'd made, but she left it all on a flash drive in the urn containing her mother's ashes. They flipped the whole house but missed it."

He smiled. "Have you looked at it all?"

She nodded. "It's a paper trail linking FEMA to nearly everything, linking Richard Hall to everything. Or a lot, anyway. If this isn't enough to bring him down then he's bulletproof."

"The attack on the President?" Jack raised an eyebrow.

The news that President Helen Morris had been gunned down shocked him, not that he'd had any huge love for her.

She shrugged. "Mariposa couldn't see that far into the future and none of the documents I've seen mentions it. But everything else is here."

"It'll do." He couldn't quite believe it, but was unable to deny what was in front of him. He laughed. "I'm impressed. Looks like it's time to pass the baton. Who needs me anymore?"

She nestled in closer. "I do, Jack."

JACK LOOKED up at Celeste and smiled as she placed the coffee cup in front of him. He took a sip, then put it down and rubbed his eyes. Though Celeste had sorted most of it, they'd been reviewing the documents all afternoon and evening. The work made him feel like he was back at university or in the early years of his career, when all-nighters spent poring over reams of documents weren't uncommon. He was too old for it now, though.

They'd struck gold. The story was damning and Jack had reached the conclusion that Richard Hall was the most dangerous man in the history of America. Though he was still technically subordinate to the President, he'd shown that meant nothing. He'd monopolized institutional power and the use of force in America, using it to keep the entire country suppressed and compliant. Only J. Edgar Hoover's FBI came close.

"You look tired." Celeste sat down next to him and took a sip from her own coffee. "Why don't you take a break?"

"Yeah, okay." Jack nodded and leaned back on the sofa. It was a ratty old thing, a castoff that had been exiled to live the last of its useful life in basement purgatory.

She touched the bruises on his face. "I wonder if we

should just burn these documents and hide here for a year or two."

Jack smiled and stroked her hair. "I'd love to, but we'd run out of tinned tuna before too long. Besides, I hate this décor too much to call it home. We'll just have to stop Hall."

While the US had seen its share of lunatics, extremists with poisonous ideology, Jack felt that Hall was the first with the unfettered power to back him up. In a year he'd created a police state without parallel in recent history, with more sophisticated surveillance than the East German Stasi and more military might than any regime in history. He had to be stopped.

She pursed her lips. "Easier said than done."

"Totalitarianism and oppression only last as long as there's a threat to make people afraid. Once there's nothing to fear they want their rights back. Plus, if we don't fight, nobody will. I've seen a lot of good people die this year, trying to do the right thing, some of them because of my mistakes. It needs to end."

He was about to say more when there was a knock at the front door, a pounding that they could barely hear in the basement. Jack tensed and wished he had a weapon, but found it strange that the authorities would knock. That wasn't FEMA's style. They were more the 'have goons kick in your door and shoot you in the face' type. He looked at Celeste. She seemed relaxed as she stood. She smiled and gave him a single nod as she started up the stairs.

He thought briefly about trying to hide the papers, but there was no point. They were both fugitives, and there were so many classified documents in the basement that if it was the authorities at the door then they'd have ample evidence of wrongdoing. He sat back on the sofa and sipped his coffee, waiting for whoever Celeste had invited into the house. He wondered if it was a relative of the owner, Mariposa, or a straggler from the resistance.

It turned out to be neither. Jack gasped when he saw who was following Celeste down the stairs. He flared with anger and pitched his coffee cup across the room toward her. Elena flinched and cowered as the cup sailed past her head and shattered on the brick wall behind her. She held up both hands as he looked for something else to arm himself with. He stood and lifted the ashtray in the middle of the coffee table. He hefted it.

He didn't get the chance to throw it before Celeste was in front of him, wrapping her arms around him and saying words he couldn't process. Slowly, the red mist receded and he could hear her telling him it was okay, that she'd planned it, and that Elena was here to help. He growled in frustration and stepped backward, which seemed to satisfy Celeste. She let go, but remained between Jack and Elena, who was still on the stairs.

"Jack, please." Elena's voice was soft with emotion. He wondered what she'd been doing in the days since she'd sold him out. It had probably involved champagne and caviar.

"Elena, if you were on fire I wouldn't piss on you." He exhaled strongly through his nose and looked at Celeste. "Why did you bring her here?"

Celeste stepped close to him again, took hold of his hands and smiled. "Because she can help us, Jack. She's scared, just like us. She wants to act, just like us."

"The resistance is in tatters because of her!"

"You're wrong." Elena shrugged. "While I may have sold you out, the only other thing I did was confirm some information FEMA already had about the resistance and its members."

"So they could kill them."

"They'd have done that months ago, Jack, if you hadn't

been hiding. Hall was waiting for you to re-emerge. Once you did, he struck."

Jack didn't care what role she'd played in the dismantling of the resistance, either central coordinator or bit player. She'd betrayed him, betrayed their cause and helped to get a lot of people killed in the meantime. Personally, he'd never felt a punch to the guts like the moment she'd shown her true colors. It had been worse than the beating he'd taken. Worse than any beating he'd ever taken.

He was about to say more when Celeste put a hand on his shoulder. She leaned in close to his ear. "Jack, give her a chance. I think you should hear her out."

He sighed. If he wasn't so happy to be alongside Celeste, against all odds, he'd have resisted her advice. He clamped his teeth together. "Why are you here, Elena?"

She smiled sadly and started to walk down the stairs again. He put down the ashtray and stood with his fists balled by his side as she joined them, and they all took a seat on one of the two sofas. She crossed her legs in front of her and seemed to consider her words carefully before she spoke. He waited, impatiently, while she seemed to struggle to find what she wanted to say.

Finally, she spoke. "Jack, I just want to say that I'm sorry. Beyond sorry. Hall imprisoned my fiancé, as you know, and he's been used as leverage against me."

"Sorry, but I don't care." He stared straight at her. "A whole lot of my friends are dead now because of the action you took."

"I know." She smiled sadly. "And I'm sorry. I made the wrong choices. But I knew you wouldn't be giving up. That's why I'm here."

"How did you find us?" Jack's eyes flicked to Celeste, then back to Elena, when finally the realization hit him. "Hickens."

She nodded. "He's been my friend for a long time, Jack. I didn't sell him out. He tracked your phone to this location, though he assures me the NSA can't do the same."

"Fuck me, did he give my number or location to everyone who asked?" He sighed and rubbed his face. "Just go, Elena. There's nothing you can do that I'd trust you to do."

"I can get a message to Hall." She dropped the revelation like a bomb. "I can tell him where you are. That must be a massive opportunity in some way."

Jack paused. A plan began to form in his head. Several times the women asked him what was going on and if he was okay, but he ignored them. It would be a long shot, but if Elena really could get a message to Hall, then it might work. He closed his eyes and turned the fledgling plan over in his head, probing for flaws and trouble spots. Hall had proven to be a detailed planner, but consistent in his habits. Predictable. It just might work.

He opened his eyes and smiled. They had to stop Hall, who now had the entire apparatus of the US government and military at his disposal. If they failed, there wouldn't be a country worth living in. It was time to take a final stand. He spent the next hour explaining the plan to them. At first, they doubted him, then they started to come around to his thinking.

When he was finished, Elena laughed. "More than happy to do my part in that, Jack."

"Wait a minute." Celeste looked concerned. "He's got the military, Jack. It's impossible."

"Not impossible, just difficult." He shared her grim expression. "We win or we die."

19

FEMA has today released footage of a man believed to be wanted fugitive Jack Emery, taken on a camera near a gas station in Chicago. The Agency and other federal authorities believe that Emery is still located in Illinois. Emery, wanted on dozens of terror-related charges, is considered to be highly dangerous and may be armed. He should not be approached by members of the public.

Federal Emergency Management Agency
News Release

Jack sat on the bench, a baseball cap covering his head and his eyes hidden behind dark sunglasses. His disguise wouldn't deter a keen observer, but he had to hope that his efforts would hold up to a casual glance by a passer by. For extra concealment, he had his back to the road. He stared out into the distance, enjoying the fact that he had little but the giant mass of Lake Michigan for company.

"Jack Emery. I knew they couldn't fucking kill you!"

Jack smiled when he heard the voice. It was barely a

loud whisper, but the speaker was close enough that Jack could hear every word. He'd know that voice underwater. He turned and his smile only grew wider. Dan Ortiz was standing there in uniform, looking a lot less scruffy than the last time Jack had seen him. The meeting they'd had in Millennium Park felt like it was a century ago.

"Good to see you, Dan." Jack reached out a hand and they shook. "You're late."

Ortiz laughed. "They had bacon in the mess this morning."

Jack scoffed. "Take a seat, Dan. I need to talk to you. I need your help."

Ortiz nodded, rounded the bench and sat down. He pulled out a cigarette, saw the look Jack gave him and then put the packet away. He shook his head. "Don't judge me."

"Didn't say a word." Jack smiled.

"Like hell." Ortiz sparked the cigarette and took a long drag, then blew it out slowly.

"Thanks for meeting with me. I know it's not safe."

"You're telling me it's not safe? I'm the one got you involved in all of this shit, Jack. I reckon we're even in the danger stakes." Ortiz shrugged. "So what do you need?"

Jack had considered his next words for the past week, but they still didn't come easily. He'd spent that time working up the plan with Elena and Celeste. They'd concluded that while it had a theoretical chance, there was a high likelihood that they'd end up dead. They'd all come to terms with that fact, but asking Ortiz to help – a man with a career and a family largely untouched by the takeover – troubled him.

More troubling still was the idea of Richard Hall continuing to tighten his grip on a country that was nearly exhausted. Whatever the risk, whatever the threat, he knew the plan and what it could achieve was worth it. Between them, Jack, Celeste and Elena had considerable talents in analyzing information and telling a story, but without the means to broadcast it they were toothless. Jack knew a solution.

"We've got everything we need to bring down Hall and FEMA. It's as simple as that."

"No, it's not, or I wouldn't be here." Ortiz slapped Jack on the leg. "Get on with it."

Jack stared down at his feet. "I have information, but no way to broadcast it."

If only Ortiz knew the half of it. He dug into his pocket, pulled out a few folded sheets of paper and handed them over. The sheets were a typed summary of events between the start of the attacks and now, with highlighter marks next to the events that Jack had managed to link to FEMA. He waited as the other man scanned the documents, a range of emotions rolling across his face. Mostly anger.

After a while, Ortiz handed them back and looked squarely at him, his eyes probing for any hint of mistruth. "I'm listening, Jack."

Jack stared back at the lake. "What's the feeling inside the Marines?"

"People are shitty we're taking orders from FEMA now." Ortiz's voice dripped with disdain. "From the same guy that shot up the 38th Infantry in Indianapolis."

"So, big fans then."

"Yeah, the boys are getting their tits out for autographs. But why do you ask?"

Jack smiled. "I have a mountain of stuff. If I can get it out, it'll topple Hall, FEMA and the State Guard. It has to. But I need your help. Lots of it."

"OK." Ortiz tapped his foot. "I'll play along. If I help you out with that, what happens? We take back the country?"

"Something like that." Jack nodded. He didn't need to tell Ortiz that his ambitions were a hell of a lot bigger than that. "But there'll only be one chance. If we fail, we die."

"I'm used to those sort of odds." Ortiz smiled. "But how can some grunts help with what you need? They're blocking our comms, so it's not like you can use the Marine network."

"Well, that's the thing." Jack turned his head to look at Ortiz, whose gaze was locked on him. "Have you ever heard of the Emergency Alert System?"

RICHARD WATCHED with interest as the man's eyes bulged and his body fought hard against the restraints. The medical professionals kept their distance from the gurney, even as the guard and priest did their best to calm the man down. Richard couldn't hear what they were saying through the glass, but guessed it had something to do with the futility of the struggle. Though the man was strapped in tight, Richard respected the effort.

He leaned forward, his face inches from the glass. He'd never seen a man die and the process of a state-sanctioned killing – calculated, clinical and just – fascinated him. It was the ultimate manifestation of the power of the state over the individual, the ultimate upholder of order against the worst crimes: in this case, the efforts by rebels to undermine his important work. He didn't like having to do this, but nor could he cower from it.

Eventually, the staff inside the room calmed the man down enough for the two orderlies to go to work. Richard was amused by the fact that they still swabbed the man's arm with alcohol, considering infection was probably a moot point for someone who'd be dead in an hour. They then inserted a pair of IV tubes into his arm, attached the line and secured the whole setup. After a saline drip and a heart monitor were attached, it was ready.

As the priest did his work, the prison officer keyed the intercom. "Administrator Hall, we're about to begin."

Richard smiled. Even though he had no role to play, the staff were clearly unnerved by his presence. He pressed the button on his own intercom panel. "Don't let me stop you."

"Okay, sir."

Richard sat back and waited as the final spiritual preparations were made. Though there had been other executions under FEMA's watch, this was the first he'd watched. He cursed as his phone suddenly started to blare. He stared down at it and felt faint as soon as he read the message. It was as if all of his Christmases had come at once. Elena Winston had texted him that Jack Emery was alive and was planning a major broadcast of information against FEMA. Most importantly, she knew where he was.

Richard's lips peeled back into a smile. He glanced up at the man doomed to die, pleased that the process had started. But his attention was now elsewhere, on Elena Winston and Jack Emery. Richard had thought she'd gone rogue, but it sounded like she was just where he needed her. He was glad that the room to witness the execution was empty. This was the opportunity to put the final piece in the puzzle. He dialed her number and waited until she picked up, then waited again while the encryption technology on his phone did its thing.

Finally able to speak, he took a deep breath. "Elena? It's Richard Hall. You've got some explaining to do."

To her credit, she didn't hide from his accusation. "I've been held up. When the two you sent failed to do the job, I was worried you'd blame me. But I know where Jack Emery is."

Emery was the last piece in a very large puzzle. "Tell me."

"He's at a house. It's just a regular, suburban place. He's

sitting on a mountain of information that was leaked by one of your staff. Mariposa Esposito?"

Richard's eyes widened and his mind screamed. Somehow Emery had got his hands on the Holy Grail. Elena couldn't be lying because she had no way of knowing. In the blink of an eye Emery had graduated from washed-up minor annoyance to the most dangerous man on the planet. With the information that Mariposa had trawled, Emery would have all he needed to put the pieces together on nearly everything Richard had been doing. As much as those actions had been necessary, they wouldn't resonate well with the broader public. Crucially, Emery had shown through the saga with the Foundation for a New America that he had the ingenuity to get the word out. He had to be dealt with.

"Give me the address, Elena."

She paused. It betrayed her nerves. "For a price, sure."

He rolled his eyes. "Name it."

"You release my fiancé." Her voice was angry. He couldn't blame her, given how badly he'd played her. He regretted it, slightly, but it had been necessary. "And leave us alone."

"Done." Richard knew the deal even before she'd asked for it. The release of one man was a trifling matter. "Your information better be good."

"The release first."

Richard sighed. "The address first. You've got precious little credit left with me, Elena. You can be smart and alive or dumb and dead. Make your decision."

She gave him the address and Richard hung up the call. He sent out a message to have Elena's fiancé released, then quickly dialed another number. Time was of the essence. As he waited, he watched as drugs were pumped into the man on the gurney. Where he might have expected spectacular convulsions, blood – *something* – instead the man's heart slowed, betrayed only by the heart rate monitor that showed it was done. As he watched the priest close the man's eyes, Richard considered that his work in fixing America was nearly done. There was only one more thing to do.

Jack Emery had to die.

ONE FELT A SENSE OF CLOSURE. Barring a major surprise, this would be her last mission for Richard Hall – the assassination of Jack Emery, the man responsible for the resistance that had kept her busy for months. She'd thought the attack on the President's convoy would signal the end of their arrangement, but Hall had contacted her with blunt instructions: kill Jack Emery, no matter how loud or costly. Loud and costly her team could do, especially for a large pile of cash.

She nodded at Two. "Go."

The small ram that Two swung at the door took just a couple of hard strikes to send the flimsy wooden thing swinging back on its hinges. As he backed away and threw the ram onto the lawn, the rest of her team surged inside. She'd left nobody on guard, this job was going to be done quickly, brutally and by the numbers. She let her team move inside before following, with Two bringing up the rear to keep their exit clear.

She moved through the house with the rest of her team. With each room they reached, a member of the team split off to make sure it was clear. She kept her weapon raised as she entered the kitchen when it came to her turn. The flash light on the end of her weapon illuminated the room. As the rest of the team started to report in, she scanned the kitchen a few times back and forth, then added her call to the mix.

The house was small, so it didn't take long. She'd made a decision to enter with maximum aggression, one member of her team per room, given it was unlikely that Emery was expecting an assault. He also probably didn't have the capacity to fight back, even if he was. While she wouldn't usually go in so loud, she hadn't had time to plan properly or get hold of the floor plans. That meant speed was their best protection.

As the last member of her team reported in, having checked the yard, she paused near the entrance to the basement, the only possible place for Emery to be hiding. Either that or Hall's information was incorrect and Emery wasn't here. But Hall had been right about nearly everything else since she'd been working with him, so she figured the likelihood of bad intelligence was fairly low.

She keyed her mic. "Okay, basement it is."

The order was confirmed in her headset. Three and Four reached for the handle, opened the door and then moved down the stairs. One followed, leaving the others upstairs. She reached the bottom of the stairs and her eyes widened as she saw the mountains of paper stacked in the middle of the room. She walked over to it as Three and Four stood alert. She gave the material a cursory glance. She'd found the information, but not Emery.

"Fucking hell, guys." She scoffed. The shock at finding so much information and the frustration at not finding Emery struck home. "Would you look at all of this?"

Three broke into a broad grin. "I wonder if there's—"

A single thud from upstairs interrupted him mid-sentence. It was a sound akin to a sack of potatoes hitting the floor. They looked to the ceiling and raised their weapons. One's mind screamed with possibilities as she froze, waiting for another sound or for one of her team to open the door, stick their heads in the basement and tell her it was okay – that someone had made a mistake. Her team didn't make mistakes. There were two more thuds.

"Move guys." She took one step toward the stairs, weapon raised, when the door at the top opened. A pair of small metal canisters bounced down the stairs and she heard the distinctive rattle of metal on concrete. She knew the green canisters well. "Oh, fuck."

The flash bangs exploded with light and noise. One tried to shield her eyes, but it was far too late. She staggered and dropped to one knee. She was blinded and couldn't hear anything around her. A few seconds later she felt a blow against her temple. She fell to the ground and screamed in pain as a boot found her midsection, again and again, until she was against something – a wall or some sort of furniture. Then she felt a barrel press against her skull.

It took some time for her vision to clear. When it did, she was lying on her side, able to see the brutal consequences of Richard Hall's miscalculation in full technicolor. It burned in her vision worse than the stun grenades. Three and Four were splayed out in front of her, a pair of corpses who minutes ago had been highly skilled men she'd considered friends and colleagues. The story would be the same upstairs.

After another moment, someone ducked down to her level and tried to speak with her, she couldn't shift her eyes from the bodies, but nor would she show emotion. She'd taken hundreds of lives, but the human mind – no matter how hard and conditioned to the trade of death – had no answer for grief when loved ones were taken. Like the finest sports stars and musicians, she'd fallen for the classic trap: trying to stay on top for a little bit too long.

She glanced at the man in front of her for just a moment, then back at her dead team members. In the recesses of her mind, the fact that the man was in uniform registered. It was a strange development, but she had neither the time nor the mental capacity to fully process the information before a hard blow hit her in the back of the head. She barely stayed conscious, then a second blow hit home.

"*Hey.*" The voice sounded like it was underwater. Underwater. And far away. "*Hey, shitbag.*"

She blacked out again.

"*Who do you work for?*" The same voice. Deep underwater.

More questions followed, but she registered only every second word and couldn't follow. Her head felt light and she had a pounding headache. She tried to sit up, but failed and retched. The two standing in front of her as she lay on the ground stepped backward as she puked and then blacked out again. She woke a few more times and briefly resisted their questioning. Then she blacked out for good.

20

Authorities are no closer to identifying or locating the six terrorists responsible for the attack on President Helen Morris, though it appears to be the same group that previously attacked the Hoover Dam. Also released today, FEMA polling data shows that, broadly, the public supports the emergency measures that are in place and that 79.2% of Americans feel safer than they did six months ago.

Federal Emergency Management Agency
News Release

J ack looked at his watch and wondered again how the Marines did this every day. It was early and the sun hadn't come up, yet as Jack stood and waited for the caffeine to kick in Fort Sheridan was a hive of activity. All around him soldiers readied their equipment and vehicles as he slurped down the last of his coffee. Truth be told, he felt a bit useless, watching as the men and women on the base worked.

Ortiz and his officer colleagues had delivered. The two battalions of the 24th Marine Regiment had made their way to Chicago under the guise of exercises, but now approximately 2000 men and women were gathered and ready to move. It wasn't an overwhelming force – a drop in the ocean against what Hall could command between the military and the State Guard – but Jack had to hope it would be enough to get the job done.

"Time to go?" He smiled as Ortiz approached in his combat fatigues. "Guess I don't have time for a second coffee?"

Ortiz nodded. "Our scouts are reporting that there's very little between us and the target. We're lucky. If they knew its importance it'd be fortified further."

"Will it work?"

"It might." Ortiz ran a hand through his hair and scratched his head. "We'll surprise them, and we'll have decoy attacks going on all over the city during the main push."

"Just have to hope we're in business before they realize what's happening, I guess." Jack shrugged. "Shame we don't have that terrorist bitch to parade around though."

Ortiz grunted. Both Jack and Ortiz had been furious at the marine who'd hit the woman in the back of the head with his carbine. The blow had concussed her and rendered her useless. Though Jack had some cell phone footage of her mentioning Richard Hall and the other attacks, he hadn't managed to get to the bottom of who she was or why she'd cooperated with Hall before she'd died. The ambush hadn't gone as well as he'd hoped, but at least Elena's fiancé had been freed. If nothing else, if the plan failed, Jack would die knowing that he'd stopped a nasty woman and her friends from further acts of terror. He'd wanted more information to hang Hall with, but anything she could have given him would have been a cherry on top of the greatest cake ever made. He had enough to crucify Hall, if he could get the word out.

"Showtime." Ortiz walked toward the main vehicle convoy. "Let's go."

Jack passed dozens of men and women hard at work as he approached the Humvee he'd been assigned to. Some nodded, some stared, some ignored him – but all of them had a crazy day ahead. He was glad that Mariposa's information had apparently convinced enough of Ortiz's fellow officers to mobilize the entire regiment. So much force didn't guarantee success, but it was more than he'd hoped for.

"This is where I leave you, Jack. You got everything you need?" Ortiz looked at him with some skepticism.

Jack couldn't blame Ortiz for any doubt he harbored. Jack had been through a lot and was about to ride into a firestorm once again. From Afghanistan to the battle against the Foundation for a New America to Syria to the struggle against FEMA, he'd seen more conflict and experienced more pain than most. Now he was asking Ortiz and his comrades to risk their lives. Ortiz wasn't saying anything, but Jack knew he had doubts.

He patted the satchel that he carried on his shoulder. "Mariposa Esposito made sure of it. I'm ready, Omega."

"Okay." Ortiz slapped him on the back. "See you on the other side, Jack. You stay frosty, buddy."

Jack nodded. His mouth was dry and he wanted more than anything to turn around, but the time for second thoughts had passed. He put his hand on the door, opened it and smiled when he saw who was inside. The shapeless combat fatigues and her combat vest did nothing to hide her attractiveness. From the flame-colored hair downward, she was a sight he was grateful to have back in his life. He smiled and climbed in.

"Howdy stranger." Celeste smiled at him. "I thought I'd surprise you."

"Hey."

"You alright?" She could clearly read his concern. When he was seated and settled, she placed a hand on his knee and squeezed it. "It's going to be okay."

He nodded, smiled as bravely as he could and placed his hand on top of hers. As the driver gunned the engine, he shifted slightly in his seat to face her. "One for the road?"

Celeste beamed. They held each other as tightly as they could in the confines of the armored vehicle and kissed deeply. His hands started to explore her body, despite the unflattering battle gear, until the driver of the vehicle turned around and cleared his throat. It was as if a trance was broken. They separated and straightened themselves out. The driver turned back to the front, focused on getting the vehicle ready.

Jack smiled. "Sorry, got carried away."

Celeste gave him one more peck on the lips. "Until later."

The driver looked at him in the mirror and laughed. Jack flushed red. He wasn't usually easy to embarrass, but the thought of career soldiers seeing his flirtations was a little much. They settled in, ready for the ride, their clasped hands the only sign that they'd shared such an embrace just a moment earlier. If he'd had his way, she wouldn't be here at all, but they all had a role to play. Jack turned and watched as the convoy prepared to head toward his assignment and his destiny.

"Comms check." He heard Ortiz's voice over the radio network.

For the next few minutes, he was distracted by vehicles checking in and diesel engines starting. It was funny, the last time he'd been inside a Humvee he'd nearly died, but now all this hardware was on his side, the crews were fighting for the same thing he was and he was alongside the woman he thought he might love. He just hoped he made it to the other side of the firestorm that was to come.

He hoped they'd all make it.

～

"Fucking hell." Callum raised his binoculars. "Fucking hell."

He'd thought his mind was playing tricks on him, but the powerful binoculars showed him the truth: there was a convoy of a dozen or so US Marine Corps vehicles rolling down the street. He lowered his binoculars, gripped his carbine and then gave a quick shout for his men to get ready. He had ten men to defend the position. Nowhere near enough.

Callum keyed his headset. "Command, this is post 457, we've got a situation here."

There was a long pause. In the time it took for a response to come in, the convoy grew from a speck in the distance to being highly visible. He could count at least twelve Humvees, enough to carry more men than he could handle. He nearly considered keying the radio again and repeating the report when, finally, it chirped in his ear.

"Be advised, 457, the entire 24th Marine Regiment has entered Chicago and elements are approaching a dozen different targets. You're to hold your position and await orders."

"Understood." The radio went silent and Callum shook his head. He called out to one of his men. "Bring me the horn!"

He gripped his carbine tightly as one of his men ran over with the megaphone. He had no idea what the 24th Marines were up to, but doubted they were on a tour of the city. He was astonished that they hadn't learned from Hall's response to Indianapolis, which had involved a far larger unit than a few thousand Marines. But he had to deal with the situation.

He waited until they closed to within a block, then lifted the megaphone. "This is Sergeant Callum Watkins, Illinois State Guard. Stand down!"

The response was swift. Callum instinctively ducked as the machine gunners on the Humvees all zeroed in on his position, but held their fire. He knew the difficult truth, that his men would lose a fire fight against the approaching convoy. They had no heavy equipment and were staring down the barrel of armored vehicles and better armed Marines.

He keyed the megaphone again. "Last chance before I have to order my men to open fire. Please, brothers."

He doubted they'd comply. Even if they stood down, their march on this building made them outlaws. They'd taken up arms against FEMA and the guard, which meant Richard Hall would crush them. Callum knew they had reasons to be concerned: the executions, the imprisonments, the squeezing of average Americans. But he didn't think this was the way to bring about change.

When his second plea achieved nothing he put down the megaphone, raised his carbine and ordered his men to do the same. Certain that fighting would erupt at any second, he was astounded when a flame-haired woman pushed her way past the Marines and held her hands up. His eyes widened as he made the connection in his mind. It was the woman he'd freed. Celeste Adams.

"Don't shoot." Her plea was laced with fear and doubt. "Please, I'm coming up the stairs."

Callum kept his weapon trained on her, even as she advanced on their defensive position and as the doubts ricocheted around his head. If he'd lacked the resolve to shoot her in the detention center, there was next to no chance he was going to do it now and spark a fire fight between the State Guard and the US Marine Corps. He gave a guttural growl and lowered his weapon.

"Let her approach!" Callum radioed to his squad. "Repeat, let her through."

Confirmation came in from his other soldiers. None of them sounded convinced, or particularly happy, but there wasn't any protest. Nobody fancied the prospect of going toe to toe with what was in front of them. Though Callum and his squad were entrenched enough that they'd cause some damage, it would be futile. There was nothing inside the building worth dying over.

Celeste Adams reached the top of the stairs and waited a few feet from Callum's position. He put his carbine down and stood, confident that his men would keep him covered. When no shots were unleashed from the Marine column, he started to hope that maybe there was a resolution to this mess. He moved slowly, walked over to her and shook her hand.

"You're mad, you know that?" Callum sighed and shook his head. "You were half a chance to get your head blown off just there."

"I know." She smiled wider. "But once I heard your voice, I had to try. I'd heard it enough times over the camp intercom."

He smiled, despite the tension. "What can I do for you?"

She shrugged. "I'm trying to save the lives of you and your men. I owe you that much. It's up to you what happens next."

Callum reached up and scratched his chin, shocked that it had come to this. He thought back to when he'd been hunting in the forest with Todd and Mike. They'd been naive then. It was hard to believe he'd allowed himself to be so corrupted by the State Guard. He'd signed up originally for some nice cash once he left the army, not to be the hammer that smashed the American people against the FEMA anvil. He didn't want to do this anymore.

He stood taller and lifted his carbine high over his head. He hoped that there wasn't a trigger-happy kid among the Marines, because that's all it would take to start a fire fight. But a shot never came. Slowly, as Callum looked around, he could see the others in the unit adopt a similar posture. The message was clear: Come and get it, but leave us alone while you do. He looked back down the stairs. The Marines were already bounding up them.

As the Marines reached the top, one unarmed man raced up to Celeste and kissed her deeply. When they broke their embrace, he laughed. "You're crazy, do you know that?"

Callum laughed hard. In front of him was the most wanted man in America. His eyes flicked between Celeste Adams and the new arrival. "Just my luck you'd end up here."

Celeste stepped between them. "Jack Emery, this man saved my life, whose name I don't actually know."

"Callum Watkins."

Emery's eyes narrowed and he said nothing for a few moments. He seemed to be considering what she'd told him against the other misdeeds he no doubt assumed Callum had committed in the State Guard uniform. Eventually, Emery nodded and held out his hand. Callum shook it. Emery seemed to be in charge of the assault and Callum could nearly feel the collective sigh of relief from his men when peace appeared to be made.

"Celeste has told me the story about you freeing her from Effingham." Emery's voice had a sharpness to it. "I don't condone anything your side has done, but thanks."

Callum nodded. "I can't expect anything else. So what now?"

"What now?" Emery laughed. "We start to end this thing."

"Here? There's nothing in here." Callum paused. "Is there?"

Emery just laughed again and shook his head. He turned and gestured to one of his companions, a Marine captain who appeared to be in command. As the troops moved forward to detain him, Callum looked to the bottom of the stairs, where vehicles sat like giant sentinels, warning that the game was up. Marines poured over the State Guard defensive positions and took his men captive.

He nearly jumped into the air when the radio in his headset chirped. "Post 457, this is command. If it proves impossible to hold your facility, you're to destroy it."

Callum laughed. He laughed hard, and couldn't stop.

His war was over.

"JACK?" Ortiz stuck his head into the office. "We're out of time. We need to go. Now."

Jack looked up from the computer. "But I'm—"

Ortiz held up a hand. "Aircraft incoming. We haven't got the gear to defend this position."

Jack knew better than to argue with Ortiz over issues such as these. The vehicles had bugged out an hour ago, moving on to the next target and hoping to sow confusion in FEMA Command about what they were dealing with. He was glad they'd been able to take the broadcast center without any bloodshed, but it was folly to think that luck could last. Two dozen feint attacks by the Marines across Chicago had opened the door for Jack and the others to do what was needed. The military force had been the can opener and Jack had found what he'd needed inside.

But even now, reports were coming in of 24th Marine

Regiment forces being harassed by drones and of State Guard forces closing in on Chicago. The entire operation had hinged on this moment. Jack had hoped he'd get a bit more time, but it would have to do. He nodded, removed the headset and held his finger over the transmit button for a moment. A million things could have gone wrong, but it had worked flawlessly until now. With a smile, he pressed the button. There were no fireworks, just a light on a console that changed from red to green.

The Emergency Alert System had been switched on in 1997 and upgraded continuously since. It was designed to allow the President to speak to the entire nation for ten minutes, or to disseminate information about more localized events such as disasters and extreme weather. Following the FEMA takeover, it had been further upgraded still, with one primary transmission center commissioned in each state capital and many other major cities. Jack was thankful that Chicago made the cut. He'd received a crash course in the system from Hickens over the telephone, prior to the assault on the station. He hoped he'd done everything right. The green light flashing on the console gave him hope he had, that the information he'd prepped for broadcast had been successfully beamed out. Out of the masses of information that Mariposa Esposito had gathered, he'd broadcast the best of it. It was enough to crucify FEMA.

Or so he hoped. He'd done all he could. It was time to go. "Okay, let's go."

Ortiz nodded and walked toward the door. Jack looked back for a second, satisfied that the green light was still flashing on the broadcast panel. Over the next few minutes, the information he'd uploaded would beam its way to every radio, television, computer and tablet in the country. The information would damn FEMA using the very system they'd used to spew their lies. It would continue to operate until someone reached the broadcast room and turned it off, but by then it would be too late.

He followed behind Ortiz and they descended to the basement, where a dozen or so marines were waiting. They were the last of the 24th Marines still here. "What now?"

Ortiz placed his carbine on the ground then pulled out his pistol and stepped closer. "Now? You're going to learn how to use this. If we get into trouble, it might save your life."

"But—"

"Turn the safety off." Ortiz ignored Jack's protests as he held the weapon out and flicked the safety off.

"Okay." Jack nodded.

"Cock it." Ortiz pulled back the slide on the handgun and let it spring back, loading a round with a satisfying click.

Jack felt like he was being taught how to drive for the first time. "Okay."

"Hold it like this." Ortiz held the weapon out in front of him with two hands. "And none of that sideways, one-handed gangsta shit, either. If I see that, I'll shoot you myself."

"Okay."

"Squeeze the trigger." Ortiz tapped the trigger with his index finger, then reset the safety and then he held the weapon out to Jack. "Take it."

Jack looked down at the weapon in horror. "I don't want it. If you're relying on me to take out bad guys, then chances are you're all dead."

"That's why you need this." Ortiz thrust the weapon forward into his chest. "I'd rather you know how to use it before the rest of us are down."

Every synapse in his brain was telling him to refuse. He didn't want to hold the weapon, fire the weapon or be responsible for the weapon. But he didn't seem to have a choice in the matter. As he looked around, there were a dozen Marines with eyes on him, apparently waiting to see if he'd stand alongside them in the conflict to come. He couldn't ask them to take up arms for the final battle if he wasn't willing to. He took the gun from Ortiz.

Jack had been in the shit plenty of times, but he'd never been in the sewers before. Ortiz had dreamed it up. Heading down there was a way to escape the airstrikes and ground forces that would be bearing down upon the city, just like they had in Indianapolis. But Jack had learnt something else in that unfortunate city. He'd learnt that Richard Hall liked to handle things personally.

The first job was done, and Ortiz had given the bug out order to all 24th Marine Regiment forces. Jack just had to hope that the first attack would open up the second.

For that, they needed far fewer men.

21

In a teleconference with reporters, Administrator Hall expressed his confidence in the ability of authorities to apprehend wanted fugitive Jack Emery, but stressed that he was a dangerous and potentially violent man, with a significant support network. FEMA would like to advise all residents of Chicago to remain in their homes, as the State Guard pursues Mr Emery and the small number of rebel United States Marines currently aiding him.

Federal Emergency Management Agency
News Release

As soon as the helicopter touched down, Richard unbuckled and climbed out. As he did, he reflected on how much things had changed in only a handful of hours. He'd thought he was flying in to deal with the attack on Chicago by the marines. But instead he faced a different issue: the hijacking of the Emergency Broadcast System by Jack Emery. Though his forces had retaken the facility, the damage had been done. Half of America had now seen some of the evidence against

FEMA. It would take a huge effort to deal with the blowback. If he could.

Outside the helicopter he was met by a five-strong armed security detail. It was excessive, but the local FEMA office had insisted. The commander of the security forces nodded. "Good morning, Administrator, we've secured the building and the Area V Command Center is ready to welcome you."

Richard nodded and as walked across the roof to the waiting elevator, he wanted to kick himself. He'd underestimated Jack Emery so much. Though Richard had whipped Emery and the resistance furiously, the man had clearly learned from each setback and each lump Richard took from his hide. He'd figured out that it wasn't the people you controlled, or the information you held, or the distribution method you had at your fingertips. Those were irrelevant.

No, real power came from those with the drive, the sense of moment – of *gravitas* – and the ruthlessness to do what needed to be done. Once Richard had decided he needed to seize power, to be the leader he'd waited decades to serve, he'd taken over America and imposed the order he considered so vital. It was also how he'd deliver the final mailed fist right to the teeth of Emery's supporters. He hoped it would be how he'd finally finish Emery, if he could find him.

They reached the main work area and Richard waited as the staff of the FEMA Area V Command Center were summoned. When they had gathered, he grasped the edge of the table with both hands. "Are we certain that all elements of the 24th Marines have now been eliminated or driven from the city?"

The State Guard attaché to the office, whose name Richard hadn't learned, nodded. "The last troops were eliminated thirty minutes ago. Airstrikes took care of the last of them. Our forces have regained control of the city, though unfortunately there was some collateral damage—"

"There always is." Richard tapped his hand on the table. "Have we found Jack Emery?"

The local supervisor coughed softly. "That's our next highest priority, Administrator."

"Wrong." Richard stood up straight. "It's your *only* priority. I don't want this office doing anything else until Emery is found."

The supervisor swallowed hard as he nodded. "You'll understand that amid so much carnage, it can be easy to lose one man. We'll inform you once we have him."

Richard smiled thinly. "I don't plan on departing until he's been located."

Richard turned and walked away from the table. He'd given them a fright, now it was time to let them work. Though his power in the organization was absolute and his word was god, there were downsides. If he was hovering where his staff worked, very little would get done. He'd made his point. He went to the staff lounge and poured a coffee from the communal pot, took a sip, grimaced at the quality and then sat.

He used the time to make some calls to his subordinates. Though Emery was the only thing on his mind, some other business wouldn't wait for a resolution to that particular headache. He was thankful that none of the individuals he called, nor anyone in the Command Center, had mentioned the information dump that Emery was responsible for leaking. He was certain they knew about it, but they'd kept quiet.

The calls were the standard time killers he dealt with every day: the President, to re-assure him that everything was under control and that the executive orders would be needed for just a little while longer. Various lobbyists and influential Americans, protesting this or that or FEMA control in general. The State Guard general staff, begging for more manpower and resources. It was all a distraction.

"Administrator?" A woman spoke from across the room.

He looked up at the distraction. "Yes?"

"We've found Jack Emery, sir. We've alerted the State Guard in the building."

"Alerted them about what?"

"Emery, sir." The woman paused. "Radio triangulation confirms he's here."

JACK NEVER THOUGHT the darkness would be worse than the smell. Even though it was a line-ball decision, he could overcome the stink of shit. But hours of moving underground with only the powerful shafts of light provided by the Marines' flashlights had made him anxious. The blackness was suffocating, akin to the cell he'd very briefly called home in China. He was tired and wet. Most of all, he missed Celeste and was worried about her.

They'd moved for blocks through the sewers underneath Chicago. As they did, the elements of 24th Marines still in the city should have started to pull back or, if they were cut off, dug in for a protracted defense. Jack had no idea if that had gone to plan or not, but the broadcast had gone out and the little band of sewer rats had gone off the radar. As far as FEMA and the State Guard were concerned, they were phantoms.

In the wake of the 24th's departure, they'd left spotters in civilian clothes to monitor dozens of locations around Chicago, possible areas where Richard Hall would arrive to coordinate the defense of the city and the search for Jack. Less than twenty minutes ago, one of those scouts had sent word: Hall was at the Clark Street building that FEMA used as its area command in the city. Hall had gone to the most obvious location. Now they just had to reach him.

Jack sighed with relief as he watched a man at the top of the ladder give the cover a firm push. He was clearly doing his best to be quiet, but it was hard to shift the heavy steel manhole cover with any sort of stealth. The man stuck his head above ground, and Jack found it odd to see nothing above the man's waist for several moments. Eventually, the Marine ducked down and gave the all clear.

Jack exhaled heavily. Ortiz had said that this would be the hardest part. If there'd been guards outside the building, it would have been nearly impossible for the Marines to force their way inside. As it was, even as they climbed the ladder one after another and he waited his turn, Jack kept his hand on his weapon. He felt stupid for doubting its necessity when Ortiz had tried to hand it to him earlier. Jack was the last to climb to the top of the ladder and pull himself up to the street.

Once he was above ground, he saw the defensive perimeter that Ortiz and his men had formed, their weapons pointed outward. He stayed in the middle of the group and followed as Ortiz's men fanned out and covered all possible directions, moving as one toward the building. They reached it with no incident, then waited as two of the soldiers scouted the lobby and returned with a report that it was all clear. Jack looked at Ortiz. He seemed disturbed by the lack of civilians, but said nothing. They moved inside.

Jack looked around the lobby. As the scouts had reported, it was dark and deserted. He frowned and felt for the gun again. A large government building such as this should have been bustling, especially given it was home to the FEMA Area Command. It should also have been guarded. All he could hope was that, with Marines assaulting the city, all non-essential workers had been sent home and the building locked down. It seemed a forlorn hope, but it had to be true. The alternative was too terrible to contemplate.

Jack was directed to wait near the door as the team started to move more quickly, waved forward by Ortiz. They had to reach the fire stairs on the other side of the lobby. He watched as the marines scanned their surrounds, including the mezzanine balcony above. When they were halfway across the lobby, every light in the area flared white hot. Jack raised his forearm to shield his eyes, even as he heard shouts and the tapping sound of boots on tiles all around. He backed away.

"*Put down your weapons!*" The shout echoed around the lobby. "*Weapons down, now!*"

Jack backed further against the wall as Ortiz's soldiers kept their weapons trained on the State Guard soldiers above them on the mezzanine level. They were outnumbered and outpositioned, but their assailants were obviously waiting on something before opening fire. Given what he knew of Richard Hall, that seemed strange. Maybe the information he'd broadcast had soothed some of the itchy trigger fingers.

"*I won't tell you again.*" Jack couldn't see the man who was shouting. "*We want your weapons and the location of Jack Emery.*"

"I'm Captain Daniel Ortiz, 24th Marines." Ortiz's voice boomed in response, with no hint of fear. "I ask you to stand down and hand over Richard Hall."

Ortiz kept his weapon raised but turned his head away from it. He caught Jack's eye, hidden from the view of the attackers, and winked once. The message was clear: they can't see you, so stay hidden. Jack wanted nothing more than to shout out, to give himself up and save these lives, but every man here had known their fate in the event of capture. Whether it was in a fire fight or in a FEMA detention center, death was certain.

"*Last chance, Captain Ortiz.*"

"Fuck yourself!" Ortiz fired.

Jack screamed as the world exploded in front of him. There was no way his voice could be heard over the roar of gunfire, the screams of combat troops and the cries of wounded men. Ortiz's team got some shots of their own off, but it was a drop against an ocean. Jack had never seen anything like it. In action movies, the heroes win regardless of numbers or positioning. Not this time. This time they were slaughtered.

He turned and ran back across the street, toward the sewer, with tears streaming down his cheeks. He fought hard to stay composed. With three steps to go, he tripped and fell, landing hard on the road. He sucked at the air, but none entered his lungs. He started to panic until, after a few moments, his breathing returned. He scrambled to his feet and to the manhole. He hauled it open and climbed down, replacing the cover.

Darkness was the only ally he had left.

RICHARD STRODE FORWARD from the elevator and inspected the carnage from moments earlier. He'd ridden down as soon as the fire fight was over, but could still smell the smoke. The scene was chaos. Around a dozen dead men in marine uniforms were sprawled in tight formation in the middle of the lobby. Their guns had been taken but no other effort had been made to move them. Emery was not among them.

He growled in frustration as he took in the scene. "How fucking hard can it be to catch one man?"

The State Guard attaché to FEMA Area V, who'd ridden

down with him, did his best to soothe Richard's anger. "All attention has shifted to finding Emery, sir."

Richard turned, grabbed the man by his collar and looked him straight in the eyes. "I'm sick of this. Find him. Kill him."

The man nodded. Richard let go and turned back to the dead soldiers. He took a few steps toward them, then stopped when he heard a cough. One of the soldiers he'd thought dead a moment ago was apparently still alive. Yet another fuck up from the State Guard troopers. He approached the wounded man, just as a guardsman hovered over the Marine and prepared to finish him.

"Don't you dare." Richard grabbed the man from behind and pulled him back. "Give me your weapon."

The young trooper looked confused, but handed over his rifle. "Sir, be careful, if you're not careful he'll—"

"Be quiet." Richard crouched down to the dying soldier. "What's your name, young man?"

"Daniel Ortiz." The soldier coughed hard once, then again. Blood dribbled down his chin.

"Here's the situation, Daniel." Richard leaned on the rifle as he crouched. "I have you and a lot of your comrades. To help all of you, I need you to tell me where Emery is."

"Go fuck yourself." Ortiz smiled. His teeth were bloody. "Just kill me. I'm not telling you shit. Neither will any of the others you've captured around the city."

Richard sighed and stood. He looked around. The State Guard troopers were searching the ground level of the building, as well as the basement and the stairs, but he had no faith in their ability to find Emery. He looked down at Ortiz again, struggling for breath and clearly fighting the pain. He pressed the barrel of the rifle into the man's stomach, right where he could see a bullet wound. Ortiz gasped and cried out.

"Where. Is. He." Richard pressed the barrel harder and

ignored the man's shrieks. But the effort was hopeless. Ortiz bled out. Richard roared with rage. "Just *find* him!"

Richard threw the weapon onto the tiled floor then stalked back toward the elevator. There was no point in him staying here much longer, among the slugs crawling around trying to please him. He could do more back in the Command Center, coordinating effort across the city to find Jack Emery. He rode the elevator on his own, using the time to think about what he'd missed, where Emery could be.

Hours passed as Richard waited futilely for his people to get results. Without Emery's head on a pike, he'd have no enemy to parade before the public, to take the attention off the information that had briefly leaked. With Emery, he could torture the other man to say the evidence was all fabricated. He made his way through four coffees and eight fingernails. He'd never felt like this before, his future so contingent on something so completely out of his control.

After yet more hours, his phone rang. He nearly screamed. He was not in the right frame of mind for this phone call, but had no choice but to take it. "Mr President."

"Administrator Hall." The President's tone was cold. "This is a courtesy call to inform you that I've revoked all executive orders relating to FEMA and the State Guard. My attorney general has also informed me that you're to be arrested on a long list of charges. I suggest you wait where you are prior to being taken into custody."

"Mr—" Richard stopped speaking when the line went dead.

He threw the phone across the room. He'd known this might be coming, but had hoped to fight it off by capturing Emery. The information that had been leaked had obviously run wild in Washington. Richard had hoped to turn the tide, but now it had washed over his head. He turned and made his way to the elevator and toward the roof. He didn't even wait for his guards. Now he had to think about survival. All he needed was his helicopter pilot.

Once he reached the roof, he was pleased that the helicopter was still there, sitting like an old friend in the night. He called out. "John! Fire it up! We're out of here."

"Hall." The voice came from beside him.

Richard knew it instantly. He turned to his left. Though the roof was only dimly lit, he could see Jack Emery emerge from behind an air-conditioning unit. He looked like hell, but he held a pistol in his hand. Emery raised the weapon and took a few quick steps toward Richard. With a shake of his head, Richard raised his hands lazily. He steeled himself for the inevitable, the irony of finally having found Emery not lost on him.

"Turn around." Emery's voice was all business. "Back to me."

Richard laughed as he turned. "Just how the hell did you get up here?"

"That's the thing with absolute dictators, isn't it? You think you control everything, but miss the detail." Emery jammed the gun into the back of his head. "Down."

Richard fell to his knees. His best chance at survival had shifted. "You realize that I'm about to be arrested? That I'm powerless? Your little vigilante job is too late."

"I don't care. This ends here." Emery's voice was cold as he pressed the weapon into the back of his head. "This ends now, you cunt."

THE PISTOL WAS SHAKING in Jack's hand as he held it to Hall's head. The other man said nothing else, apparently at peace with what was to come.

So much emotion and fury was flooding through him, he was unsure what to feel. He'd waited for hours in the sewers, unsure about what to do. He'd thought about fumbling through the sewers, until he found daylight and freedom, but that would have wasted the lives of the marines who'd fallen. He'd known he still had a role to play, even if there was nobody else left to help him and very little chance of success.

When he'd fought the Foundation for a New America, he'd been content to sit in a hotel room while the FBI wrapped up the threat. But this time was different. Even though the choicest pieces of Mariposa's information were now percolating around the country, and he was certain it would be enough to topple Hall, he still had a score to settle. He had to be sure that this was the end of it.

He'd waited until night, then climbed out of the sewer and crossed the street. Then, instead of going upstairs, he'd spotted something – a window-cleaning rig outside the building. Silently and in darkness, he'd enjoyed the wind through his hair as he rode it to the top. On the roof, he'd waited, hoping that Hall would emerge and head for his helicopter.

Now, he had the administrator right where he wanted him. Right where he'd wanted him for months. His finger squeezed the trigger slightly, but Jack held off when he heard the *thock-thock-thock* sound of helicopters drawing closer. They moved quickly and soon there were two circling above. Jack could barely hear himself think over the noise.

"*My name is Special Agent Roberto Garcia, FBI.*" A voice boomed over the sound of the choppers. "*Richard Hall is to be arrested and charged with treason and multiple counts of first-degree murder. Put down your weapon.*"

Jack shook his head at the irony. He'd fought so hard for nearly a year to fight Hall's control and got nowhere, but now he had a choice about how to do it. Whether his inner circle was breached or not, Hall still had a great deal of power all across the country. There was no guarantee that Hall would end up in the slammer if Jack let him live.

"Listen to him, Jack." Hall's shout could barely be heard over the noise. "Put your faith in the people, in the justice system. You don't need to do this."

Jack had been a reporter for ten years and had covered enough injustice to know the system got it wrong sometimes. On the other hand, if America was to have a chance of rediscovering itself, its freedoms and its moral purpose, then men like Richard Hall needed to be brought to justice, not executed.

Jack lowered the weapon, tossed it aside and stepped back, even as FBI agents began to rappel down onto the roof. He closed his eyes and took a deep breath.

It was over.

EPILOGUE

"**A**ttention passengers, this is your captain. We're about to enter a small patch of turbulence. I'd ask that you return to your seat and buckle up for a few minutes."

Jack sighed and opened his eyes as the aircraft started to shake. He was already in his seat and buckled up, but after the pilot's announcement, he was no longer asleep. He'd been sleeping fairly lightly recently – the slightest noise or flash of light enough to wake him – much to his annoyance. While this wasn't surprising, given the events of the past few years, what he'd never considered before was how many minor irritations could be found on a plane flight.

Even Air Force One.

He was flying from Los Angeles to Washington DC in time for the State of the Union address. The President's chief of staff had invited Jack along. He'd buttered Jack up, telling him that the President wanted him as an honored guest and that the President would be pleased to share a meal with him on board the aircraft. It hadn't happened.

The turbulence lessened and he turned to Celeste. She was still asleep. Jack closed his eyes and started to drift off again.

Just as he was nearly out the cursed chime sounded again. "Jack Emery, please report to the President's office for your appointment."

Jack's eyes shot open, more quickly than the last time. He prodded Celeste and she woke with a start. Jack leaned in to kiss her on the cheek. "Just going to meet with McGhinnist."

"Okay." Her voice was groggy, and he knew she was no good in the moments after waking. "Good luck."

Jack made his way through the aircraft. Once he arrived at the office, he exchanged a few pleasantries with the Secret Service agent stationed outside, even as the agent used his radio to report Jack had arrived. He obviously heard what he wanted to in his earpiece, because the lock on the door give a heavy *clunk* and the agent pushed the door open and stood aside to let Jack inside.

President Bill McGhinnist was seated behind his desk. Though this was not the first time he'd met world leaders, or even Bill McGhinnist, it was the first time he was both one on one with the President and also likely to be the major topic of conversation. Jack waited nervously as McGhinnist finished signing some paperwork, then looked up with a broad smile.

"Mr President?" Jack had planned what he'd say to the most powerful man in the world, but it had escaped him. "Thanks for inviting me to meet with you."

"Come on, Jack." McGhinnist stood, walked around the desk and slapped him on the back. "How many times do we need to save the country before you'll start calling me Bill in private?"

"A few more times yet, given your new job, sir." Jack laughed.

One of the pleasant surprises in the aftermath of the arrest of Richard Hall and the return to normalcy had been finding out Bill McGhinnist was alive. Somehow he'd survived the assault on the New York resistance cell and gone to ground. Along with Celeste, he was one of the few involved who'd survived Hall's decapitation of the resistance. A lot of good people hadn't. Jack mourned them all.

Hall was still on trial, but the daily court reports showed little chance of him being freed. Though he'd had a mandate to take over the country, he'd gone a mile beyond it. Every day new information emerged about the atrocities Hall and his organization had committed in the name of order and safety, and it sickened him. FEMA had already been gutted and the State Guard abolished.

In the aftermath, Jack had traveled to Europe with Celeste, to visit her family in the UK and get as far away from the States as he could while it healed. At the first elections following the collapse of FEMA control, Bill McGhinnist had been elected in a landslide for the Republican Party. Though he'd seemed a reluctant candidate, the public had bonded with his call for a whole lot of fresh air through Washington.

Jack had worked closely with McGhinnist to end the threat of both the Foundation for a New America and FEMA, but those interactions had been brief and for a sharp purpose. He'd had no real time to get to know the man beneath the bureaucrat, who now happened to be President. Jack couldn't guess what McGhinnist had up his sleeve, but he wasn't sure he'd like it.

McGhinnist gestured toward a lounge chair, then took a seat himself. "I've got to be upfront. I didn't just ask you along for the ride."

Jack kept his features even. "What can I do for you?"

"I need you to come work for me, Jack."

Jack didn't hesitate. "Not interested."

"I'm not asking, Jack." McGhinnist's features hardened. "Your co—"

"I'm Australian, don't forget."

McGhinnist laughed and his face softened. "Fine, *the* country needs you. While I think we've purged most of the cancers, I can't be completely sure."

"Well, I did try to shoot Hall." Jack shrugged. "The FBI stopped me. Even given that, I still nearly pulled the trigger."

"A shame, if you ask me. But don't worry about Hall. He's sorted." McGhinnist sipped his coffee. "I need you, Jack. I need you on my side full time."

Jack leaned forward in his chair. "Why me, though? There're better people for the job."

"No, there aren't. You've got a knack for this stuff. But more importantly, you're also above reproach. You've saved America from itself and its leaders twice. I need you on the payroll."

Jack stayed silent.

"The first time, it took us to war with China and we nearly had a large chunk of Congress controlled by maniacs. You put a stop to that, though not without cost. The second time, it was our own agencies attacking America while pretending to save it, using the very laws designed the safeguard us all. Again, you stopped it."

"At great personal cost." Jack's voice was soft.

"I know that."

Jack sighed. "Okay, so theoretically, what's the job?"

McGhinnist smiled. "Winding back the clock twenty years. While terrorism is a serious threat, it pales in comparison to the loss of our freedoms over the past few decades. To sleep soundly at night and keep the shadows at bay, we've unshackled a much greater darkness. It is too open to abuse and must be put right."

Jack didn't disagree. Since 9/11, the Patriot Act and its various add-ons had combined to form a miasma of abuse. Civil rights had been curtailed. Bureaucracy and red tape had been allowed to stifle good sense. A minor increase in security from the unlikeliest of events had been given primacy over everything that made America what it is. And, while he doubted it could be unwound entirely, there were definitely improvements that could be made.

"Put right..." Jack's voice trailed off.

"Reviewed and abolished where sensible. I'm talking about a full, independent inquiry into the laws, regulations and actions of government that have gone too far, and a combined effort of my entire administration to fix it."

Jack would have doubted the words if they came from the mouth of any other person on the planet. Governments the world over were pleased to take more power on the slightest pretext, but didn't like to give it up. Curing the addiction of America's government to this power would be difficult, if not impossible, but Bill McGhinnist had done his absolute best to fight both the Foundation and FEMA. He mightn't succeed, but Jack knew he'd try.

"You don't need me for that."

"You're wrong, I do." McGhinnist sighed. "I'm the former Director of the FBI, I helped to devise and enact some of the laws. Others? They're too blinkered to see what needs doing. I need someone who has been proven to have America's best interests at heart, who's smart and who can lead this change."

"Me."

"You, Jack."

"Okay." Jack stood after a moment and held out his hand. "I'm in. But I think you're crazy brave. If you pull this off, they'll need to make some space on Mount Rushmore."

McGhinnist stood, beaming, and shook Jack's hand

with vigor. "When I agreed to run, I hoped you might agree to join the team. You won't regret this."

"So, what's that make me?"

"Special Advisor to the President of the United States of America. It'll look good on your CV, though it's not quite a third Pulitzer."

"Two are enough."

"Indeed." McGhinnist laughed. "Keeping an eye on the review will be your first job, but after that I've got some other things in mind."

"Fine. When do I start?"

"Well, I'd actually planned to announce it in about..." McGhinnist checked his watch. "An hour? I have to say *something* at the State of the Union."

Jack stared. He hadn't expected his appointment to be quite so public, quite so soon. "Okay, sir."

"Bill."

"Okay, Bill." Jack laughed.

"Plus I've got a medal or two to pin on your chest."

ACKNOWLEDGMENTS

Vanessa Pratt. My everything.

My Praetorian Guard is the beta readers who help me carve out the worst of the excesses and missteps, while amplifying the explosions and intrigue. Gerard Burg, Dr Kirstie Barry, Andrew McLaughlin, Emily Swann and Ashley Pratt have my thanks. Special thanks to Dr James Barry, my go to guy on all things Middle East.

Giant high-five to the Momentum team – Joel Naoum, Tara Goedjen, Ashley Thomson, Patrick Lenton and Michelle Cameron. They are the Beatles of Australian publishing and I love every second working with such a dynamic and energetic bunch. I appreciate all of their hard work and look forward to more adventures.

Haylee Nash at Pan Macmillan plucked me off "the pile" and dropped me in a bucket of deadlines, courtesy of a three-book run. She has my thanks for all of the support and for the belief she shows in my writing. She's also wonderful to work with. I wish her all the best with the little one due about now.

I get the best editing and cover design in the business.

Dip of the lid to my editor, Kylie Mason, who did a great job yet again. She's a fantastic wing-woman and I treasure her input. She made the book better and Jack can't wait to spend more time in her capable hands. Thanks also to Xou Creative, for once again rocking the cover.

I need to also mention the other authors, reviewers and boosters who have accepted me into their community with a giant warm group hug. I've been blown away by the advice, generosity and good fun that has come my way, whether over drinks or online. I'll do my best to pay it forward.

A small army of family, friends, colleagues and acquaintances have encouraged and supported me since this adventure began. There's too many to name, but all I can say is thanks. This can be a lonely business but it's nice to have such a great bunch to share the excitement with.

Finally, thanks to readers who enjoyed *The Foundation* enough to stick with Jack on this ride. I hope you enjoyed it. To the new arrivals, welcome!

ABOUT THE AUTHOR

Steve P. Vincent lives with his wife in Melbourne, Australia, where he's forced to write on the couch in front of an obnoxiously large television.

When he's not writing, Steve enjoys beer, whisky, sports and dreaming up ever more elaborate conspiracy theories to write about. Oh, and travel.

Steve has a degree in Political Science and History, with a thesis on global terrorism. He's received instruction from the FBI and the Australian Army.

You can contact Steve at all the usual places:

stevepvincent.com
steve@stevepvincent.com

Printed in Great Britain
by Amazon

39566045R00179